SEEDS OF DECEPTION

a novel

Arlene L. Walker

Seeds Of Deception

ISBN 978-0-578-49283-4

www.arlenelwalker.com

arlenelwalkerauthor@gmail.com

Fleetwood Publishing

For AJ, my precious sugar-biscuit,
Even before you were born, I knew this would be for you.

Chapter One

I f poverty was slavery, then wisdom was wealth. That was the revelation that came to Sput Louie McClendon as she glared at her husband across their paltry potato field. Benjamin tended the vines carefree and untroubled, like the two of them weren't in the middle of a spat.

No matter. Sput had waited long enough. She was tired of living life just a notch above slavery. That morning, she would have her druthers. Damn her husband. Damn the Cherokee Indians. Damn the white man's treaty.

She just had to be wise about it this time, and make her wishes seem less like a demand, and more like a request.

But maybe Benjamin didn't know they were in a spat. He should. All three of their sons sure knew it. They knew it when she'd slammed down a tin plate of wild onions and cornbread on the breakfast table. They'd looked at her wide-eyed, then wordlessly scarfed down their meager portion, and skedaddled out of the house. Skedaddling was something they never did. When it came to chore time, they moved slower than honey-laden bees.

Benjamin jerked his hand back and forth, motioning for Sput to bring more water from the well. With skin the color of corn silk, he looked more Cherokee than Negro. The only visible trace of his mother's

Negro blood was the waves and curls in his hair that, without that blood, would have been straight and stringy. Sput mindlessly fiddled with the head rag that covered her wiry hair, then hauled her bucket towards him.

It was Benjamin's covetable Indian blood that would put them in line for an allotment of land, and all that land possession promised with its open arms and toothy grin. They would no longer be squatters. They would no longer have to wait for the Cherokees to come through on their treaty promise of land to their former slaves. They would be full-fledged members of the tribe. Leastwise, Benjamin would. Sput Louie would have a death grip on his coattails.

Of course, she would first have to get him to beseech his blood father to claim him. That was her goal for the day. No small feat, that. Just like cattle wouldn't graze where sheep had been, Benjamin wouldn't go anywhere near the man who had fathered him.

"Like trying to thread a needle in the wind," she mumbled as she plopped her wooden water bucket down in the dirt next to him, then gasped in surprise at herself for allowing her thoughts to bubble up into words.

Benjamin twisted around and squinted up at her. "You say somethin'?"

She rocked from one moccasin-clad foot to the other and shook her head no. Not yet.

He looked up and down her small five-foot frame, then reached up and took the dipper tied to her bucket. He ladled water onto vines nearly barren of spuds. "That's all the water you brung?" he asked and blew out a flustered sigh.

"Ya-huh." She snatched up her bucket.

Benjamin rose, and trudged over to the second of their three small fields, while she returned to the well to pulley up more water and shore up more nerve for their imminent showdown. Meanwhile, it was time for him to resume teaching their son L.B. how to mound farm the Cherokee way so he wouldn't starve once they were both bone dead.

L.B., the youngest of their three surviving children, was crouched over one such mound in a field full of five-foot-wide mounds. Laughing Boy—so named because as a baby he seldom smiled and constantly cried—had Sput's skin coloring, a rich butternut brown. Unlike his mother, though, he had more forehead than face. His lower lip pushed out further than his upper, and his eyes held constant the innocent expression of a four-year-old child, even though he was fifteen.

Hoisting her newly refilled bucket on her shoulder along with a stronger resolve for what she had to say and do, she marched straight towards them.

"Ben," she yelled louder than she'd intended. "I need a word with you."

Each foot stomped with determination until the unexpected happened. The earth pushed back.

It stopped her stride.

She shot a quick glance towards her earthly protector, and mumbled a quick "Lawd," to her heavenly one.

Benjamin rose to his feet, turning this way and that until he'd looked in all four directions. When he turned back to her, she saw the look of alarm on his face. He had felt it, too.

A feeling of *asgina* passed between them, what the Cherokees called bad spirit.

She let down her bucket and sunk to her knees.

Out in the sticks, you felt visitors before you saw them, so she pressed her palms firmly to the ground. A man-made rhythm vibrated her hands and knees. It rose through her squirrel-skin moccasins, rode under her skirt and up her stockingless legs. It shook her bones like a rattlesnake's warning.

Listening as hard as she could, she heard a crackle-clank sound along with steady hoof pounds.

"Rider in a wagon," she yelled in warning. "Reckon one, maybe two horses."

L.B. seemed oblivious to the rumble in the ground and the *asgina* in the air. He was too busy pushing pole beans into the outer rim of his foot-high mound so that they formed a perfect circle around the corn stalks sprouting in the middle. Just like his Pa had taught him. He didn't look up until Benjamin placed a hand on his shoulder.

"Run get my gun, Son."

L.B. stood. "But, Pa," he pleaded through his thick tongue, bean seeds still in hand. "I never get to do nothin' everybody elth be doin'. Alwayth got to do different."

Benjamin was firm but gentle. "Do as I say now, Son," he said, without an ounce of chastisement in his tone.

L.B. hung his head but obeyed his father. He ambled towards their one-room abode, the toes of his time-worn Brogans flapping like loose clapboards in an angry storm.

Gazing towards the horizon with unflappable focus, Sput used the flat of her hand to shield her eyes for a better look.

There were no roads this far out in Feather Falls. The only official road in the history of the town was Rabbit Run, so-called because, at one time, rabbits overran the thoroughfare. It was barren now, the hares having been killed for food long ago. Rabbit Run Road was like the spine of a leaf, with veins of footpaths or wagon trails veering in and out in various directions to and from the forty or so households that made up the tribal township. One such wagon trail, carved through the woods over time, passed right by the McClendon home.

That was where Sput spotted the lone man in a four-wheeled buggy pulled by a stout Appaloosa.

"Maybe somebody needs my healin' graces." She tried to sound more hopeful than fearful. Indians rarely sought her medicine anymore, though. Thank God her black brethren still did.

Benjamin took the gun from a still sulking L.B. "More likely another land grabber." He headed towards the front of their lopsided shanty to the sentry position. Sput and L.B. fell in line behind him.

There were three kinds of people who might come calling in Indian Territory in 1886: The land-rich, the land-poor, or the land-greedy.

The land-rich would be the Indians, either Creek, Seminole, Chickasaw, Choctaw, or Cherokee. Each tribe had their own separate territorial land, unlike smaller bands like the Delaware, or the Caddo, who had to share a slice of a bigger tribe's pie. It was said that the Cherokees had the largest wedge of that pie, rumored to come in at ten million acres. That they wouldn't honor their treaty promise to share just a tiny chunk of that with the people they had once held in captivity stuck in Sput's craw. Not holding land in a territory where land was abundant was like being thirsty in the midst of water.

The land-poor would be, for the most part, those former slaves—now called Freedmen—who had chosen to stay and fight for their fair share after the War Between the North and the South had freed them. The Cherokees had consistently denied them not only allotments of land, but also the things associated with the land: bread money, grass money, whatever they were calling the monies earned from the lease of grazing land to Texas Cattlemen. That treaty promise was the main reason Freedmen still stayed. Any Freedmen coming to call, though, would more than likely be on foot.

The land-greedy could include the likes of whiskey peddlers working outside the law, train robbers hiding from the law, or land grabbers looking to skirt the law. Most would be white. All would be considered "intruders." All would, sooner or later, come to the same side notion of coveting Indian land.

As the wagon gained ground through a copse of cedars, Sput was able to distinguish the buttoned-down suit the driver wore. There was only one man who had such a grand opinion of himself that he would dress so highfalutin in such backwoods country.

For most of her life, Sput had pictured this man meeting his maker in one fashion or another. Sometimes she was the instrument of death. Other times, she imagined it being at the hands of another.

She reached for the ever-present amulet hanging from her neck, her fingers feeling for the smoothness of the bird bone baubles that decorated it, while her gut twisted trying to puzzle out the reason for the visit.

Sput shot a look of dread to Benjamin, who passed one right back to her.

"Old Crow," he said, through tightened teeth.

Chapter Two

Goliah T. Lynch, known as Old Crow behind his back, was a man of considerable coin. He was arguably the most powerful mixed-blood in Feather Falls, being half-white and half-Cherokee. He was also the man who had owned both Sput's and Benjamin's families during slavery. A constant reminder of that was the "L" branded onto their upper right arm.

The couple hadn't known each other back then. They were children growing up on separate farms run by the Lynch family, and the Lynches forbade the different slave families who worked the various farms from consorting and, thereby, conspiring.

Sput wanted to spit bile. She knew Benjamin did as well. She'd seen the havoc Old Crow could wreak. When the battles of the Freedom War encroached on Indian Territory, Old Crow leased land in Texas and sent a gaggle of slaves to plant his crops there for the duration of the war. He didn't dare send his money-making medicine woman with them, but he had no qualms about snatching that medicine woman's ten-year-old daughter and sending her to tend to any sick slave in her stead. Sput never saw her Ma and Pa again.

She shivered as she shook off the memory.

That her two older sons were not around gave Sput some small solace.

"Here come the boys." Benjamin jutted his chin towards the prairie to the left of Goliah Lynch.

Damn it, Sput thought.

She followed his nod. Sure enough, there was Hunter Big, her oldest, trailed by Archie, her middle son. They both knew of her and Benjamin's loathing for Goliah. They'd cut their teeth on it. Hunter, in particular, had an unsafe lack of fear in regards to him. Both boys would be able to sense the cloud of dread hanging in the air, ready to burst and make good its threat of rain.

Hunter Big was a bison of a man. He swung a rope-tied red fox from his left hand and carried a bow in his right, while his ever-present pet ferret circled his neck like a moving collar. He wore woolen pants topped by a cow-skin vest that barely contained his robust chest. Sput could see the feathered flights of the arrows he carried in his quiver peek out just above his wooly head. The slingshot he'd carved from a piece of white oak hung from his belt and had most likely been used to fell the fox.

Just like Benjamin, Hunter Big knew by heart the rise and fall of the land. He strode wide and shrewd towards them now, his moccasin-clad feet deftly maneuvering across the tallgrass prairie, while never taking his eyes off of their impending visitor.

Trying to keep up with him was Archie, Hunter's twin brother. They neither looked alike nor were alike. Archie had inherited Sput's physique, and was as small and slim as a dried herring. He was the only member of the family who had managed to amass any schooling—three scattered years in his stretch of two decades on earth—supplemented by reading the Bible, the newspaper, and anything else he could get his hands on that contained the printed word. Hunter, on the other hand, saw no need for the alphabet if it couldn't back him up in a bear fight.

The twins reached them in tandem with Goliah. The three boys flanked their parents like a protective covering as they watched Goliah's wagon roll to a stop at the rock-lined edge of the dirt yard.

"*Osiyo*." Benjamin greeted first, holding his shotgun in the crook of his arm. He pressed the barrel downward with his other hand, as though it might rise and shoot Goliah of its own accord.

At the Cherokee greeting, Goliah flinched like he had been pinched. His complacent expression quickly hardened into a searing scowl. It was no secret that Goliah blotted out his Cherokee side as much as he trotted out his white side. One way he did that was to keep his once-black, heavy hair cropped short and hidden under his Boler. Another was to shun his native tongue in favor of the Queen's English.

"I have a hundred head of new cattle coming in," he said, skipping any semblance of social pleasantries.

No surprise to Sput there.

The barrel of the shotgun flipped up as Benjamin slid the butt to the ground.

"Well, suh," Benjamin began.

What was a surprise to Sput was hearing her husband refer to this particular man as "sir." She whipped her head around to give Benjamin a questioning stare. Was that a smile she saw stretching at his lips? A nasty shiver went down her spine, as her ire heated up. She took a deep breath and curtailed her displeasure into a stifled grunt that, hopefully, only she heard. She needed to calm herself because she understood all too well the dire straits in which they found themselves. It was her whole reason for being that day. She also understood how desperation could make a man like Benjamin sacrifice his skin in order to save his bones.

"I—I don't have a mule no more——" Benjamin continued.

"'Cauth we ate him." L.B. hooked his thumbs around the shoulder straps of overalls that didn't quite reach his ankles.

Sput reached around Hunter, who stood between her and L.B, and swatted him on the arm. "Hush now, L.B. Let your Pa talk."

"But we ate him lath Chrithmath." L.B. was never one to leave a story unfinished. "He died firth. Then we ate him."

Benjamin was not sidetracked. "But if you supply a horse," he went on as if L.B. hadn't said a word, "I can rope a steer, brand it, and castrate it with the best of 'em. Never lost a steer to a snippin' yet."

Archie jumped right on board with the idea of any one of the McClendons being hired out—even to this man—though Goliah had yet to declare such an intention. "They don't call Pa Snippin' Ben for nothing—um, I mean, anything." He hesitated as if standing at a schoolroom chalkboard ciphering arithmetic. "I mean nothing." His eyes rolled upwards like the answer was in the clouds. He quickly settled on what must have been his idea of the correct word. "Um, I mean nothing. Yes, that's what I mean." He began making circles in the dirt with the toe of his shoe.

"And Hunter here," Benjamin pointed with a proud nod of his head, "he can break a bronco into a cow pony in no time, if you need that done, too. I reckon you might?"

Benjamin seemed not to notice or care that Hunter appeared unmoved, and Goliah unimpressed.

"And Archie can rope and ride a salty one all day long," he said, rounding out the recitation of McClendon family skills. "What you got comin'," Sput's husband rambled on, "lanky longhorns? Shorthorns?"

Although Archie had a job at the Sentinel Newspaper one day a week, neither Benjamin nor Hunter had been hired out for some months now. Sput knew desperation reeked through everyone's clothes. Even with Archie's thirty-cent-a-week salary, they had been hard-pressed for means far too long. Filthy water could not be washed, and Old Crow was as dirty a drink as ever there was. If you were parched enough to drink such dirty water, you had to deal with the muck that came with it. She blinked back her reservations about it, while Benjamin rambled on as peppy as a kid about to get a peppermint.

"You got Durhams? Or Berkshires?"

Sput scoured Goliah's face because she didn't know what to make of his prolonged muteness. His skin was as white as parchment paper, and the lines that creased it were like narrow gorges in a dried up field. His eyes were a mix of copper and gray. Silver lashes framed one of them, topped by a silver brow. That oddity was like a beacon from a benevolent God to be wary of this man.

Goliah began a slow, guttural laugh. "I'm not looking to hire you." His laugh grew. "I'm looking to evict you." He was in full guffaws by the time he doubled over on the bench seat of his wagon and slapped the reins against the buckboard with glee.

Sput's mouth went so dry it couldn't even court a swallow.

"You runnin' us off this here land?" Benjamin's eyes narrowed.

Hunter nudged the ferret now sitting at attention on his shoulder. It obediently followed orders and scampered to the ground.

One quick side-glance and Sput was alerted to Hunter's body going rigid as he dropped the dead fox to the ground, too, then shoved it to one side with his foot. Her hand instinctively struck a position of command across his abdomen as if to say, *don't make a move or say a word. Your Pa will handle this.*

Finally emerging from his fit of laughter, Goliah straightened up. "Yes. You're going to have to move."

"Again?" Benjamin barked. "It's been only three plantin' seasons since Deer Jim threw us off our last place. Sayin' he needed that land."

"Ya-huh," Sput grumbled.

"We done made improvements on this here land." Benjamin stood as straight and firm as a stake in the ground.

Goliah chuffed, as his eyes swept across not only their slapdash shack of a home that leaned to one side but all of their various sheds and shanties surrounding it that had been built with every throwaway piece of mismatched, misshapen lumber and boards they could gather. It screamed of hard times. He cleared his throat. "Now, you know a freedman can't plant residential seeds within a quarter mile of an Indian. That's a fact per the treaty."

That damn treaty, Sput thought. It gave former slaves the right to the use of a particular plot of land from which they could not be moved, as well as the right to vote, but no one was enforcing those parts. They never brought up the treaty unless they were using it against the freedman instead of for him. Besides, she thought the quarter-mile rule applied to everyone, not just coloreds.

Benjamin twisted his mouth to one side. "Cain't tell what a quarter mile is if folks keep movin' their fence line."

"Well, now." Goliah's thin lips gave way to a lopsided grin that seemed to mock their very existence. "I don't have to proffer an explanation. You know I have land all over Cherokee country. Always have. Always will." He cleared his throat again. "As a courtesy, though, I'll tell you my new herd is arriving on the Katy any day now."

Though none of the McClendons had ever ridden a train, Sput was familiar enough to know that "Katy" was the nickname for the MK&T railroad that ran through Indian Territory connecting Missouri, Kansas, and Texas. Texas was where most cattle hailed.

"And this land you're on," Goliah continued, "is smack in the midst of some fine grazing land. Cattle like nothing better than bluestem, and your grass here is as high as a newborn calf." He looked admiringly towards the low prairie sprouted with tall grass.

Hunter turned his back on everyone, while Archie remained slack-jawed.

"You have a day to vacate the premises."

Hunter swung back around as if yanked by a rope.

"A day?" Benjamin asked, in unison with the twins.

Sput looked around for L.B. It was about that time that she would expect him to toss out one of his Bible verses just to be included in the conversation. But he was no longer beside them. No sooner had she wondered where he was than a cane chair came flying out of their front door solving the mystery of his whereabouts. It rolled bottom over top, past the brush arbor that served as their porch, and onto the dirt yard. L.B. didn't even wait for it to roll to a stop before he rushed back inside, shoes flopping hard and loud.

The ragged chair with the broken-cane bottom landed right at the hooves of Goliah's horse. The spotted Appaloosa gave a short squeal as Goliah slowly turned it and his wagon, and coolly trotted away. Just in time to avoid a flying kerosene lamp long ago dry of oil.

Benjamin's whole body seemed to drain of life in the matter of a minute. His head drooped so low it looked like his chin was piercing his chest. His arms hung by his side loose and lifeless. The only thing that kept his shotgun from falling to the ground was the natural curve of his now limp fingers.

Sput averted her eyes, unable to watch the anguished face of the man who had been her salvation after slavery when she had nowhere for her and her newborn twins to go, the man who had protected her from the treachery of frontier life, the man who treated her like his *galvquodi*—his precious—the man who had guided her for more than half her life, the man who had just been evicted by his own father.

Chapter Three

G oliah T. Lynch was well pleased. With himself. He'd completed one of his two chores for the week, and it was just Wednesday. He jaunted bright-eyed towards the town of Feather Falls to complete his second task.

First, he'd evicted that bastard family of his. Easier than peeling a cat, and not nearly so noisy, he thought. He chuckled as he slowed his wagon in front of Malloy's Store-haus. He hadn't even had to lie about it, either. He did have cattle coming in on the Katy. Feather Falls Township was nothing if not a broad sweep of land chock-full of good grazing grass, and he could have chosen any of it. It was just his pure luck that the mis-born had the misfortune to set up house on a prime piece of prairie.

With a smug smile tingling his lips, he bounded down from the wagon like he wasn't a middle-aged man. He looped the lead rope into a slipknot around the hitching rail and proceeded towards Malloy's.

Malloy's Store-haus was a general store built of a shingled roof held up by four walls of walnut weatherboards. The sign over the double doors—like most business signs in Feather Falls proper—were painted by the town ironsmith, a German immigrant named Gunter Friedenberg. By Friedenberg's hand, storehouse became store-haus, livery became liveree, and ironsmith became ironschmidt.

When Goliah, the self-appointed town spokesman, went eyeball-to-eyeball with Friedenberg on the point of his spelling, Friedenberg responded that he and the other white proprietors had permits from ruling authorities—both the Cherokee Government as well as the U.S. government—to operate businesses in this godforsaken town, and that they could spell the name of their stores any way they saw fit, and what difference did it make because most Cherokees couldn't read, anyway. Present company excepted, he had said and patted Goliah on the back.

Goliah couldn't argue the point. Or wouldn't. It peeved him to no end that learning the English language was not a priority for the tribe, especially among the full bloods. How would they ever outgrow their image of being barbaric savages if they didn't speak English?

It wasn't like Feather Falls had a plethora of visitors. The locals only made their way to town on Saturdays, and that was just to trade amongst themselves at the open market. Even if an out-of-towner did pass through, there was nothing to invite him to stay; no boarding house, and certainly nothing like a hotel, though passers-thru had been known to use the livery stable as such in wintertime. It wasn't a big city like Tahlequah or even Vinita. It had no silversmith, no stonecutter, no salt-maker, and no gunsmith. This was Feather Falls, small and sluggish, an unincorporated town that never promised to be more than a twig in a land of timber.

The forty-seven-year-old Goliah sprung up the wooden steps and entered the store to pick up his wife's hat that he'd ordered all the way from Chicago. That would complete his second chore. A green felt hat with long black plumes just might lure Philura out of her Paregoric haze long enough to accompany him to the big marriage ceremony. Attending the wedding of the niece of clan elder Two Bird was going to be the highlight of his month. Though Two Bird was a plague on Goliah's life worse than syphilis—the full-blood's constant questioning of his actions vexed him like an open sore—he thought the old Indian's niece surprisingly smart for marrying not just a white man, but a white man who also happened to be a lawyer for the tribe.

The wedding was still two weeks away, but if Goliah was to launch a successful bid for a seat on the Cherokee Council some day, hobnobbing with other great men was the backbone of any political career, and lots of bigwigs would be at this particular ceremony.

When he entered the small gallery at the front of Malloy's, Brendan Malloy was nowhere to be seen. The store was empty of patrons. Goliah retraced his steps back out to the plank board sidewalk that lined the main road. Only a handful of denizens milled about town. A couple of men were talking to the sheriff outside of the wheelwright shop, one woman and her child were about to enter Ames Undertaking, which doubled as a furniture store. That's when he spotted Brendan Malloy nailing a broadside to a post outside of the mail hack. Goliah knew nothing about any broadsides being authorized for posting, so he headed towards the hack to investigate.

The mail hack was not an official post office. That was in Vinita. Whenever someone from Feather Falls went to Vinita to get their mail, they'd also pick up and drop off back at the mail hack any other posts destined for residents of Route 2, Feather Falls' official mailing address.

Goliah noticed other broadsides hammered up across the road, and down. He stopped at the one in front of the livery stables.

CHEROKEE ENROLLMENT NOTICE it read at the top.

> *Enrollment Commissioner John W. Wallace will be in the Cherokee Nation, from July 19 to July 29, Inclusive, for the purpose of accepting verbal as well as written testimony from adopted Delaware, Shawnee, and also Cherokee Freedmen as to why they should be recognized as rightful citizens of the Cherokee Nation, and participate in per capita payments.*

Goliah snatched it down.

"Under whose authority are you posting this?" he asked, as he intercepted the proprietor on his way back to his store.

Malloy was a rotund man with a robust voice and red hair. "Bollocks, man," he said in a sing-song Irish brogue. "And a fine 'How's yer form' to ye, too." His nose wrinkled into the beginnings of a snarl.

"How do you do?" Goliah delivered the line in a perfunctory tone. "Who authorized you to post these?" With his knuckles, he thumped the back of the stack of papers Malloy held to his chest.

"Why, 'twas Agent Talbot, of course, fella."

Clem Talbot was the Indian Agent, the United States Government's eyes and ears of the goings on in Indian Territory. Some considered Talbot—a former captain in the Union Army—a spy who was always counting the Indians, creating censuses and rolls for this, that, and whatnot. Goliah, though, saw him as his personal pipeline to inside information on the Federals, what they were thinking, what they were up to, what they wanted from the Indian. That is, when he could catch Talbot dry of whiskey, which was not easy. Now Talbot was trying to count the Negroes? So they could get Cherokee money? And he had not been forewarned?

Well, he would see about that. Once the Freedmen got a per capita payment just like the Cherokees had already gotten, they would never leave. They would remain the scourge of Indian Territory, and the Cherokees had been punished by their presence long enough. After all, slavery was over. Why didn't they go back to where they belonged?

"What are ye lookin' so concerned about, fella? Yer alright." Malloy swatted Goliah on the back. "It's the niggers that's knackered. They're as broken a lot as ye ever seen. What do ye care about a small dog when yer a mountain lion?" He rolled the remainder of his broadsides up and stuffed them under his arm, then headed inside his store.

Goliah crumpled up his copy and shoved it into his pants pocket.

As he stormed past Malloy and the entrance to the store, Malloy yelled, "Hey there, fella. What about this hat ye ordered?"

Philura's hat would have to wait. Goliah turned right at the corner of Malloy's building, then caught himself when he looked up and realized he should have gone left. He about-faced towards the office of the Cherokee Sentinel Newspaper situated behind the general store. That was where he would find his friend and editor-in-chief Billy Bean Stick. Maybe Billy could shed some light on this matter. He would know what suddenly brought about all of this Freedmen enrollment nonsense.

They want to give niggers part of our money now? Why now? Goliah wondered. What was next, an allotment of land?

This mountain lion, he thought, would maul some small dogs to death before he ever let that happen.

Chapter Four

In the aftermath of Goliah's visit, Benjamin remained rooted in the yard like a tree on the shore with the waters around him rising higher and higher.

His gaze bounced from here to there, and back again like a crazed cat. He looked everywhere, except at Sput Louie.

He walked to the edge of the yard away from her and towards the potato field like he was pacing it off, but then changed his mind and came back. Stopping abruptly, Benjamin hastily righted the tattered chair that L.B. had tossed out with such ferocity, then started the same disturbing stride all over again.

All three of the boys silently huddled together watching their Pa pace, and their Ma look perplexed.

Sput thought to go to Ben, put her arm around him, let him nuzzle in the comfort of her neck. But affection was not the Cherokee way, and so it was not their way. They'd grown up with the mores and traditions of the tribe. No physical affection unless they were joining blankets, which they hadn't done in a few years now. That was as much her fault as his, though. With five babies created by their union having fallen stillborn, and their only daughter Lily having suffered an ungodly death by fire at the tender age of five—for which Sput blamed herself—it was like their coupling was cursed, desire dimmed. On both their parts, she presumed, because he never came to her anymore, either.

She had never seen Benjamin so flummoxed as he was at that moment. Sput had also never seen him become a casualty of his own father's deviltry. Throughout their years together, she'd heard about it in bits and pieces. She'd sewn them together to make a full story quilt. Still, there were blank patches.

Bloodline was a sour subject in the McClendon household. She hated to pour oil on already troubled waters, but they had been tossed off the land and made homeless in the course of a morning. Things needed to be done and done right away. They had to find a suitable place to camp until they could build a new home. Building anything new was a problem in itself since they had no permission to access the timber that abounded. They needed to gather any of their crops they could harvest, most likely none, as it was too early. And they had to bundle up all of their belongings and move them to the new location without a cart or a wagon to pack them in, or a mule or horse to pull it.

First and foremost, though, the head of the family needed to shake off his stupor.

When Benjamin's pacing brought him in Sput's vicinity, she took the opportunity to do just that. "Beggared by your own father," she groused, and shook her head in disgust.

Benjamin's stride came to a sudden stop like he'd reached the edge of a cliff and could go no further without falling to his death. A guttural sound escaped him, a garbled groan she'd never heard before. It almost scared her. It was like the *gyyyaaaahhhggg* hadn't come from him but some animal trapped inside him.

He turned and pierced her with a look that caused her to step back. "Well, beggin's what you been wantin' me to do all along, ain't it?" His chest began a slow heave that barely contained his bubbling anger.

So he had known earlier that they were in a spat and had correctly guessed what it concerned. Or maybe deep down, he just knew what was needed now more than ever. As much as he didn't want to, he would have to officially present his claim of Indian blood in Citizenship Court, which Indians could do at any time. Such a claim would garner him an allotment of land right away. To prove it up, though, he would have to drag Old Crow clucking and yapping, because such an assertion carried less weight than the fluff of a feather unless his father claimed him, too.

"We down to the bottom, Ben." A little spittle flew out when she enunciated his name. "Nothin' but a little maize left in the larder, and nobody's got work for you or the boys. Ain't made money off my medicine in a while." Her eyes wandered to the lean-to Benjamin had built as her healing hut. It had sat unused for weeks now, a reminder of how useless she felt outside of her family. "And now," she spoke slowly to calm her breathing, and still her thumping heart, "we ain't got no home."

"You see what that man just did?" Benjamin glared at her, waving his hand in the direction in which Goliah had beat his hasty retreat. "Like you say, he done beggared me. You. Us." His eyes darted towards the boys who were suddenly looking in every direction but theirs.

She fumbled for the right words. "Ya-huh. Old Crow's lower than a belly-crawler in a mud rut. Everybody know that." That was her effort to commiserate, to empathize, to let her husband know that whatever she said or did next, she was on his side, and they were in this together.

"And you want me to go to him," he said, "and try to *reason* with him?" His chin rose up, allowing him to look down at her with disdain. "On bended knee, I 'spect."

Sput adjusted her headscarf so that the knot in front was centered again. Somehow, in all the ruckus of the morning and all the sweating underneath, it had gone askew. She didn't care about her head rag, though. She began re-tying the knot, anyway, while she debated whether or not to say what she wanted to say. It only took a second to decide. "You coulda asked him when he was here," she blurted. "I thought you would have."

"Argghhh, woman." He slapped the back of his neck and began rubbing it like he'd just been stung by a bee. "You don't even—"

She jerked her hands down from the scarf. "Don't be mad at me, Benjamin McClendon." Her lip began to tremble. "You listen here." She unthinkingly clutched two handfuls of dress in her fists. "I...I am not the one who put the cry in your hate."

Her words were sharp enough to pierce. She ran her palm across her face as if that could somehow erase the hurt she now saw on his. His entire body shuddered like a ripple of lightning had slashed through him.

With his hairless jawline gone rigid, Benjamin slowly took the tip of his thumb and jammed it into the only part of his bare chest visible through his buckskin vest. "This man don't want nothin' to do with Old Crow." He hesitated, then said, much more quietly, "And Old Crow don't want nothin' to do with no nigger son."

Whenever they'd had this argument before, that idea, that sentiment, that truth was what halted the horses. They never got around to the fact of exactly how Benjamin came to be half Cherokee in the first place.

"I remembers that man," he snarled. "He might act like he forgot, but I remembers." He stared into the distance as if measuring his words. Choosing and picking ones that danced around his heart without stomping on it.

In the growing silence, Sput allowed her mind to go blank and willed herself to want for Benjamin to find the right words.

"Comin' around for my Ma like that. I was just a little boy. He—he would do things to her. Wrong things. Bad things. Hurtful things. Right in front of me." He banged his fist against his chest. "And then he look over at me and smile while he did it." A tear appeared in the corner of his eye but stubbornly refused to fall.

Not wanting to see his hurt, Sput hung her head to the side. "The *asodlvdi*," she mumbled, the Cherokee word for rape.

Rare was the occasion they talked about their time as slaves, but they never discussed the *asodlvdi*. This rough little nugget was the most Benjamin had ever revealed about that time of his life, other than to say that his Ma had told him Old Crow was his father.

It was disconcerting for Sput to see how much deeper he was affected by this particular part of his past than she had previously thought. Many things had happened to them during captivity. Every former slave had a story to tell. She and Benjamin tried to tamp down their old memories because ill will did no one any good. They put one foot in front of the other and kept moving forward. She knew he had been hurt by his blood father, but it usually showed up as a grudge, a resentment, or something beyond bitterness but just short of anger. Whenever Goliah's name came up, or they encountered him in town and cut across the road to avoid even walking past him, it always evoked ire. Never self-pity.

Benjamin stared at the spot on the ground Goliah's wagon no longer occupied. Maybe he was flashing back to his time in bondage.

Being enslaved left you with a certain mindset. After it stripped you naked of your dignity, it bore a hole in your soul and your spirit. It shucked the customs and traditions from your homeland and slashed away at your pride and your self-respect. It shamed you. It burrowed a hole through your trust in man with each ramming shove until all of the good inside you ended up whittled pieces of wood scattered to the wind. Then as it withdrew, it had the nerve to look down on you with an unapologetic eye as if it were your fault.

"He should have to pay for the *asodlvdi*," Sput said, trying to bring her husband back from wherever his mind had withdrawn.

Benjamin released a long sigh. "If I could hate that man more, I guess I would." He turned a softened eye towards the boys who were still standing together. "Hunter?"

Hunter hustled over.

"I want you to go see if you can find a place for us to roost for the meantime. Maybe find one of them houses some of them white intruders done abandoned when the tribe found out they was squattin', and run 'em off."

A perplexed look washed across Hunter's face. "In the meantime?"

"Archie, you go with your brother."

Archie came running over as well, with L.B. following him like a baby duck follows its mother. "Yes, sir, Pa."

"And when y'all get back, see what's ripe." He nodded to the two fields of crops that would have fed them for a few months had they been allowed to mature. "If anythin'. Even if it's just one cob."

It was Archie's turn to wear the puzzled expression. He and Hunter exchanged glances. "But Pa, it's gonna take more than a day to hunt down new lodgings."

"A day is all we got, Son."

L.B., looking like a beaver in need of a dam to build, asked "You want me to do thomethin', Pa? Huh?"

Benjamin reached up and rubbed the top of his young son's head. "You stay with your Ma and help pack up the place."

It did Sput good to see Benjamin standing tall again, looking alive and alert, the self-assured head of the family. Must have helped finally getting that bit of nastiness off his chest. They should have talked that out a long time ago.

"But I don't wanna thtay with Ma, Pa." L.B. folded his arms across his chest and collapsed into the chair he'd tossed onto the yard. His butt promptly busted through the already torn bottom, and he was stuck with his legs straight up in the air like a dead bug.

Archie nudged Hunter with his elbow. Hunter turned his head away too late to hide his widening grin. Sput ran to try and assist L.B., but it was Benjamin's eyes, lit with an inner glow, that gave them all permission to burst out laughing. It was a much-needed relief from a day that started out with a promising morning sun but had quickly descended into a dismal noonday. At least they could still laugh.

In his battle with the chair, L.B. only managed to squirm himself deeper into the hole, finally toppling it and himself over, decisively losing the skirmish.

While the three men took over the rescue efforts, a thought occurred to Sput. If the twins were going to hunt for a house, and see to the crops, and she and L.B. were going to pack up their meager belongings, that left only one thing for Benjamin to do.

Now a free man, L.B. dusted himself off and proclaimed, "If the thon thet you free, you will indeed be free."

Chuckling, Benjamin said, "The Son didn't set you free. The father did." Seemingly a little more lighthearted, Benjamin headed to the tanning shed attached to the east side of their house.

Sput followed him into the five-by-three-feet structure made up of four pine poles that held up a sloped roof of twisted twigs. He reached up and lifted a calfskin pouch off of its hook. He pulled the long strap over his head and rested it comfortably across one shoulder, exposing the image of a sunflower he had painstakingly embossed on the strap. He marked all of his tools and trappings in this manner, as a brand of sorts, the possible bag included.

A possible bag was what Indians used when traveling. It held anything they might possibly need during an outing. In his bag, Benjamin usually kept a piece of Sput's persimmon bread that would keep for a year, which was why it was always on hand. Sput thought there was a chance he might have a piece of deer jerky in there, too, but probably not. That would have been eaten a while ago. She knew for sure that he had a snippet of each son's hair so that they would be with him always. But mostly, he used it to store anything of value he might come across in his travels. But to where was he traveling? Could she hope upon the prospect that he was really, actually, finally going to ask Old Crow to claim him?

He didn't reach for his long-blade knife, so he wasn't going hunting. Besides, Hunter had already brought the day's supper home. They would eat well that night. Plus, Benjamin already had his short blade sheathed on his belt. As she moved in further, he must have seen her questioning eyes, because he winked at her. "Cain't go bear hunting with a switch."

Sput blinked hard. "If you goin' bear huntin', you gon' need a bigger knife than that." She nodded at the short blade in his sheath that some folks called a scalping knife.

He slowly shook his head no. "This," he patted the calfskin case, "is always for just-in-case. Won't need it for where I'm goin'." He pulled his kerchief from his back pocket and wiped sweat from his brow, without sullying the sunflower she had embroidered on it.

She bit her bottom lip in anticipation. "Well, where you goin', is it a secret?"

Again, he shook his head no. "Goin' to tackle the devil."

Chapter Five

That evening, a savagely red sunset cast an ominous glow over the land while Sput awaited the return of her menfolk. It was a beautifully eerie sky, and she'd never seen a twilight quite like it.

Perched in the rocking chair she'd dragged to the front yard, she was swinging and swaying, marking time until everything that was on the line could be resolved. She knew it would be. Benjamin had finally decided to do the right thing and confront that devil, Old Crow. It was taking longer than expected, though. She knew it wouldn't go smoothly, but she hoped he was giving Goliah a serious what-for.

When the crimson rays in the distance suddenly shaped into a silhouette, Sput lurched out of her rocker.

It was about time. As Sput's gaze bore down on the bleary blob, it advanced and expanded. When it split into twin shadows—one big, one small—she stomped her foot and plopped back down in her rocker.

Benjamin, not the twins, should have returned first.

Her mind was full of excuses as to what was keeping her husband. Maybe he'd gone to see Two Bird first, his friend and town elder. Benjamin always sought his counsel in times of trouble. Two Bird was not only the tallest man they knew, but also the wisest. He always had sage advice no matter the dilemma. However, Two Bird lived in the opposite direction from where Ben had headed.

On the other hand, maybe Ben had gotten himself into a fix with Old Crow. She would be to blame for that. Still, she wouldn't worry just yet. Benjamin could handle himself. But if he hadn't returned by the time the moon had completely chased the sun away that would be cause for concern.

As her sons neared, Archie was hunched over in a sorrowful stride. Hunter's broad shoulders cut an able-bodied figure against the horizon, but his forlorn gait told her everything she needed to know. Even Sinker, the ferret, was sprawled motionless across Hunter's shoulder like a wounded soldier being carried home from battle.

When they reached Sput, she said nothing. She let her silence ask the question her mouth couldn't quite bring to bear—*have you seen your Pa.*

Hunter shrugged. "Nothin'. Didn't find nothin'."

Instead of releasing the breath she had been holding, she sucked in more air. "Did you come across your Pa?" Her overfilled lungs pushed her voice an octave higher.

Archie looked up. "He ain't here?" Archie always tried to use proper English. Unless he was tired or addled, or both.

It was Sput's turn to shrug and feign indifference as if she hadn't been worrying up a thunderclap of a headache all day.

The twins began dragging towards the house, Hunter in the lead by a hair's breadth, as usual.

"We'll find a place tomorrow," Sput said, as she gazed across the once-again empty horizon. "You boys go see what can be harvested like your Pa said, now."

They both stopped, but only Hunter responded, as if by some unspoken agreement between the two brothers. "Cain't we eat first?"

"Best do your work first. It's gon' be too dark to see anythin' pretty soon. Besides, supper's cold. I'll heat it up right good and hot by the time y'all done."

Sput had already skinned and parboiled the red fox Hunter had snared that morning. She'd wanted some poke greens or wild yams to throw in the pot as well, and had sent L.B. off to find such. All he came back with was two pockets full of chinquapin nuts, and a Mason jar with three dying bees.

While the boys ambled towards the field, Sput stoked the kindling underneath the pot hanging from the cooking crane in the front yard. By the time she coaxed the embers into a full-fledged fire, she heard a ruckus coming from the mound field.

Straining to see, she saw Archie grappling with ferocity trying to wrench himself free from his brother's hold. Hunter had him pulled into a backward bear hug so that only Archie's lower arms were free to flail against the vigor of Hunter's strength. It was Hunter's typical way of fighting so as not to hurt his little brother.

L.B. came running out of the house, past Sput and towards the ruckus. He hated to see his brothers in fisticuffs, and always took it personally when they fought as if it were somehow his fault.

Sput, though, did not move.

The twins had had their differences on just about everything since before they'd learned to talk. They usually settled them before they drew blood, though. Sput thought it was better that they get their anger out before their Pa came home. She considered herself a better mother than a wife because she knew how to handle her boys. She let them go at it.

Archie scrambled his feet hard against the dirt. Being smaller, he had to fight smarter, proving true the old Indian adage that even a small mouse has anger. She could see that small mouse was angling to push his big brother towards the bang board on the corn cart. The bang board was a high side-panel used during harvest to deflect ears of corn thrown by the shucker. If you hit it just right, the cob would ricochet into the cart. But Archie used it to bang Hunter's back into it instead, and they both boomeranged to the ground.

In the scuffle, Hunter fell sideways and hit his head on a pointy rock. With a look of shock on his face, he grabbed the back of his head, while Archie clambered up and away.

Hunter must have seen blood, Sput thought, but there couldn't have been much. Nevertheless, it was time to break it up. They needed some *dohi* in their lives right about then, some peace.

Before she could reach them, Hunter lunged up and went towards his brother again, but L.B. weaseled himself in between them, while Sinker darted his narrow body in and out of the way of their footfalls. Maybe the little furry thing would trip them, but maybe they would step on him. Sput hurried her pace. By the time she reached them, Hunter had pushed Archie away and backed up from the fracas. "Archie wanna burn the crops, Ma," he appealed to her upon approach.

Sput mindlessly clutched her lambskin amulet. "And why would we do that?" She turned towards Archie to await an explanation.

L.B. answered for him. "No one can tame the tongue, for it ith full of deadly poithon," he said with his own untamable tongue. L.B. had never learned to read, but he could remember a Bible verse after hearing Archie read it to him just once. He would squirrel it away in his memory, then crack it open at his whim. Most of the time, his selection ill fit the situation, and they would just ignore him.

"So Old Crow won't profit from ours, and Pa's hard work," Archie huffed, still winded from the tussle. "That's why."

The twins called Benjamin Pa even though they knew he was not their blood father. Their father was a fellow slave Sput had known only briefly during her exile in Texas. She was twelve or thirteen by then, and so was Willie Lynch. They'd grown close when she treated the cancer on his leg by applying sticky beggar lice to it like she'd been taught by her Ma. But then Willie got wind of the 1st Kansas Colored Infantry recruiting slaves to fight in the Freedom War, and he ran off to join them before either of them knew she was with child. She had never seen him again.

"That's food you talkin' 'bout, boy," Hunter said. "Them's God's gift, and I'm not..." he flat-handed Archie upside his head to the beat of his words, "...gonna..." THWAP "...let..." THWAP "...you destroy it." THWAP, THWAP, THWAP.

Archie ducked with each swat and tried to block the blows with his forearm until Sput put her hand on Hunter's offending arm. He obediently stopped.

"You think Old Crow won't know who set fire to these crops?" she asked.

"The cobs are thin, Ma, and the silk's still wet," Archie protested.

Hunter felt for more blood on the back of his head. "It's good enough to take to the Green Corn Festival."

"That's a whole month from now, Ma." Archie's eyes pleaded with his mother. "It's gon' be hard brown corn by then. He gave Hunter a side-eye. "Old Crow's hard brown corn."

Sput didn't even have to look at the mound field. She had figured as much. The crops were useless. To them. "Well, that's it then, ain't it?" She turned to leave. "Ya-huh," she said in answer to her own question.

#

After the boys had eaten and dragged their bedrolls from the house to the coolness of the brush arbor where they usually slept in summer, Sput went to her herb garden. In their third and last field, she harvested what medicinal plants she could. Only the heartleaf, skullcap stalks, wild Sienna, and her giant comfrey root were ripe enough for pulling.

By the time she finished, the moon was in its midnight position. Still no Benjamin. She brushed worry to the wayside.

She crept past the boys already asleep under the arbor, probably anticipating an early rise. They lined up as neatly as beads in a necklace. Her arms were full of herbs ready to be hung to dry in the moonlight. She was grateful for her bounty. It was the only thing that had gone her way all day. Except for Benjamin finally seeking his father's help. Although it remained to be seen whether that went her way as well. At this point, she didn't care if he came home with or without the promise of an allotment of land. She just wanted to know that he was safe and hadn't fallen in the way of some gang of thieves holed up on Devil's Ridge, or found himself—God forbid—on the business end of the gun or knife of some train robber, horse thief, or bushwhacker, all of which were plentiful in Indian Territory.

To the wayside those thoughts went as well.

As she entered the house to trim and tie the herbs, one of the floor-boards beneath her feet wobbled loosely. It made a knocking sound. Sput shrugged it off. She had bigger things to worry about and didn't have to fret fixing that now. That would be Goliah's problem.

Pruned and tied by their stems, the herbs were finally ready to be hung upside down from the nails on the arbor's rim specifically placed there for herb-drying purposes. Once outside, she reached up to feel for the nails quietly in the moonlight so as to not rouse the boys. She didn't feel any.

Moving her hand down further, then further still, she wondered whether she had misgauged where the nails were. Each and every one of them was missing.

A thought struck her, and she re-entered the house to give the loose floorboard more scrutiny. There were empty holes where nails should have been. She walked the rest of the one-room house, giving the floor a close inspection and saw that nails were missing from just about every puncheon plank.

What was happening here? Where were all the nails?

All of their belongings were packed in burlap bags and neatly tied bundles piled against the wall. Digging through the stack, Sput found the tin can that Benjamin reserved for nails scrounged from old discarded furniture, or mined from the Feather Falls chuck yard where people discarded their unwanted odds and ends. He'd even found a few cast iron spikes left over from the railroad construction over in Tahlequah and had fashioned one of them into a door latch. The tin can usually contained a smattering of nails. Now, though, it was full. From their house, she surmised.

This had to be the work of Archie.

Back outside, she glanced over at Archie who promptly rolled onto his side and faced away from her. Had he been waiting and watching for her reaction? And was he waiting for praise or punishment?

Not a modicum of anger could she muster. All Sput could do was shake her head at him. He had probably figured, and rightly so, that they would need the nails to build their new home, wherever that was to be. Wooden dowels just didn't hold as well. And if Archie couldn't kill the crops, at least he could sabotage the house.

She started towards Archie, but something stopped her. She understood his reasoning. Life was not fair, but at least her sons had been born free. Did they even know how blessed they were? They would never be chained like an animal, and for that, she would always be thankful. Life had been unfair to her as well, but what was she to do about that? More than that, what could she do? She was but a small mouse herself.

Turning towards the useless mound field where hope no longer resided, a sting of sorrow pierced her heart. Sorrow for her lot in life, sorrow for sending her husband on what seemed more and more like a wild goose chase.

Then an idea poked its way into her head.

Looking at the bundles of herbs in her sweaty hands, she fathomed one thing that she could do. Her mother, Ma Bay, had taught it to her as a child when Sput was her *tsila*—her apprentice—learning the skills of a medicine woman. It involved a concoction of rhubarb leaves, mixed with a little wormwood, and a pinch of comfrey root thrown in. And what else? Anything that would poison crops and make it look like a natural death.

Chapter Six

Two Bird stood six-foot-eight and had a voice that boomed like boulders down a mountain. He was also the only man in Feather Falls who wore a dress.

Be that as it may, the form-fitting bodice with the box-pleated skirt in no way interfered with his choking the man he now had clinched in the crook of his massive arm.

The blond-hair—as Two Bird referred to every white man, even if they had red hair—flailed like a minnow in the maws of a pike. His captive squiggled and squirmed. He dusted up clouds of dirt in Tincy Long Bone's front yard with the heels of his fancy shoes to, what? Knock Two Bird off his feet? Two Bird almost laughed at the thought. However, he was not a laughing man, and this was not a laughing matter. Especially when the blond-hair still would not relinquish the polished wooden box.

Tincy Long Bone, the whole reason behind the scuffle, grabbed at the infamous contraption. *"I want no paper likeness of me so it can be buried face down in the dirt,"* she spat in Cherokee.

Not the least bit winded from the one-armed scuffle, Two Bird said for a second time, *"I desire it very much that you give her the picture box."* This time, he said it more politely than he probably should have, given that the man's hair was leaving a grease spot on his purple paisley dress. After all, this was no summer sack dress he was wearing. A whiff of the man's hair pomade stung his nose as Two Bird reached around with his free hand and tried to knock the box out of his hands and towards Tincy.

The blonde-hair yanked it out of Two Bird's reach. "Clem...Clem... help!" he yelled to the man who had brought him to Cherokee country but was now too far away to hear him. "I... haven't even...taken...the photograph yet."

The English words fell on non-English ears. To Two Bird, the English language sounded like the noise of a silver spoon rattling a tin can, slapping against the bark of a tree. By speaking it, the cameraman had demonstrated not only his ignorance of the language of the people whose country he was intruding upon, but of their customs and beliefs as well.

"Let...me...go," the man managed to squeeze out.

Two Bird could have easily lifted him off of the ground and completely cut off his air, but he did not want to kill the man. He had come to Tincy's that morning to honor her husband who lay dying in the house behind them. Shortly after he and other clansmen had begun gathering in front of her house—some sitting in chairs, some on the ground—the two blonde-hairs arrived. The Kodak man and the Indian Agent. Agent Clem Talbot had gone one way dragging his measuring stick in the dirt. The cameraman headed in the direction of the circle of men at the very moment that Tincy had come out to serve her guests meat skin soup.

Just as the blond-hair put his hand in the middle of Tincy's chest to stop her mid-stride, every Indian gathered there rose, ready to come to her defense. However, Two Bird's long legs got him to her first. The others let him handle it.

Agent Talbot finally heeded his cohort and came running. Talbot had a thick dark mustache that hid his lips, and a thick round belly that Two Bird thought made him run like a grandmother.

"*Wait, let him go,*" Talbot huffed in stilted Cherokee. "*Let him go, Two Bird.*" His labored trot came to an abrupt halt just two feet short of the tussling trio. "*He has permission from the tribe.*" He looked at Two Bird's arm like he wanted to peel it from around his friend's neck, but couldn't figure out how.

Two Bird snorted. An editorial on what he deemed to be the misguided notions of tribal leaders and any permission they might give to a ghost-faced blond-hair.

"*The popular press thinks Indians still lives in tipis.*" Talbot lifted his black felt derby and scratched his head as he watched the cameraman's face turn red. "*We need to correct that for the good of the Indian.*"

"*I spit on words burned onto paper, and those who trust them,*" Two Bird said of the white man's newspapers. "*Cherokee have never lived in tipis.*"

"Precisely *what makes pictures necessary, to prove how civilized Cherokee are, to preserve real Indian life before it fast disappears.*"

"*Shuh.*" Two Bird lifted his chin and looked down his nose at Talbot. "*Cherokee need prove nothing to no one. Cherokee are not here to teach white men the ways of the Indian. We are not the makers of things known,*" which is how the tribe referred to teachers. He tired of constantly having to explain tribal ways to outsiders who shouldn't have been there in the first place. "*Be it remembered, we are the original people. Only the Cherokees can preserve the Cherokee way of life.*"

With that, he released the blond-hair. His face now crimson, the man slithered to the ground like a stunned snake. Two Bird picked up the hem of his dress and stepped over him as if he were steering clear of hog swill.

Agent Talbot shook his head at his comrade. "Just give her the damn photograph, Thad," he grunted in English. "We'll take pictures somewhere else." He fell in line behind Two Bird who was heading towards Tincy's house.

The cameraman, still holding the box with one hand, wiped his eyes with his other hand, and gawked at the giant in a dress. "Was that a man or a woman?"

With the blond-hair distracted, Tincy reached down and snatched the box away from him. She backed up to a safe distance a few feet away and turned the box upside down. She shook it, and nothing came out. She threw it on the ground and stomped on it. She beat it, sat on it, and when it didn't crack, or break, or split open she spat on it.

Despite all of the commotion, Two Bird felt himself being trailed. He stopped and turned so sharply that Talbot ran smack into him, causing the agent to bounce back a step. Two Bird did not laugh at the weakling who had the stench of day-old whiskey fuming from his breath. Clearly, the agent had more to say, but Two Bird didn't want to hear it, let alone smell it. Unless it was about the reason for Tiger Tec Hee's imminent death, and what the agent was going to do about it. He doubted they would do anything. That just meant one less Indian in the white man's way.

Two Bird himself stepped back and trained a suspicious eye on Talbot. *"Each time Cherokee land is measured,"* he looked at the notched stick in Talbot's hand, *"a count of the Indian cannot be far behind."* He had seen the Cherokee Nation plotted and platted many times before. Each time, it seemed the white man found more and more land to be deemed surplus. Every time Indian land was deemed surplus, it was then sold or leased to the United States government on behalf of the Cherokee under the guise of benefitting the Cherokee. That was the lie freely given by the white man and freely swallowed by tribal leaders. Two Bird knew better, though.

Surplus, he repeated in his mind, because he loathed letting an English word pass his lips.

"Well," said Agent Talbot, *"you are half right. There is a new stipend to be gifted, so land must be surveyed, and a new roll must be created."*

"A debt owed is not a gift given," he protested, not understanding nor caring enough to ask what the agent meant by "half right."

"But *it is almost twenty dollars,* Per capita, U.S. Dollars," Talbot added in English at the end, like he was throwing in a small stick of candy to sweeten a large jar of pickles.

"Per capita" and "U.S. dollars" were just two more English terms Two Bird had come to understand out of necessity, and against his will. Yes, he could use the money. He turned and looked at the men who had resumed their positions in the sitting circle. They could all use it.

Yet, with that money came more white intruders, he was sure. Pretty soon there would be more whites than Indians living in Indian Territory.

Whites who did not have to answer to the Cherokee, and could break Cherokee laws with impunity. It was disruptive to all of the tribes in Indian Territory that whites fell under the jurisdiction of federal law and could not be touched by Lighthorsemen, the Indian arm of the law. Where was the power in that? Two Bird wondered. Where was the sovereignty in that?

"*Is the white man counted in such a way?*" Two Bird doubted it.

Agent Talbot's eyes met his with a steadfast stare. "*Actually, yes. Such a thing is called a census, and it happens every ten years.*"

Two Bird looked away as he weighed this new information. It seemed that they counted Indians every two or three years. In fact, they had received a per capita payment just a couple of years before. It was fine for the white man to count white people if such a thing was true. Why count the Indian, though? Blond-hairs always made the Indians their business, like they were children who could not manage themselves. It made no sense. His gut instinct was not to trust this blond-hair, or any other one, for that matter. He would not help string his enemy's bow.

He pulled his lips tight.

Two Bird was not a man of many words, but when he did speak, you never knew if he was going to coddle you like a kitten or cut you like a razor. When dealing with blond-hairs, it was usually the latter.

"*When rough edges are shaved off of the truth,*" he said, "*it then becomes a lie.*" And he knew this man was lying about something.

Chapter Seven

Sput Louie awakened the next morning curled on her husk-filled pallet with the tin cup still in her right hand. Fearing what she'd find when she opened her eyes, she reached out with her left, and blindly cast about for her husband.

Just as the cup was empty of her crop-poisoning concoction, Benjamin's side of their pallet was empty of him.

If he had been there, though, *uyo ayelvdi* would have been the first thing out of her mouth. Apologizing in his favored language should make the bitter better. Benjamin always said the Cherokee language sounded like purple dragonflies sipping from a sea of orange sweet milk. Sput couldn't quite picture that image, but it sure sounded pretty, and she guessed that was the point.

Yet she wasn't at all sure what she had to apologize for. Maybe the things she'd said to him, the deep-rooted hurt she'd caused to come to a head. Whatever it was that made him not come home the previous night, humbling herself to him would be a good way to a fresh start.

That was assuming nothing untoward was the cause of his absence. Then it occurred to her that every now and again, Benjamin would disappear for a night to clear his head. Especially when there was a problem to be solved. He liked to walk on the wind, as he called it, and think on his woes.

Today felt different. Not just because they had to be off of the land by nightfall, though that was a major concern. Her gut churned, twisted, knotted inside. It wasn't from hunger.

Rising, she opened the front door expecting to see the boys still asleep under the arbor. She was going to announce breakfast would be on soon, but found that all three of their pallets—which had been rolled and propped against the door—fell in on her feet. Her sons were gone. Resuming their search for a place to live, no doubt, trying to fulfill their Pa's orders since they'd had no luck the day before. She was relieved they appeared to have taken L.B. with them.

So without bothering to eat breakfast, or changing out of the clothing she'd fallen asleep in the night before, Sput decided not to wait for Benjamin to return but would go out and find him. Who knew? Maybe she would run smack dab into him on his way back.

Until then, she would hunt for her husband at all of his favorite haunts.

First stop was Two Bird's, the wisest man she and Benjamin knew. He had been one of the first people she'd met when she returned home after the Freedom War. Two Bird had already been Benjamin's confidante and he'd quickly become hers. She figured maybe Ben had gone there seeking the sage's counsel.

As soon as she climbed the steep hill to his cabin, though, she remembered what she'd heard about Tiger Tee Hee. Two Bird would likely be at his house comforting him as he lay dying. Sure enough, she found no one home except the mixed menagerie of wild animals inexplicably drawn to Two Bird's house even when he was elsewhere. It was like the coons and coyotes were tethered there by the elder's lingering scent.

Sput understood that. She, herself, had thrown on one of Benjamin's old shirts over her clothes before she'd left that morning. She loved his smell of liniment and fresh forest pine.

After coming to naught at Two Bird's, she trudged over to the sweat lodge near Clinch Creek where Ben sometimes went to clear his head and pray. But there was no lingering scent of kinnik-kinnik, the inner bark of the red willow Benjamin would have burned in order to let the smoke carry his prayers to God, and no sign of the turkey feather he would have used to aid its drift. All she found there were willow poles bowed together and tied at the top to form the skeleton of the dome-shaped hut.

The next stop was Lake Watanuga. Benjamin liked to take the waters there. She had hoped to find his clothing spread out on boulders at the water's edge and a naked Benjamin in the water. She found neither. Aside from the squeaking clicks of water beetles, the scene was eerily lonely.

By mid-day, she figured she'd walked at least ten miles, though it felt like twenty. At a loss as to where to search next, she decided to take a rest at Ma Bay's old stomping ground and Sput Louie's present one.

Ma Bay and her young apprentice Sput Louie had discovered the Ugly Tree during one of the rare occasions they'd been loaned out to tend a sick slave on a neighboring farm. Ma Bay liked the dreary tree because she said it reminded her of the baobab tree of her ancestral homeland in Africa. The story she reveled in telling an inquisitive young Sput was that the baobab tree was never happy. It was a fleshy tree that hated its wrinkled bark so much that it complained to the Creator that its skin looked like an old rhinoceros. When it saw a slender, graceful palm tree, it cried out that it wanted to be taller. When it saw the flame tree blooming with red flowers, it wanted blossoms. When it saw the fig tree, it began to pray for fruit. God became so angry that He yanked the baobab up from its roots and replanted it upside down to keep it quiet. Its bottom roots became its top growth, and it was truly hideous, just like the Ugly Tree Sput Louie now saw up ahead through a stand of pines.

The Ugly Tree was set alone and apart from the other evergreens as if it had committed some egregious forestry offense and was sentenced to die alone in exile.

Three times as tall as a man, and two times as wide, the dead gray pine had not given life to a leaf in all the years Sput had been going there. Its stunted branches and truncated top made it look like a headless beast whose arms had been chopped off.

Tired and footsore, Sput rested her back against the beast and did what she always did upon first arriving at the Ugly Tree. She silently thanked Ma Bay for finding the tree, and the Lord for saving her life there.

She'd been rescued at that very spot right after the War when all the slaves had been granted their freedom. Sput was about thirteen years old by then. After setting out on her long walk from Texas—where she had been sent to slave for Old Crow during the Freedom War—she headed straight back to Feather Falls to reunite with her Ma and Pa.

Soon after arriving in town with her two babies in tow—one tied on her back, and the bigger twin on her hip—she found other former slaves milling about town homeless, broken and dispirited. They were all looking for something, waiting for something, hoping for something. Feather Falls was in a state of flux. Sput likened freedmen to frogs trapped at the bottom of a well, unable to get out and move on with their lives. They weren't looking for a handout, just a hand up. Although all coloreds were willing to work, very few former Confederate Cherokee were inclined to pay for that labor since it had previously been unpaid. Negroes wanted to be as self-sufficient as people who had been free their whole lives. Because freedom was not tantamount to equality, though, they were starting miles behind everyone else.

Some, however, were on a mission like her, looking for family from whom they'd been separated or sold. Asking everyone she encountered whether they'd seen her parents or even knew Ma Bay and Boslan Lynch, Sput soon learned that they had both died during a cholera outbreak while she'd been away.

She cursed Goliah Lynch that day as she'd done on so many others. But she couldn't wallow. She still had a family, her only family, her twins. She kept moving one foot in front of the other.

Sput had roamed here and there, looking for work, and scrounging for scraps to feed herself and keep her milk from drying up. At night, she would sleep behind buildings like Malloy's store-haus, or sneak into someone's horse barn and be gone by daylight. It was either that or sleep under trees, behind bushes, in logs, using her baby sling as their only blanket.

One day, desperate, weary, and tired of wandering, she remembered Ma Bay's Ugly Tree. She headed there to contemplate a plan for what to do next.

When she finally found it, it was just as she had remembered. The tree looked as lost and forlorn as she felt. She took some comfort in that, as she closed her eyes and sat with her back against the bark rutted with dry rot. Its texture was as rough as her life had been thus far.

With a baby latched onto each breast, suckling futilely, she drifted off to sleep.

Startled awake—by what, she couldn't immediately discern—her eyes darted up, down and all around until they landed on a man. He was standing to her left, holding a rope connected to a bony horse that sagged in the middle.

"Are both of them boys?" the man asked, removing his flop hat just as brusquely as he'd asked the question.

Even though he had surprised her by his sudden appearance, for some reason, she was not afraid. He was a boy of maybe sixteen, she guessed, but had a man-like face. The man-boy's eyes were copper in color, and kind in expression. Still, she squeezed her babies tight to her bosom and nodded yes in answer to his question.

The man-boy pulled what looked like a piece of deer jerky from his shirt pocket. "Here," he said, tearing off a chunk of the dried meat and shoving it in Sput's face.

Small things talk loud, and his offering of food was a kindness that said a lot about the stranger. Hungry, but having no free hand with which to grab the mouth-watering morsel, Sput tried to pull her bigger as-yet-to-be-named baby from her breast.

"Ow," she cried, as the further away she pulled him, the tighter he clamped down, and the longer her nipple stretched.

She knew the smaller one—also nameless—was weak and needed whatever fluid her breast had left, so she was reluctant to pull him off first. But she had to if she was going to eat. He put up no fuss as she gently laid him on his back in the dirt, and took the hunk of meat.

The tall man-boy promptly picked him up and tenderly dusted him off. His eyes went from Sput to the littlest baby, to the big one, and then back to her with a look of disbelief.

"Are these boys *dinitlawa?*" he asked, using the Cherokee word for twins. "That big one there done sucked up all the size from this here one." In the world of the Cherokee, twins were regarded as special and thought to have unusual powers. So he seemed to ogle mother and sons with renewed vigor.

His fixed stare made her feel as if he knew something about her, like who she was, what she wanted, from where she hailed. After all, he had rightly presumed she understood Cherokee.

She knew something about him, too, though. Clearly, his facial features were at odds with each other. The narrow nose said one thing, but his lush lips told a different version of the same story. That story was that this Indian was half-Negro.

"My sons gonna help me work the farm," he said matter-of-factly.

Sput stopped chewing and looked all around. She assumed he had arrived alone, but now second guessed that presumption. "Where your sons at?"

"Ain't got none."

"Where your farm?"

"Ain't got one of them, neither."

Sput raised one eyebrow, but then shrugged and took another pull on the jerky.

"Gon' have one right soon, though," he said, "a farm. They gon' give all the Freedmen use of they own land. Any day now. They even wrote it down in one of them there treaties."

Sput pressed her lips together, then pinched her big baby's cheek, forcing him to finally relinquish her nipple. As soon as he did, she quickly closed her shirt over the exposed breast, and pushed herself to a standing position. She adjusted the bigger baby on her hip and grabbed the smaller one back from the man. "These here is babies, sir. Cain't work no land you ain't got, noway."

"Ain't seen you around these parts before." He put his hat back on.

"Been in Texas." Then a thought gave her pause. "What about the women, the free women? They gets land, too?"

He shrugged. "Don't rightly know." Then he nodded at her babies. "Where's they *edoda*?"

"Don't rightly know where they Pa is."

The stranger smiled. Not with his lips, but with his eyes.

"I got a place to stay," he announced. "You and your boys more than welcome there if'n you need it."

Grabbing the rope lead, he turned his horse and pointed him away, preparing to leave.

Her ears prickled, and she took the tiniest of steps forward. She wanted to ask what kind of place it was. A hut? A brush shed? A lean-to? Instead, she asked him, "Your wife like it there?"

"It's a roof and four walls," he replied, as if he'd read her mind, heard her thoughts, knew what she needed. He paused and rubbed his horse's snout. "That's good enough for now. 'Til I get a wife." He looked off into the distance, but not before he'd shot her a quick side-glance.

She thought about all the nights she and her babies had slept out-side in the wilderness, alone and unprotected. Should she go with this man? Even for a night? While she got her plan together? She didn't even know his name.

"You can stay as long as you want," he added, gently stroking his horse.

Sput pursed her lips. "Why should I go with you at all," she heard herself say, despite his soft eyes and the prospect of food, lodging, pro-tection. "You probably livin' in a brush shed." She gave him the side-eye while she waited for an answer.

He chuckled. "You a spitfire, huh? What your name, gal?"

"Sput Louie. What your name?"

He smiled with his lips that time. "Well, that name just say it all, don't it, Sput?" He tilted his head to the side, as if he'd never been asked his name before, and needed to formulate a suitable answer. "I used to be Isaac. That be my slave name. Benjamin now, though. Ain't settled on a last name yet."

Sput nodded her approval. Like lots of other former slaves had done already, she, too, would change her name. The last one, anyway. She would never be known as a Lynch again.

"It ain't a brush shed, neither," he went on to explain. "Walls are wood, sure enough, but the roof—well, it's a old wagon canvas. Keeps bird droppin's off your head, though, and no dew will settle on you in the night."

Sounded more like a box shed than a brush shed, which wasn't much better. Still, it had one more roof than she had, and she was tired of having her babies wake up damp every day.

Benjamin watched her struggle to put her little one back into the sling tied to her back.

"I can make you a cradleboard if you like," he said, stepping forward to help slide the baby into its wrap, while she balanced the other one on her hip.

With her babies secure and ready to continue their aimless journey, Sput stood there and waited for him to mount his horse leave. It appeared as though he was waiting for her to shove off first.

Finally, Benjamin backed up a couple of steps closer to his horse, keeping his eyes on Sput the entire time. At the spot where there should have been a saddle but was instead a blanket, he hunched over and laced his fingers together setting forth a proposition in the form of a simulated stirrup as their was no real one.

She paused as if feeling the weight of her babies for the very first time, and wondering how she'd walked all the way from Texas carrying them all by herself. How much longer would she have to roam? If her memories of Indian Territory served her, she might get through summer living out and about, eating wild greens and the occasional varmint, but the coming winter would be hard and white.

In the lengthening silence, she took the baby from her hip and laid him face down on the horse's neck at the nook where mane met blanket. Holding him in place with one hand, she grabbed the mane with the other, put her foot in Benjamin's finger-laced stirrup, while he pushed her up to straddle atop the horse.

They'd been together ever since.

Until now, she thought, as a screech of paroquets broke her from her reminiscences. She no longer had babies in her arms, and Benjamin was certainly not there. She was alone at the Ugly Tree once again.

Squinting skyward, she took in the flock of noisy green-breasted birds with tawny orange heads and forked tails. They glided in waves of tranquility. She stood to better behold the swiftness of the lines of the flying formation, and the solidarity of the clusters. They made a sharp turn all in unison. The cluster split, and then merged again. Birds that fly together survive together. She and Benjamin had survived together, were surviving together, would still survive together. As soon as he came home, she thought.

That's when she saw it.

It was dead center of her line of sight. Not in the sky, but hanging from a twig at the top of the Ugly Tree. Something white. Something small. Something man-made.

But how did it get way up there?

Curious, she decided to climb the tree for a closer inspection. She hiked her skirt and placed her foot on first one branch collar—the only surviving remnant of the branch—and then the next. Like climbing a rickety ladder, she proceeded slowly, carefully, in case the collars were deadwood that might break away under even her light weight.

The higher she got, the clearer the item became, and what she could make out of the object confounded her.

It was a kerchief embroidered with a bit of yellow and green purposely tied to the tree with two overhand knots, one on top of the other. Who would do that? And why?

The more she stared, the clearer the decorative pattern became. And then she was truly astonished.

It was a sunflower. Just like the sunflower the McClendon's used as their brand.

She removed it from the twig and felt the weight of something inside it. She hurried back down to the ground. Gazing at it in the palm of her hand, she realized not only was the embellishment like the McClendon's sunflower, but it was the McClendon's sunflower. And she had embroidered it herself.

On Benjamin's kerchief.

She remembered seeing it hanging from his back pocket as he'd left for Old Crow's place the day before. That meant that between then and now, Benjamin had been there. At the Ugly Tree.

Her heart flooded with relief that he was okay. She could put that worry to bed. But was he okay? If he'd had the opportunity to tie this kerchief to the one place he knew she'd eventually come, not only was he okay, but he was trying to tell her something. What, though? And why wouldn't he just come home and give it to her in person, say it with words?

The objects inside were light and delicate.

Carefully untying the knots, she opened it and saw something she'd never seen before, something she didn't recognize, but something Benjamin evidently wanted her to have.

"What the devil are these small things?"

Chapter Eight

As soon as Sput Louie got home, she planned to lay the oblong items out delicately down on the table on top of their kerchief like they were golden eggs.

Before she entered her house, though, she circled it twice, checking all four directions to make sure her sons were not on approach.

No sign of them. It was only mid-afternoon, so they probably wouldn't be back for a while, unless they'd been fortunate enough to find a place to set up house. For some reason, her instincts told her to keep the news of the kerchief and its contents secret until she figured out what they were and what they meant. If life had taught her nothing else, it had taught her to follow her gut.

Pausing at her front door, she listened first. No sound or movement came from within. It was too hot for them to be inside the windowless house in this heat, anyway. She, herself, wanted to leave the door open but thought it ill advised. She would have to suffer through the swelter.

After dragging a ladder-back chair up to the table, she investigated the clues laid out before her, scrutinizing every inch of them. She gently rolled the gobs from one end of the cloth to the other. She thought it out, over, and through. What were these things and what was Benjamin trying to tell her with them?

The only odor she detected smelled like sweat from hard-working men, mucus from colds and coughs, mixed with the tang of herbs and liniments. But that was probably from the four walls of her house.

Maybe it wasn't a *what*, he was trying to tell her, she mused, but a *where*. First, though, perhaps she should try and figure out the *why* of it.

She studied them without touching them. No meaning shone through. Trying to decipher this was like trying to bite her nose. The answer was there, but just out of reach.

Without warning the door burst open.

Startled, Sput jumped up so fast she knocked her chair over backward.

L.B. entered huffing and hollering. "Mama, Mama." He danced in place, rocking side to side. "We found a hole in a rock."

Hunter entered next, doffing his hat. "Ain't exactly a hole, Ma, and ain't exactly a rock," he explained, then his eyes immediately flashed on the kerchief and what lay on top of it. He frowned. "You eatin' pawpaw fruit?" he asked, in a tone of disbelief.

Sput Louie's mouth fell open while the rest of her body froze in place. She had been too slow to scoop up the handkerchief, and now it was too late. She cursed herself for being slower than an old horned ox. So she just casually stepped forward and gathered it up like it was nothing. When she did, she considered the objects in a new light.

Pawpaw fruit, she repeated in her mind, as she nonchalantly folded the kerchief back over the items. They certainly had felt like they might be fleshy inside, and their outer covering looked as thick as the skin of the pawpaw.

Pawpaws were plentiful in Feather Falls. You couldn't tromp through too many forests without passing under one of the tree's leafy canopies. It had too much of a flowery aftertaste, though, so Sput didn't much care for them. Hence, the question from Hunter.

On the other hand, maybe it wasn't pawpaw. Sput would have to pull it apart to see if there were seeds inside, and she didn't want to do that. Not just yet, anyway. Besides, even salt looked like sugar at first glance, so it could be something else.

She coolly slid it into her skirt pocket, careful not to squish the precious cargo.

L.B., the knower of all things Benjamin-related, asked, "Ith that Pa kerchief?"

Luckily, Archie snailed through the door before Sput had to answer. "Is what Pa's kerchief?" He looked equal parts haggard, puzzled and frazzled.

"What's this about a hole in a rock?" Sput asked, to shift attention away elsewhere. She righted the chair, then sat down and gave them her full attention. She was both curious and suspicious.

"We found a place, Ma."

"It's just for the meantime, though," said Archie, repeating his Pa's words.

Hunter Big said in a quiet voice, "It's near the Cocteau bottoms."

Sput was alarmed by his tone and the way he avoided her eyes. "Ain't that where Tawny lives?"

Tawny was a sixteen-year-old girl that the townspeople considered friendless, a term the Cherokee used when describing orphans. With no family, friends, or favors to bestow, Tawny grew up and discovered favors of the flesh. She went from friendless to friendly, and folks began calling her a night woman.

L.B. said, "Uh-huh. He thweet on Tawny." He reached for his mother's pocket. "Can I have thome of your pawpaw fruit, Ma?"

Sput swatted his hand away. "Bottom land? And nobody live within a quarter mile of it?" Sput asked, doubtful that such a prime piece of land was available.

"Not bottom-bottom," Hunter explained. "It's a little hilly."

Sput shook her head. "It's a dugout, ain't it?"

A dugout was a primitive manner of living, one step below a box lean-to. In the old days, Indians called it an earth lodge. Sput hadn't been forced to use one as shelter since her trek from Texas.

At one point during that odyssey, when her birthing pains began, she'd found an abandoned hillside dugout. Laboring alone for two days with no food or water, Sput delivered her first babies.

She recalled having to pile rocks high enough to block the entrance to keep sniffing animals away from her birthing blood.

Now years later, here she was going back to where she started.

"We can use our old wagon canvas to cover the openin'," said Hunter.

It was the same cover Benjamin had been using for a roof when she'd met him. "I've lived in them before," Sput said, dismissing further conversation with her sharp tone. She supposed it was better than the old daub-and-wattle dwelling of yore made of woven boards and stinky cow dung. Like Archie said, it was only for the meantime, until they could gather the materials to build a proper structure. That was the plan. And hopefully before then, Benjamin would—

L.B. interrupted her thought. "How lovely ith your dwelling plathe," L.B. offered. "Thalm 84."

Psalms were L.B.'s favorite thing to quote. "Not even a little bit lovely, Son," Sput bemoaned. "Not even a little bit."

There was a bold rap-tap-tap-tap on the door. Whoever it was would be the second visitor in as many days. That was two more than they'd had in the last three months. The knock sounded desperate. She hoped this time it really was someone seeking one of her cures. Someone who could pay.

When Hunter jerked the door open, though, it wasn't anyone seeking her medicinal prowess.

It was Goliah's skull.

Chapter Nine

Aftering handily dismissing Clem Talbot with his sharp words, Two Bird angled away from the agent and crossed Tincy Long Bone's yard towards the house where Tiger Tee Hee, fellow elder of the Wild Potato Clan, lay in his final hours.

The house was a flat-top, shaped just like the blond-hair's camera box, if that box had been battered and run-down, and had a mud-and-stick chimney on its side, and only one window.

Tiger's head wife, Dark Ana, met him at the door. Ana's complexion was a much redder hue than the average Cherokee, and she was so old she could have been Tincy Long Bone's grandmother.

Women sometimes wore their deceased husband's shirt for a year in remembrance of them. Two Bird noticed Ana already had on Tiger's red and brown plaid shirt. *"Has he walked on to place of long rest?"* he inquired solemnly.

She shook her head. *"There is breath yet in those old lungs. He still talks."*

Two Bird nodded his understanding, and relief that he hadn't arrived too late. *"Tiger was never one to leave a thing unsaid."*

Ana agreed. *"He talks overlong. Always did."*

There was no judgment in her words. Just lifelong experience with her husband's spirited side. Ana's eyes began to redden as she stepped aside to allow Two Bird entry.

What Two Bird had heard about Tiger Tee Hee's injuries did not prepare him for what he saw next. He did not recoil from many things, but this was something even he hadn't seen in his fifty-five years on earth.

Tiger lay on a plush pallet of hand-tufted rugs, with the top of his head split wide open. The layers of flesh peeled and parted down the middle in a perfect line from crown to forehead. The wound was as long as a man's middle finger and wide enough to fit a newborn's fist. The top layer of skin had had four days to curl back and expose deeper layers of pink, yellow, and one of pond-water-green. Two Bird wondered if the sliver of white he saw at the bottom was Tiger's skull.

The story was that Tiger was transported to three towns in two days, and saw four doctors following his injury, with nothing but a kerchief to protect it from the elements. When each doctor determined that there was nothing to remedy such a deep wound, he returned to Feather Falls. There, he traded his pocket watch for a casket at Ames Furniture, and with the money left over, settled his family's account at Malloy's Store-haus.

Such a story might one day become folklore told around a campfire, but Two Bird would be able to confirm it as truth, because there Tiger was, awake and alive. Like he couldn't smell the putrid odor of rotting flesh that emanated from his scalp. Like an ax hadn't been brought down on his skull. The only thing Two Bird wouldn't be able to explain was why there was flesh drying and dying without any blood dripping or pooling.

"Yuh." Tiger looked up at Two Bird looking down. "*Timber thieves… thought I had need…of a part in my hair.*" A phlegm-filled cough made its way to daylight.

Somehow, Two Bird managed a faint smile as he took a seat on the floor next to his old bald friend. It was heartening to see the old man's sense of humor still intact.

"*The final catchers,*" as the Cherokee called the lighthorsemen, "*will find the cowards who did this to an old man trying to protect the land,*" Two Bird said.

A knowing look passed between them as the empty words hung in the air. Tiger had stumbled upon a band of blond-hairs cutting trees for timber on Cherokee land. When he questioned them, they answered with an ax. They would be long gone by now, probably over to Arkansas-land.

"Nearly finished with this life." Tiger's chest rattled with each labored breath. *"Pain no longer. Just thirst."*

Two Bird picked up the calfskin gourd laying next to him and turned it up at his old friend's lips.

Tiger struggled to swallow the liquid that smelled like a brew of stink gut tea, and then pushed it away. *"Just enough to keep body and soul together while I say what must be heard."*

"Shuh," the younger of the two elders said. *"You are stronger than the vine of a live oak."*

Tee Hee's demise would not be Two Bird's first live death. He had seen many take their last breath, starting when he was a boy, and the Cherokees were forcibly removed from their ancestral homeland in North Carolina and marched by U.S. Army escort to what is now known as Indian Territory. Many men, women, and children succumbed to the cold weather, the long walk, the absence of food, and the presence of disease. His grandfather and three older brothers had been among those who died. Still buried along the trail somewhere. Many tears were shed along the way at the loss of their homes, the loss of their loved ones, and the fear of an unknown destination and what kind of life lay ahead of them. And so it became known as *Nunahi-duna-dlo-hilu-I*, The Trail Where They Cried.

Yet there would be no tears today from Tiger or Two Bird. They'd had nearly fifty years to acclimate to this land. *"This is our home now. We have been here longer than we have not,"* Tiger loved to say. Indeed, some Cherokee knew only of this new land, and nothing of the old country. The Old Ones like he and Tiger, though, remembered.

Whenever the old were dying, they called upon their loved ones to gather around so they could share lessons learned from a long life.

"By a thin thread, the Cherokees hang," Tiger said in a hoarse whisper. *"Blond-hairs give us tonic made of money. Indians swallow it...thinking it*

will fill the belly better than boiled corn." He shook his head. *"Different from our way of life. Thin-bloods...chase blond-hair's influence. Everything they do, they want us to do. A-dapt. A-dopt. As-si-mi-late. These...are the* English *words blond-hairs use to draw away the soul of a people."*

Though he agreed, Two Bird's back stiffened at Tiger's use of the white man's words. Still, he knew to sit quiet and listen hard.

"In the long ago time, blond-hairs...did not rule Cherokee." Tee Hee waved a dismissive hand across his face. *"Cherokee ruled Cherokee. Our tribe...must go back to that. Much work is yet to be done."* He swallowed hard and loud.

Two Bird shifted in his seat on the floor. He adjusted his dress, smoothing it over his knees while Tiger continued.

"Along the Hiawassee River, they stole our land. Rich, fertile land... because they desired it. What you do not give... to the Great White Father in Washington, he will take. Their hunger is never...satisfied. They give us this land." He coughed, and whatever he coughed up, he struggled to swallow back down. *"But if it is ours,"* he paused, *"why do they still have hands in it?"*

Tiger's eyes darted towards the gourd. Two Bird took the hint and gave him another sip.

"Blond-hairs are not wanted here." His voice was a bit stronger. *"We are punished by their presence. This soil belongs only to blood Cherokee. Not white man. Not colored man."* He pointed a long, crooked finger at Two Bird. *"You must stop them from taking our land."*

Two Bird put his thumb to his chest and raised his eyebrows in a quest for clarity. *"I must stop them?"* He could try to keep one or two tribal members of their clan in line, or people like Goliah who were from the same town. He enjoyed that immensely. Nevertheless, to be able to wield any amount of influence beyond Feather Falls was not an undertaking, but an overtaking. *"Blond-hairs have an army."* He shrugged. *"Mixed-bloods grow that army."*

"Mixed marriages...bleach out the brown of the Indian. True," Tiger agreed. *"And mixed-bloods...sometimes have mixed allegiance. They dishonor their tribe in this way."*

Goliah Lynch and his ilk immediately came to Two Bird's mind again. As far as he was concerned, they carried the stench of the white man's greed on their breath. *"Mixed-bloods are the ones that betray us."*

"Mixed-bloods are thin-bloods. They think they are clever, true. But... they have lost their way. We must get back to traditions of Keetoowah and our full-blooded forefathers. Stick to ways of the Old Settlers or the Cherokees will be no longer."

Throughout the years, some had encouraged Two Bird to follow a political path and run for council member, but such a role was not for him. To his way of thinking, in politics, there was too much disregard for facts. Surely there was another way. *"I am but one man,"* he said. *"How can one man be a force in a tribe of many?"*

With his wrinkled finger, Tiger reached out and traced a circle on Two Bird's chest. Two Bird looked down wondering what the old man was trying to draw. The sacred circle? A likeness of the sun?

When the old man drew eight short lines extending out from all sides of the circle, Two Bird knew without a doubt what it was.

"When spider webs unite," Tiger Tee Hee said, *"they can tie up a lion."*

Chapter Ten

Senix Lynch had skin the color of burnt corn, hair a yellowing gray, and a well-muscled body despite his age of—Sput guessed—nearly fifty. He was the only freedman in Feather Falls who still went by his former master's last name, probably because soon after the war, Goliah Lynch had made him his right-hand man in charge of all of his operations from crops to cattle. That meant he was Goliah's most trusted worker, his head man, his skull.

But why was he at her house, Sput wondered?

The skull tried to look past Hunter, who had answered the door, and into the house. "Is Benjamin here?"

Hunter stepped aside, and Sput Louie stepped up to the threshold so Senix wouldn't come in and step on one of the nail-less floorboards. "What you need him for?"

Senix removed his straw hat, exposing a hairline shaped like a horseshoe that left him bald in the middle. After visually assessing Hunter, Archie, and L.B. one by one, he asked Sput, "Can we talk outside?" He motioned behind him with his fraying hat.

Crossing her arms over her chest, Sput followed him out to the yard. The hair on her arms stood as straight as quills on a fretful porcupine.

"I come to warn you," Senix said when they reached the edge of the yard lined with rocks instead of a fence. "Benjamin, too. If he around here." His eyes darted about the property.

A ripple of nerves shuddered down Sput's spine. She neither confirmed nor denied her husband's presence because she felt somewhere deep in the marrow of her bones, this visit had something to do with the kerchief.

"Warn him?" Sput noticed a red sumac shrub sprouting from the ground, probably started by bird droppings. She bent down and pulled off a few of the bobs to use later as a spice. "Warn him 'bout what?" She rolled the fruit in the palm of her hand, feigning boredom, hiding concern.

As if he were about to divulge the most sinister of secrets, Senix looked from side to side. Then he stared at her with his lips parted, and his eyes softening. Benjamin had always said that Senix had eyes for her. That he just wanted to lie at her feet and soak up her shade. Sput had laughed and told him to get away from her with that foolishness. But then he said that beauty was not always the draw. Sometimes, a man prized a good woman.

"To tell you the truth, Miss Sput," Senix said with a pointed stare, "I'm warnin' you."

"Warnin' me? 'Bout what?"

"Mr. Lynch's prize horse was stole yestidy."

The sumac bobs slipped from Sput's hand. "Ferd?" she asked as she stooped to scoop them back up.

Ferd was a blaze-faced roan with white socks circling three of his four fetlocks. Many admired this distinction, Sput among them. Benjamin, too.

"Yep. Stole right out the barn." Senix shook his head in disbelief. "You know how Mr. Lynch love him some Ferd. Finest horse around. Always puttin' it up against other horses."

Sput sucked in a breath while her mind began to whirl like a spindle. "And that got to do with Benjamin, what?" She raised a brow as the spindle toppled by a sudden realization. "You tryin' to say my Ben stole him?" She pouted her lips. "My husband ain't no thief. Never stole nothin' a day in his life." She put her hands on her hips. "A blacksmith don't need no ax, and Benjamin don't need no horse. Not a stolen one. And why would he steal a horse, anyway? Where he gon' hide it? We ain't got no barn. What he gon' do with it where people couldn't see he had it? How he gon'—"

Senix held up both palms to halt her ripping into him. "I ain't sayin' he did it." He paused. "Mr. Lynch is."

Sput scratched her cheek in contemplation.

"He done gone and told the Annie-horse Thief Society, too," Senix said.

"Annie who?" Sput pronounced *Anti* the same way Senix had.

"The Annie-Horse Thief Society and they don't fool with folks. Most of them was in that there Knights of the Golden Circle before the Freedom War, so you know they just lookin' for a reason to have a nigger hangin' from a tree, blowin' in the wind."

The shudder in her spine moved around to her gut and grew into a full-on tremble. She tried to block the image of Benjamin dangling from a tree. Like if she couldn't picture it, it wouldn't happen. Still, it shoved its way into her mind.

"Lord, if they got a whole society for it..." Her words trailed off as the spindle of her mind picked up its twirl again. "But wait. Why he think Ben stole it?"

Senix gave her a sideways glance. "Seems Benjamin paid a little visit to Mr. Lynch yestidy. You know somethin' 'bout that?"

She didn't know enough about it. She wished she did. All she knew was that Benjamin had gone there, apparently left there, and went by the Ugly Tree to leave her a clue in a kerchief. Whatever that had to do with Ferd the horse or Goliah his owner was a puzzlement that made her head hurt. "Why would I know anything about it? Ben his own man. He don't tell me where he goin', when he comin' back, or nothin'." She clasped her amulet. "Maybe he had business with Goliah. Maybe that horse just ran away. You sure Ben even went there?"

Their attention was momentarily drawn to the house as her sons came out and sat under the brush arbor. All three pairs of eyes were fixed on her and Senix.

"Now, Miss Sput," Senix said in a mildly chastising tone. "I know you been thrown off the land. Ben ain't got no business with Mr. Lynch except to move off his property." He clucked his teeth. "Besides, Ferd was a trick horse, sho nuff, but he couldn't open no barn door."

"Well, Ben ain't no horse thief," she countered again, "But Old Crow, on the other hand, is a well-known liar."

As much as Senix might have a spark of fire for her, she knew he did not cotton to the use of Goliah's nickname, which is why she'd said it. Old Crow was the same kind of evil every day—Sunday's not excepted—and Senix had an unnatural loyalty to him that Sput could not understand. She had heard that Goliah's father had publicly punished Senix's father, a runaway slave at the time, by tying him to a post and whipping him to death in full view of all the slaves, including Senix, his siblings, as well as his mother. Was Senix beginning to question that loyalty, Sput wondered? He was, after all, going behind Old Crow's back to warn her.

The skull put his hat back on. "Well, the whole Society gon' be lookin' for him. So—"

"They won't find him with no horse."

Senix tipped his hat and ambled towards his wagon, then abruptly turned back. Once again, he looked from side to side as if he had yet another secret to divulge. "I ain't supposed to be here." He stared her dead in the eye.

"I ain't seen you." Then she thanked him to hurry him on his merry way. "*Wado.*"

Watching him ride away, she considered the possibility that Benjamin could steal a horse. She didn't know what to make of it. And what about the kerchief? And the clue inside? She could not make out head nor tail of the situation, nor arm, nor leg, nor any other part of the body.

Suddenly, a coldness washed over her.

If something had happened at Old Crow's place, and Ben did make off with that horse knowing full well he couldn't keep it, that meant only one thing.

Benjamin wasn't coming back.

Chapter Eleven

Two weeks later, in the dimness of their hillside dugout, Sput Louie could barely make out the money Billy Bean Stick had tossed at her feet. She saw enough of it on the dirt floor, though, to know it was useless Cherokee scrip worth only two bits on the U.S. dollar.

Short of being paid in dollars, she'd rather have earned her fee in a good length of cloth, half a basket of eggs, or the promise of milk for a month. Her boys loved milk more than bees loved trees. Though they rarely ever got any.

Of course, Bean Stick had given her none of those things, just a handful of the worthless paper. That he'd thrown it at her as opposed to handing it to her was a sign of his lack of respect for her medicinal talent. This was after she'd fashioned a frond from mullein leaves and used it to apply her milkweed decoction to his gonorrheal eruptions.

She deserved at least a bony milch cow for that deed.

Sighing with resignation, she didn't complain. Such was the life of a colored medicine woman, no matter how clever she was. She was just glad someone had sought her good medicine. Grateful, too, that Bean Stick had seen fit to hire Archie down at the Sentinel a couple of years before, even though it was just one day a week.

Archie had left for work at dawn that morning, and Hunter and L.B. made themselves scarce when they saw Bean Stick riding up. Archie must have given Bean Stick directions, because the dugout was not easy to find unless you knew where to look.

There were others, though, who had known where to look. So many men had ridden close to the dugout, circled the dugout, posted themselves in the trees across from the dugout. Every time she saw them, she breathed easy, because that meant they hadn't yet found Benjamin. He was safe. Somewhere.

She could hear Billy Bean Stick in the corner of the cave struggling to fasten his trousers over his portly middle. She would not let him see her pick the money up. However, pick up the money she would, as soon as he was gone. Maybe Malloy would—if only begrudgingly—let her trade the wretched currency at the store-haus. She would try that, at least.

Bean Stick paid her ignoring him no mind. He probably hadn't even noticed. Coloreds were almost an invisible people, ghosts of the past, not to be acknowledged unless needed for something. Partly because, Sput figured, they were a constant reminder of the things the Cherokees lost after the Freedom War, namely free labor, but also the devastation war had left on the land; and partly because they were now considered a burden on the Indian.

Sput pulled back the canvas cover that now served as a door to the dugout. Bean Stick bent down and exited into the bright torrid sun.

"*Wado*," he said, thanking her without tipping his hat or even looking back at her.

She was not impressed by this thin-blood's use of his native tongue when it suited him. Especially since she'd gotten a gander at his very, very small *watoli*.

As soon as Bean Stick was out of sight, Archie bounded light and breezy from around the far side of the hill into which the dugout had been carved, eagerly waving a newspaper at her.

"What you doin' home?" she asked, astonished to see him back so soon.

His eyes glowed as he rushed towards her.

"I was hiding out back until Mr. Bean Stick left."

"What you hidin' for?"

"I got something to tell you. To show you. I mean to read to you." He shoved a rumpled copy of the Sentinel at her.

At the Cherokee Sentinel, Archie was a printer's devil by trade, a chore-boy charged with setting the type and inking the press for printing on long sheets of foolscap. Whenever he could, he would sneak home a copy of that week's paper that had been crumpled between the rollers, caught in the grippers, or discarded for ink smudges. Archie would read it to his family by the firelight, and they would listen to news about a world that hardly ever concerned itself with people who looked like them. Archie was always curious about the goings-on of the outside world, and he tried to fan the fire of his family's interest, but that interest had been beaten down to indifference by having to eke out their daily existence.

The Sentinel reported everything from scuttlebutt about the U.S. government's desire to turn Indian Territory into an actual state, all the way to social news like *"Mr. Friedenberg's mother is visiting from St. Louis."*

Negroes, she knew, were not newsworthy. The only time coloreds were mentioned was if it involved a crime.

"Conductor Hit in Head—Colored suspects at large" read one such headline. The short article that followed had been about a few boys in Wybark, a colored township in the Creek Nation, chucking rocks at the MK&T Railroad as it passed through their town, probably because no coloreds had been hired to work the new line.

"What's that newspaper sayin' now?" Sput asked, just to get Archie to stop waving it in her face.

"Freedmen are now gonna get bread money and be bona fide members of the tribe, Ma." He paused, as if waiting for Sput to catch up to his enthusiasm.

Sput's interest in anything at all had been lagging since Benjamin left. The first week in the dugout, she seldom rose from her pallet, dooming herself to wallow in the yawning abyss of his absence. She almost never went outside, except to cook what had been snared for supper, and then she barely ate any of it. It wasn't until the heat wave hit and made being inside so unbearable that she had to come out. Even then, she dragged around like a bag of rocks was tied to her feet.

"Bone a what? Say what now?"

Seemingly undeterred by his mother's glaring lack of enthusiasm, Archie explained. "Per capita payment, Ma. See, it started with this here editorial by Mr. Bean Stick all the way at the back of the paper." He flipped the paper over to showcase the last page as if Sput could read it. "And then I found this here broadside on the ground in town." He pulled from his back pocket a crumpled paper streaked with mud marks.

Sput scratched her head. "What you talkin' about, Son?"

"Mama, Mama, just listen, here." He cleared his throat. "'*Negroes, Niggers and Ninnies,*'" he paused and looked up from the Sentinel. "Uh, that's the title."

"Ya-huh," Sput said, twisting her mouth in complaint.

Archie resumed reading.

> "*Negroes, Niggers and Ninnies*
>
> "*It doesn't matter what you call them they are a leech in the pond of humanity. We Cherokee have generously allowed them to live on any unclaimed lands, and we even pay them a decent wage to work for us. Now, the federal government, the now United States of America, wants to invoke Article 9 of the Treaty of 1866, and encroach on our benevolence by insisting that we enroll the Negro and allow them to share in our per capita payment for lands 'ceded back to the Union,' as they describe it, but were actually lands taken from the Cherokees at the end of the war. Now, all the non-Cherokee have to do is appear before the appointed person and prove they were born in The Cherokee Nation, or returned here within six months of the signing of the treaty, and our beloved Indian homeland becomes a Negro promised land.*
>
> "*We all know that treaty was forced upon us as punishment for the minuscule faction of Cherokee who sided with the Confederacy in the War. The proof is in the pudding. Nowhere else in the South, from Texas to the Carolinas, have former slave owners been required to share anything with their ex-slaves. Why*

should Indians have to share their bread money? That should be between the United States and the Negroes, Niggers and Ninnies. We don't have a dog in that fight. They've riled up the Negroes, and now they're agitating for Indian money and Indian land.

"I am here to tell you and anyone within spitting distance we don't have to adopt the Negro and give them all the same rights we have. There's no such thing as a colored Cherokee; there's only Cherokee, plain and simple. The Shawnee are not Cherokee, and neither are the Delaware. We don't have to stand for this, and in my humble opinion, something must be done."

Sput Louie drew her hand to her cheek at the vile names written by the man who had just sought the healing graces of someone he considered a nigger and a ninnie.

"Now, this paper here..." Archie un-crumpled the broadside that stretched nearly as long as his arm, "...says all you have to do is be a freedman and prove you returned to—let's see, now." His eyes darted across the paper until he got to the bottom. "'There will be citizenship hearings held where any Colored can present proof that they resided in, or returned to Indian Territory on or about February 11, 1867.' This Wallace man is coming to town. You just have to meet up with him, and he'll fill out the affidavit—that's how you enroll—for you," he explained. He folded the notice more neatly this time and tucked it into the breast pocket of his suit coat, which he always wore to work even in vest-weather. He patted it like he would a baby being put to sleep.

Archie continued, as he looked off into the distance. "This means you'll be a bona fide—"

"They said all that before, Son." Listening to him ramble on, Sput was proud that at least one family member could speak proper English and knew big words like *agitate*, but she had interrupted him anyway. She then removed the red and blue medicine sash that hung around her neck and folded it into the left pocket of her skirt because the right one was full with Benjamin's kerchief. "Been sayin' it ever since I been free. Empty talk. That's what that is. 'Gon' enroll the Negroes, give 'em land, give 'em rights, give 'em money,'" she mimicked. "Ya-huh." She gave a long hard blink and raised her eyes to a memory. "They let Benjamin vote in one election, though. First one after the war, it was." Then she turned her eyes back to Archie. "And not a one ever since."

"But," Archie began to reason with her, "This here is the United States government doing it, not the tribe."

"Even worse," she said. "White folks can make a seven look like an eight, and a eight look like a seven." That she didn't know what either one looked like was not her point. "They fooled the Indians with that already. I don't trust a one of them blue-eyed devils. Listenin' to a liar is like drinkin' warm water. It go down easy, but it don't quench the thirst."

Archie blew out a dry sigh.

"And Cherokees, don't get me started on them." Sput was on a tear. "They act like we 'bout as useful as a pocket on the back of a shirt, even though the white man think the same 'bout them. So go on away from here with that foolishness." She shooed him away with a swish of her hand. "I'll believe it when I see it."

"But you cain't see it if you don't sign up."

Sput Louie had had enough of the Indians and their land, or the white folks' land, whoever's land it was. She couldn't tell for sure. Indians thought it was theirs, but white people ran it like it belonged to them. Whoever's land it was, that land was the reason her husband was no longer with his family, she was sure of it.

"But Ma," Archie said, not giving up. "Pa ain't here. We got to do something."

The twins were becoming more angry than confused about Benjamin's seeming abandonment of the family. Hunter seemed easily vexed as of late, and Archie had stopped mentioning his Pa at all. Sput was surprised at his bringing him up now.

She looked at the newspaper in Archie's hand, and then back at him. She flung her hand, dismissing her own growing anger.

"That ain't news."

The only news she was interested in was why Benjamin left her that kerchief. But that, too, was becoming old news.

Chapter Twelve

As soon as Sput turned to reenter the hillside dugout, she caught sight of Hunter and L.B. angling towards her and Archie. Tawny was in between them with Sinker the ferret, oddly enough, riding *her* shoulder this time. So close to Hunter was she that the ferret could hop from one of them to the other. Sput was distracted for a moment wondering whether Tawny was still drinking the roux she'd given her to prevent babies from sprouting. It was the best thing for a woman in her line of work to do. Maybe the girl thought she didn't need it anymore since she'd taken up with Hunter. Maybe she'd stopped being a night woman. Who knew? All Sput knew was that the female persuasion had to make their way the best way they could when they didn't have a husband to fend for them.

Just like Sput now.

"*'Siyo,*" Tawny greeted.

Sput responded in kind and moved to sit in one of the rickety hickory bark chairs outside the entrance to the dugout, while Archie brought the newly arrived up to date on the newspaper article.

Tall, lithe Tawny playfully snatched the paper from Archie once he finished. She began flipping through all four pages of the Sentinel. "Everybody could use some bread money." She turned her back to Archie when he tried in vain snatch the paper back. "Too bad I was born after the war."

Tawny was one of many mixed-blood children routinely abandoned to the Cherokee Orphan Asylum because of the father being Negro, and their Indian mother being forced by her clan to give up the dark-skinned child. Plenty of people in Indian Territory stood with sad stories as their backbone, so Sput didn't look on Tawny with pity.

Hunter, however, looked at Tawny with envy at that particular moment. "You know exactly when you was born?"

Tawny nodded. "The missionaries at the asylum said I was born in 1870. That makes me sixteen this year," Tawny said proudly. "But they didn't know what month. So," she hesitated, with just a tinge of sadness coloring her boastfulness, "I guess no, I don't know exactly when I was born."

Once Archie learned enough arithmetic, he'd been able to figure out how old he and Hunter were. Just like Tawny they would never know the exact month because Sput didn't know her months.

That was the main problem, she thought, with the whole enrollment thing. How would anyone who couldn't read, write, count, or know the months of the year—or even the number of the years—cipher whether they returned to Indian Territory by the deadline printed in the broadside?

She needed Benjamin there. Right then. He could become a citizen of the Cherokee Nation just by proving his bloodline, and they'd be moved out of the dugout by tomorrow. No ciphering necessary.

But Benjamin wasn't there. That left her the only freedman in the family. If she didn't even *try* to enroll for the bread money and help uplift her family, what kind of mother would she be? She was the head of the McClendon household now.

"I'm gon' do it," she blurted.

Everyone stopped what they were doing, and gaped at Sput Louie, except for Tawny, who continued perusing the Sentinel, and L.B. who had already wandered away with his bug jar in one hand, and the lid in the other.

"Huh?" Archie asked.

His face was bright with hope, and Sput knew why. He wanted the family to have use of their own land, sure enough, and this was the path to it. He'd also wanted to start his own school ever since the Cherokees closed down the one for coloreds because it had less than the minimum requirement of twenty-five pupils. He saw this as an opportunity for that, land on which they could build permanent structures instead of lean-to's, land that they couldn't be uprooted from, land that would be in their family forever, land that would be Archie's grubstake.

"Ma Bay always said, 'if you want a thing done, you'd best do it yourself.' I'm gon' enroll," she said, and then scratched the back of her neck. "But, Son, how would I prove it up?"

Tawny folded the paper in half and pointed to the bottom section of it. "Well, lookie here. They—"

Archie cut her off. "You gonna need some witnesses, Ma, people who can say they saw you back here before the deadline, people who can say you were from here in the first place, people who knew you were sent away to Texas by your—by Old Crow, but came back here just in time."

"People like who?" She immediately thought of Benjamin.

"Lemme think now." Archie looked skyward. "What about Emarthla?"

"Ya-huh." Sput nodded her agreement with that possibility.

"And—and Famous Johnson," he said, seemingly pulling names from the air.

Sput frowned. "No, not Famous Johnson. You cain't tell whether what he say is a half-truth or a whole lie."

Hunter looked perplexed. "That old man that be tellin' all them wild tales?"

"That old man is a hundred and twenty years old," Archie countered. "You don't think he knows everybody and everything?"

"He sure claim he do," Sput said.

"Hey," Tawny interjected, more loudly this time. "There's an advertisement in here for an interpreter. The Shawnee and Delaware who don't speak English will need a translator in order to enroll."

Archie smirked and snatched the paper back from her.

"Four dollars a day," Tawny exclaimed, shrugging off Archie's actions, while she switched her long black braid from one shoulder to the other.

Hunter shot Archie a glare. "That's more than you make down at the Sentinel, huh, little brother. What you make, 'bout thirty cents a day, ain't it?"

"That's thirty cents more than we had yesterday," Archie said in a matter-of-fact tone that bespoke no brag, just fact. "Now, that right there," Archie tap-tap-tapped the paper with his finger, "is a government job. They wouldn't hire a woman for that just because you can speak Shawnee. Lots of folks speak Shawnee."

"I speak Cherokee and some Delaware, too. It won't hurt to try." Tawny looked to Hunter like a child would a parent. He gave her a sharp nod of encouragement.

Archie shook his head from side to side. "First of all, you'd have to wear a dress."

He ogled her long brown legs that stretched from underneath her short buckskin skirt until Hunter gave his cheek a one-handed shove. Somewhat playfully, but also somewhat seriously.

"A regular dress." Archie shook off the shove and continued. "A long one. Got to reach your ankles. Maybe made of satinette, like they have in that Montgomery Ward Catalog."

Everyone stared blankly. No one spoke.

"What?" Archie's voice cracked. "I snuck a peek at the catalog when Bean Stick sent me over to Malloy's one time to fetch his sundries."

Tawny put a finger to her chin. "I bet Two Bird might have some extra cloth for a new skirt."

Sput nodded. "Two Bird." She'd all but forgotten about him. He, too, could vouch for her to get on the Wallace Roll.

"He's at his niece's wedding today," Tawny said, a light of excitement growing in her eyes, "but tonight will be the first smiling moon of June." She nudged Hunter's big elbow with her bony one.

Hunter's head tipped back. "Ahhh," he said, smiling. "The fish-kill."

"I could ask Two Bird at the fish-kill," Tawny said.

With everything that had been going on with the McClendons, the annual town fish-kill had completely slipped Sput's mind, and apparently everyone else's, too.

Sput mindlessly slid her hand into her pocket while the others went on chatting. She gently cupped the kerchief so as not to disturb its contents. Finally, she would get to show it to Two Bird, and get his assessment of not just the gobs, but the whole situation with the Anti-horsethief Society, too.

The orbs were smaller now, shriveling daily in the summer heat.

As she continued fingering their size and shape, several thoughts took form. There was something oddly familiar about them in their wrinkled state. The way they felt in her hand evoked a vague memory that had nothing to do with pawpaw fruit. What exactly it did have to do with, she couldn't quite place.

Closing her eyes, she tried to block out the conversation of the others. With the pad of her thumb, she traced the outline of the gobs, but abruptly stopped. All of her thoughts, every bit of speculation she'd engaged in regarding the gobs was suddenly distilled down to a single idea, one odd notion, one peculiar possibility that beat back all the rest and knocked and nudged its way to the forefront of her mind.

Her eyes popped open, wide with horror.

Chapter Thirteen

Two Bird ducked to enter the Feather Falls Town House where the wedding of his niece Sky Spirit was to take place. The throngs of attendees parted to let him through. His latest dress design did not go unremarked upon as he strutted around the circular room smoother than the second hand on a gold watch.

Feeling the press of admiring eyes following his every move, he slowed to a saunter so as to facilitate their adoration, and soak up their not-so-silent praise.

"*Ja-ja,*" one woman exclaimed to another. "*No bodice has ever been— how say in* English—ruched *in such a way.*"

"*Iyee-Iyee-Iyee,*" he heard another woman say excitedly, "*The flair of his skirt. How did he do it?*"

"*Gu-gwe, gu-gwe. Do you think those are store-bought buttons?*"

"*From* Montgomery Ward Catalog, *it may be,*" one young lady informed an elderly one.

Not from Malloy's store-haus, Two Bird thought upon hearing it, but did not satisfy his onlookers by saying out loud. They were critter teeth he had hand-painted himself and placed strategically down his sleeve to help mask his muscular arms. The dress had been ruched in the middle to make his waist appear smaller than it was. His creations always reflected a blend of the traditional Cherokee style of dress, which included items from nature's bounty—though he rarely used skins any-more—and the more modern muslins and silks. Cloth was easier to work with, and much more versatile than skins. Though Two Bird held sacred many Cherokee traditions, in fashion he held no aversion to modernity.

"What price would you ask to make a dress like that for me?" asked one of his cousins and long-time patron as he swaggered past.

"We will talk." He waved her off as he took his seat on the end of one of the long benches that lined the walls. He was preoccupied not just with the wedding, but with news he had heard about Goliah Lynch. Not only was he accusing Benjamin McClendon of being a horse thief, but he had turned the McClendon's off the land just to turn around and lease that same land to Texas cattlemen. Two Bird hated gossip, but that he had listened to with both ears. Though the tribe could sell or lease a section of land, leasing by an individual was strictly prohibited, albeit haphazardly enforced.

Having accepted the challenge Tiger Tee Hee had issued from his deathbed, Two Bird surveyed the room in search of Goliah. He wanted to see if he would deny the plain truth that this is what happens when one man controls too much land; someone else has to do without.

The same double doors through which Two Bird had entered earlier were suddenly flung open. He turned to see if it might be Goliah, but it was only the bride and the groom.

More *Ooh's,* and *iy-iy-iy's* went up from the guests as the betrothed couple strode to the center of the circle of benches. He approved of the praise the bride's dress was receiving, but he did not approve of Sky Spirit's union to a blonde-hair. Too many of them were marrying Indian women, diluting Indian blood, and usurping Indian land. Nor had he signed the required petition her husband-to-be had to submit setting forth the signatures of ten of the bride's relatives who did not object to the union.

Nevertheless, the Clerk of the District accepted the petition, certified the ten names, and issued the license to the Methodist minister who was to perform the ceremony.

The ceremony. That was a tradition—or the lack of which—that sent a slow burn through Two Bird's veins as he watched it begin in the middle of the circle.

Instead of the groom giving the bride a ham of venison to symbolize his intent to keep meat on the table, and the bride, in return, giving the groom an ear of corn as a token of her intent to be a good wife and partner, they exchanged vows, professed oaths, minced words.

Where was the ceremony in that? He shook his head at the loss of yet another Cherokee tradition that lay dying on the roadside, gasping for air. Tradition was betrothed to history, was it not? They were a pair, a sort of husband and wife themselves, Two Bird thought. They went arm in arm, and should always be honored. The youth today, however, had other ideas.

He sat with his arms folded, and shook his head. He was glad the ceremony was only half in English. That way, he would be only half offended.

Sky Spirit was his favorite niece, and that was why he had succumbed to her entreaties to make her ceremonial dress. It was his only concession to the union, other than his attendance. He had made the dress appropriately of a gray serge he had loomed himself with a two-up, two-down weave, and trimmed it in a rose-colored satin which he had gone all the way to Tahlequah to purchase. Its basque was tight-fitting with many small buttons of hummingbird bones down the back. The skirt was full enough to form a slight train behind but short enough in the front so as not to trip her as she paraded around the room after the ceremony, addressing each person at the wedding party.

"*Uncle,*" Sky Spirit said, as she made her way over to him, with her new husband in tow. "*Where is Aunt Rogers? Did you not tell him there would be no picture-taking?*"

Rogers was Two Bird's *adalii*, his wife for all intents and purposes, and was therefore addressed by the clan with the reverential "aunt" even though he was a man.

Two Bird ignored the judgment he saw in the groom's cold, flat eyes, and the way he tightened his jaw at the mention of Rogers. He knew ghost-faces did not tolerate men choosing to be with other men, but Two Bird couldn't care less. Such relationships went unremarked upon among the Cherokees. They were a private people. What happened inside one's home was the business of no one else. Like tribal members who chose to have two, three, or even four wives, if a man wanted four times the trouble, so be it. Two Bird had his hands full with the one.

He stretched out his hands and pressed them on the crowns of each head of the newly wed, affecting a bow of obeisance. *"May comfort and warmth be found in one another. May your lives be long and prosperous, Sky Spirit, and..."* He stopped short and turned to the groom. *"Again, your name?"* he asked, knowing that Jasper Polk spoke not one word of Cherokee.

Sky Spirit looked up, blinked hard, and then gave Two Bird a chastising roll of her eyes as she removed his hand from her head. *"Uncle, you know his name to be* Jasper Polk. *And from now on, I will be known as* Polly Polk." She stood. Her husband, following her lead, rose as well.

Two Bird's face remained stoic. *"Sounds like a disease."* He put his hand over his heart and contorted his face. *"I have been stricken with the Polly Polk,"* he said. Then added a half-hearted *"Ahh"* for dramatic flair.

Before she could respond, Jasper Polk led his bride away, probably suspicious that what Two Bird had said was in no way flattering to him.

Whatever happened to the naming ceremony, Two Bird wondered, where the elders of the clan had the privilege of picking the name? He himself had had a name change in such a fashion.

As a boy, back when the Cherokee clung to the woods and waters, and before villages gave way to towns, he had been called Aseven, being the seventh son of a seventh son. The number seven was sacred to the Cherokee. There were seven clans, seven ancient ceremonies, seven directions. Even the Cherokee National Council House in Tahlequah was constructed of seven sides, as was the Feather Falls town house.

This fortune of birth afforded him an inherent status within his clan. Seventh sons had a reputation for being the cleverest of people. Some, like his father, used this skill for gambling instead of good, but Aseven's interests lay elsewhere.

While watching his grandmother Kogee sew one day, the skill with which she created clothes tickled his boyish curiosity, so she began to teach him her craft.

"Hunting duties with the men of the clan first," his father and uncles had asserted gently, giving due deference to the matriarch of the family.

Aseven was a gifted marksman with his bow and arrow, but he also had an eye for the stitch. Kogee, eager to foster any talents her special grandson had, began teaching him a simple stitch, sewn straightforward with waxed thread attached to a hog bristle needle.

Over time, though, he began to complain to his grandmother. *"Such a stitch is good for moccasins only,"* he pouted.

She put him off. *"Even a bear must walk on all fours before he stands upright."*

Once Aseven could measure and cut his own patterns, he added a distinguishing flair to the shoes by adorning them with buttons and bones in a pattern unlike the diamond shaped design the Cherokee traditionally used. Those of the village who were too busy to make their own shoes often traded favors or goods to the family in return for the fruits of his handiwork.

As the seasons passed, he still was not happy being limited to simple footwear. An idea came to him that required his being paid in more than favors and goods. He said to anyone in his village that wished to own his wares, *"Money talks. Cherokee it speaks."*

He saved the money he earned, planning to travel to Tahlequah to see what he could purchase by way of sewing wares, but then Malloy opened a trading store in what would eventually become Feather Falls. He brought with him needles made of wiry metal and bolts of all different kinds of cloth.

Grandmother Kogee then graduated him to the backstitch, the chain stitch, and even taught him the featherstitch for decorative embroidery.

Aseven soon began to neglect his daily chores of hunting and fishing and wanted only to create from cloth. When his grandmother saw the needle case he had hand-carved from Maplewood into the shape of a fish that had a detachable head so as to slip the needle inside for safekeeping, she stopped teaching him, and began watching him.

She quietly looked over his shoulder as his advancing skills and nimble fingers began to fashion women's skirts embroidered with images of a winter wren, a yellow Mockingbird, or a blue warbler. When he sold them to the women of his clan, they would comment on how nice the pieces looked trimmed in ribbon ties or turkey feathers.

The women's homages pleased him, but there was still an unrest within his gut, a dissatisfaction in his bones, an itch in his heart. He puzzled over it and reflected upon it. It weighed upon him so much, that one day, he put down his sewing and fasted for seven days straight until a blessed vision came to him.

That image came to him in his sleep. It was a clear blue lake under a midnight moon. The moon's rays stroked the ripples of the lake, and they blushed a silvery sparkle. When he looked into this glistening body of water, it reflected everything around him like a looking glass. Everything reversed. Right was left, up was down, top was bottom. The moon became the sun, the future became the past, ugly was beautiful, and a curse became a blessing.

When he awoke the following morning, it was then that he realized there was only one way to quell his inquietude.

Picking up his sewing again, he worked feverishly for days, stopping only to eat a small meal or sleep a short time.

He felt his grandmother watching from a distance. When he turned to try and catch her looking, she would quickly turn the other way as if in search of something in the totally opposite direction.

When the garment he had imagined was made real, he took it and bolted all the way down to nearby Lake Watanuga. Alone there, he untied his breech-clout and stepped out of it. Not caring whether anyone might happen upon him, or what they would think if they did, he merely wanted to see his reflection in the water. He unfolded the bundle he had carried with him and took out his newest creation; his usual skirt, only this time it had a bodice attached that hung loose like a sack. He stepped into it. If his measurements were correct, he would be able to pull it up over his waistline.

They were, and he did.

However, Aseven had experienced a growth spurt since his thirteenth birthday a few months prior. His arms were now much too brawny to fit into the sleeves. He pressed his lips tight in a bitter smile.

Eyes towards the sky, he pondered his surroundings, taking in the high drama of the tall trees, first in confusion and then in clarity. He began to rock to and fro, balancing from heel to toe until the idea that was forming grew to fruition.

He peeled the sleeves off stitch-by-stitch, careful not to tear the material around the double-reinforced shoulder seams. When he was finally able to push his arms through the arm hole, he turned to the water to see his reflection, but he also saw the depth of what lay beneath. There, he saw a vision of himself floating on high, his head topped with a crown of clouds matching the blue and white sleeveless dress that looked beautiful on him. He gave himself a crisp nod and a sharp wink. He felt light. He felt free. He felt like himself for the very first time.

The young boy picked up the hem of his dress and began to dance around humming a tune, when suddenly, Grandmother Kogee rushed from the bushes behind him. Though she was much slighter than he, she yanked him by the wrist as if he were as small and limp as his sisters' old cornhusk dolls. She marched him back to the home of his parents where his mother was cooking in the front yard.

Upon first seeing him in the dress, his mother dropped her wooden cooking spoon and fell on her haunches in the mud behind her. His father, coming from the rear of the log cabin with a possum primed for cooking draped over his shoulder, stopped mid-stride, and the lifeless critter slithered down his arm and folded onto the ground.

Aseven's entire body trembled. Had he done something wrong? If he had, surely his father and uncles would discipline him by scratching the backs of his legs with the sharp teeth of a garpike. But wasn't he too old for such a punishment?

He tried to yank his wrist from Grandmother Kogee's clutches, but she had more strength than her small frame let on.

While the Cherokees cherish youth, they also trust old age. When Kogee thrust his arm high into the air and announced, *"A new naming ceremony this boy needs,"* it was not questioned.

According to custom, a baby's name is bestowed upon the seventh day after its birth. If later in life, that person's character changes, though, or significant events or achievements occur, a new name might be given. Like the girl who survived a bear mauling later became known as Bear Legs. Or the warrior who killed many men in battle became known as Ten Killer.

In Aseven's case, Grandmother Kogee declared, *"The spirit of two birds has this one, one male, one female. He shall now be called Two Bird."*

Now, in the Feather Falls townhouse, as Two Bird watched Sky Spirit and her new husband scurry away, he doubted whether any elder would have ever chosen the name Polly Polk.

Chapter Fourteen

Two Bird watched as Goliah finally entered the Town House and immediately honed in on the groom. Greeting Jaspar Polk the English way, their hands fit together like a hook and eye clasp when they shook. It was just like him, Two Bird thought, to focus his attention on the blond-hair, and not speak two words to the bride even though she was standing right beside them.

She would have, in the old days, been highly revered, as the Cherokees were at one time a matrilineal society where women were head of the household, and children were related to the mother, not the father. Not so much anymore. Goliah and his sort helped usher out that convention with their European influences that placed more value on men than women.

Some mixed-bloods wanted so badly to be white. That is why Two Bird felt he had to keep an eye on the cunning. People who were as sly as Goliah Lynch could move without changing locations. He bore watching.

Goliah had most assuredly ushered Benjamin out of Sput Louie's life in a sudden and swift manner. Two Bird was also led to believe that Goliah was forging a path to become some big bug politician. He was not fit to be even a town delegate, much less deserving of the aggrandized rank that a member of the Cherokee National Council enjoyed. Unjustly enjoyed, to Two Bird's way of thinking, for all the good they did. Half of them would lie, and the other half would swear to that lie.

Now Goliah was going to hear some facts from him.

With his ire rising like a flaming forge at the mere sight of the man, Two Bird smoothed down his taffeta sleeves and aimed towards the bride, the groom, and the double-dealer.

"*Fencing Indian land is banned,*" Two Bird said bluntly.

The bride led her groom away in an abrupt backward withdrawal.

Goliah's eyes darted towards the only exit to the room, his one silver brow reminding Two Bird of the stripe down a skunk's back. The skunk seemed to realize it was too late for a hasty retreat. Instead, the varmint nodded towards the fleeing bride and groom.

"Now, there's a pair with a fine prospect of happiness behind them, wouldn't you say?" He gently slapped Two Bird's arm in jest.

Two Bird had no trouble remaining unamused in the face of what he surmised was a lame attempt at humor. And in English, no less. With a swift swipe, he dusted off the part of his sleeve Goliah had touched. "*This land belongs to us all,*" he said, in the language of his people.

Goliah's expression went from unusually pleasant to terribly pinched. "*It is written where?*" he asked with narrowed eyes, succumbing to Two Bird's use of Cherokee.

A small victory. Good, Two Bird thought. Because he was not about to let any thin-blood close his eyes to his *Tsalagi* side. "*Tongues wag. They say you have turned Sput Louie off her land.*"

"*You speak out of both sides of your mouth. If this land belongs to us all, how is it then 'her' land? And what is your disagreement with me this time? The land, or your favorite* nigger?"

There was no Cherokee equivalent for the word "nigger," but the English term was well-known in Indian Territory.

"*She is without a husband now, but this you know.*" And, Two Bird wanted to say, if you had rightfully claimed him as your son, he would still be there. But to interfere in another's personal life was neither the Cherokee way nor Two Bird's way. He had probably already said too much in that regard, but the McClendons were his friends. The land, however, was not personal, but tribal.

Goliah's face turned as pale as a raw biscuit. His features tightened, then smoothed back out, as if he had considered an unpleasant notion, and just as quickly dismissed it.

He stealthily scratched at his groin, making Two Bird wonder if maybe he had contracted the dirty woman's disease. He let the notion pass and proceeded to more important things than Goliah's well-known penchant for night women. *"Men talk,"* he continued.

Goliah's eyes, as beady as black-eyed peas, flitted about the room like he was on the lookout for incoming arrows.

"They say you have plenty of land. You need to take Sput Louie's *small share, why?"*

The pale color in Goliah's cheeks quickly curved towards crimson.

Two Bird continued. *"Talk says you will lease Indian land to Texas cow chasers. That is also against Cherokee law."*

A tetchy sigh blew from Goliah's lips. *"I have more cattle arriving by train soon, yes. They are from* Texas, *yes. But they are mine. My intent is to fatten them and sell them. Is making a profit against tribal law?"*

There was a time in the old country when Indians used the land for sustenance only. Then the blonde-hairs became their neighbors and brought with them the idea of farming and ranching for profit. To get more profits, one needed more land, and the Indians had the best land. Thus, the Indian Removal from their lands along the Hiawassee River to this part of the country. Two Bird had never warmed to the idea of using land to gain wealth. That had never been the Cherokee way.

"A boat does not go forward if each one rows his own way. All Cherokee must row together."

"Look." Goliah crossed his arms. *"It is clear you desire the old ways, but these are new circumstances. The leasing law will be the first order of business once I am on the council."*

What was clear to Two Bird was that greed could be the only new circumstance of which Goliah was speaking. *"Be it remembered, man is not here to get rich, only to get by."*

"Then *why*," Goliah asked, flicking his fingers, *"is bread money to be gifted to Freedmen?"*

Two Bird stretched his neck back in disbelief. *"Bread money is for Freedmen, also?"* So that, Two Bird thought, is what the Indian Agent meant when he said there was a new stipend to be gifted.

Goliah shook his head and smirked. *"This particular bread money is for freedmen only."*

He glared at Goliah long and hard. So Agent Talbot had tricked him. He quickly replayed the conversation in his mind. When he had questioned him about his measuring Indian land yet again, Talbot had said he was "half right" without explaining the other half. That is how the Great White Father always played it, with half-truths and whole lies. He should have snapped that blond-hair like a string bean.

Two Bird had no objection to Freedmen's use of Indian land as long as land was in abundance. However, bread payments were a separate issue. They were usually small and always infrequent. He breathed in deeply and let it out resolutely. *"Not if I have a say."*

Goliah shrugged as if to say you don't have a say.

"The fact is, *your freedmen have hired an attorney. That attorney accuses the tribe of wrongdoing."* He tapped Two Bird's chest with the back of his fingers like a brother giving friendly advice. "So *your favorite Negro family may soon take profit from Cherokee coffers because* Washington *is stepping in now."*

"Wa-shing-ton *may be the capitol of ghost-faces,"* said Two Bird, stepping back far enough to discourage any further touching, *"Tahlequah is the capitol of Cherokee Nation."* Then he spat on the planked floor as if he'd tasted something bitter.

Goliah smirked. *"Which do you think is of higher rank?"*

Two Bird blenched, then said through clenched teeth, *"You think you fly above the hawk."*

"What I think," Goliah narrowed his eyes, *"is that you should stick to dressmaking,"* his eyes swept up, then down the length of Two Bird's outfit, *"and leave politicking to others."* His words were clipped, their edges sharp.

"Ukshana." Two Bird mouthed a sharp derogation of his own, just as Goliah turned tail, and shuffled away like he had a red-headed wood-pecker lodged in his ass.

Chapter Fifteen

On the following Saturday, a crisp morning sun saluted every family in Feather Falls as they draped their blankets and spread their shawls over the grassy shores of Lake Watanuga.

The townspeople pushed nearby rocks and fallen logs into haphazard seating circles where—after the day's festivities—men would gather to smoke, talk, and drink. Some would drink coffee. Others might sneak in spirit water. Young girls harvested kindling to use in the cook fires, while young boys like L.B. prepped for a game of stickball in a clearing. A few men set up canvas arbors to shelter the elderly from the sun, while a handful of young mothers set up a tent for sleeping babies.

No spoken invitation had been necessary. No formal announcement made. It was simply the sighting of the first crescent moon of June that served notice on the townsfolk that a fish-kill would be held the following Saturday. It was said that the smiling moon, as the crescent was called, coaxed the fish to flip, cajoled them to flutter, and drew the people down to the pearly ripples of the lake where they would catch the day's meal with sport and skill.

For the competition, Indians gathered upstream, while coloreds congregated downstream, and the town's white business owners mustered on the opposite side of the lake away from everyone. They had self-segregated less by design than by desire. People just naturally migrated to others like themselves. So Goliah aligning himself with the town's whites didn't surprise Sput at all. He was probably over there eating light bread instead of frybread, she thought. It didn't matter. That one day of the year, all were united by one common goal, to catch the biggest fish and win the grandest prize.

The grand prize was not something that could be seen with the eye, or touched with the hand, but something that was known in the bones, felt in the heart. The purse paid was that elusive intangible called respect. Respect for one's skill in capturing the creatures and the bragging rights that came along it. The winner would be a talked-about legend for at least a year.

The previous year, Hunter Big had won by spearing a flathead catfish that had the bonus of having a fat sturgeon clamped in its maw when he wrested it from the water. Snagging two fish for the price of one had made Hunter twice the legend.

Tawny had won the year before that. The only woman who had ever won as far as Sput could remember, and she hadn't had to lull her big-mouthed bass into a drunken stupor to catch it.

The Cherokees preferred to mesmerize their prey with a motley mix of fish intoxicants, like Devil's Shoestring, or the roots of the buckeye bush. As did the Freedmen, having been taught it during their enslavement. That timeworn technique would stupefy the fish until they forgot they were fish and thought they were men needing to surface for air. When they floated to the top, they became easy pickings.

Sput Louie fanned the air with her shawl as she spread it under the shade of a papershell pecan tree, and unpacked the bean bread from her wooden bucket. She wished it were *kanuchi* instead, but she'd had no sweetener to mix with hickory nuts to make the tasty treat.

Nevertheless, she was glad to be away from the dusty rayless hole-in-the-hill home to which she had been relegated. She took a moment to close her eyes and inhale the aroma of fresh coffee wafting around the picnic grounds. Not that wheat coffee she and Benjamin were used to, either, but real coffee. From beans. She let the scent of the beans and the warmth of the day settle around her. It was good to be amongst people again, albeit, without Benjamin.

Sput Louie anticipated a productive day, nonetheless. Everyone she needed for one thing or another was in attendance. Like potential witnesses to help her get on the roll, including Two Bird, to whom she would also show the kerchief.

She resisted the urge to touch the treasure, which she now kept in her bosom, while she scanned the lakeside for her lanky friend. She spotted Two Bird upstream yanking from the mud a cluster of devil's shoestrings that were as long as he was tall. She would make her way over there soon enough.

First, though, she joined the other colored women who were filling burlap bags with buckeye bush.

"Osiyo," she said to everyone, then knelt on the spot next to one of her favorite people, Emarthla. "It's somethin' awful powerful about plungin' a bag of buckeye underwater and beatin' the bejeezus out of it with a stick." Sput looked towards the lake where a few of the men were knee-deep in the water beating the bags with vigor, sifting the peculiar poison into the water to slow the fish down.

Emarthla watched, too. She was slightly younger than Sput, though considerably larger, and her complexion was the color of a smoky lantern. "You picturin' Benjamin or Old Crow when you commence to beatin'?" She knelt back down in the dirt, and let out a throaty laugh that puffed her cheeks up so they looked like brown pumpkins.

Sput's spine straightened as she dropped her bag and slowly stood. She put her hands on her hips and shot a pointed stare down at Emarthla. News traveled fast in Feather Falls, so she figured everyone had already heard about the whole McClendon family saga by now, horse and all, but no one had alluded to it until then.

Under Sput's glare, Emarthla froze in her busy work with the buckeye bag. As did the other ladies around them. When she slowly looked up at Sput, her eyes pleaded forgiveness for the gaffe.

"Not my husband. Ever," Sput said with finality.

Emarthla deflected Sput's stern tone by turning her attention to an inbound Hunter Big. She promptly licked her lips.

Sput stretched out her overfilled bag towards her first born.

"It's all set, Ma," Hunter said, accepting the bag. "The men gon' come around in the next couple of days for a go-doo." He knotted the top of the burlap, securing the intoxicant inside.

A go-doo was a Cherokee tradition whereby men got together to go and do whatever a neighbor in need required, whether that be a barn-raising or a house raising, or a crop harvesting if extra hands were required. Indians didn't do it so much anymore, but Freedmen still practiced the tradition.

"And who told you to do that?" Sput asked.

She might accept help from someone like Two Bird. He was considered family. But she would rather hold the hot end of a poker than ask anyone to call a go-doo just for her. Of course, Benjamin probably wouldn't have minded. His pride only reared its head when Old Crow was involved; hers was an ever-present albatross.

"Ma, that dugout is darker than the inside of a cow," Hunter groused. "Pa aint' gon' wanna come back to that."

And there it was, proof that her sons fully expected Benjamin to return. If one son had hope, the other two did as well. Even after nearly a month of him missing. She, though, was less hopeful, especially if her guess about the kerchief's contents was correct.

"Besides," Hunter said, his chin dipping down, "Tawny gon' move in with us."

Sput couldn't say she hadn't seen that coming, and her lack of expression said so. She knew they would wind up in a wedding. She also knew—but quite often needed reminding—that Hunter was a man with ideas of his own, not a boy who did what his mother told him to do. "And you'll be rightly married?" she asked, anyway.

One of the first things former slave couples did upon being let free was get married properly, with a preacher and paperwork. She and Benjamin had done it. Even if they couldn't read the certificate, they wanted the same rights as everyone else.

Not Hunter, though. He shook his head. "Don't need another man's say-so to call her my wife."

Emarthla shook her head in agreement, even though she'd been legally married three times and was on the hunt for a fourth. "If ain't nobody claimed that land you on by now, y'all good for it. Decent spot to build on, bein' near water and all. I just hope they can find enough timber here and there, and not have to clear too many trees for the house. You know Indians act like the trees belong to them instead of God."

Sput conjured an image of what a new house might look like, though she usually didn't want to get ahead of herself. "Sure would be nice to have two rooms instead of just the one." Especially since there would be increased coupling going on, she thought. Who was she fooling? Coupling, period. "And a raised floor," she added. "Never had one of them before."

Houses with a crawlspace beneath kept the cold from seeping up into the floors during winter, and the heat in summer. Of course, extra timber would be required for that luxury.

"That mean we can do it?" Hunter asked, with the *please* coming from his eyes instead of his mouth.

"Ya-huh," she said, with a sigh.

Hunter almost smiled. "I'm gon' try to gather enough wood for two rooms." He shook the burlap bag excitedly. "And a crawlspace."

Emarthla harrumphed. "Almost ain't eaten, young buck." She looked him up and down and sucked her teeth. "Don't try. Do. Go do. Go-doo." She chuckled at her own joke, though no one else did.

The other women merely nodded in agreement, like a council granting approval of a treaty. Hunter took his Ma's consent and ran off with the burlap bag and a budding grin straight to Tawny, who was staked out at the babies' tent.

Sput swatted at a crane fly as she watched him bypass the men at the shoreline. The medley of voices wafted up soft and sibilant. The longer she stared, though, the more she realized the sounds were strong and vociferous.

She bore down a bead on the cluster of men as they crowded around none other than her second born.

#

Archie held a copy of the Sentinel high in the air, gesticulating like a politician giving a speech. Sput made her way down to see what was going on. Emarthla fell in line beside her. The council of women followed them both.

"The law on paper don't match the law on the land," she heard Famous Johnson say. He hawked a wad of his homespun chewing tobacco against the inside of the tin spittoon bound to his cane with a wrapping of twine. The can was expertly positioned so that his spittle never missed its mark. The spittle clanged decisively, putting a seal on his proclamation. "I ain't fallin' for it. Somethin' 'bout it ain't right."

"Yeah, they makin' it too hard to enroll," Sput heard one man say as the throng of women reached the circle of men.

"Like trying to get in a house that ain't got no doors," said another.

"They don't really want us in."

Someone else added, "They say we gots to prove we was a slave. Well, what else was I? President of these United States?"

"Like we swam here all the way from the homeland."

The crowd, composed of various shades of brown-complected people, chuckled.

"Some of us freedmen is more Indian than those half-whites."

"Uh-huh, in spirit and in blood, since we was taught to live the Cherokee way, dress the Cherokee way, talk the Cherokee way."

"Didn't know nothin' 'bout the Homeland. Wasn't even allowed to say the word *Africa*."

Heads all around nodded in agreement, including Sput Louie who was reminded that, as a child, her mother had insisted that Sput address her as Ma Bay because it was close to her hidden and forbidden African name of Mbena.

"What y'all buckin' for?" asked Green Brown, who had migrated to Indian Territory from Tennessee after the war. Such immigrants were called State Negroes or *wachinas*, and they were just as unwelcomed as white intruders. "Back in Shelby County, we didn't have no rights."

He chawed down on the snuff stick hanging from his mouth. "Wasn't much different than when we was slaves, except we could finally get a piddlin' wage for our work. Back then, we thought freedom was better than Jesus."

"That didn't last long," someone groused.

"Like fruit that died on the vine."

"Hell," said Green Brown as he skillfully maneuvered the twig of snuff from one side of his mouth to the other using only his tongue. "I woulda took one acre and a *picture* of a mule." Snickers went up. "Broke that promise like it was a egg." With his foot on a log, he leaned on one knee and dusted off his worn, but store-cobbled shoes. One big difference between *wachinas* and freedmen was the *wachina's* penchant for store-bought attire as opposed to homemade.

"Had to live by our bare hands and common sense," someone agreed.

"Didn't give us nothin', no means to live by."

"Not even a big-eyed hoe tool."

More laughter.

"If I was y'all," Green Brown continued, "I'd sign up, fill out, lay down, and roll over if somebody was gon' give me a—what you call it?"

Archie stuck his chest out. "Per capita payment," he said. "Bread money."

"Well, they not givin' nothin' to you," came a voice in the crowd. "It's only for those who slaved for the Indians, and you just got here, Green."

"But they might give my woman some money, ain't that right, sweetness?" Green looked at Emarthla and cast a wink her way.

Sput Louie couldn't even look at him. Green Brown had rebuffed everything Emarthla had offered except what she put in the supper pail she took to his shack every Sunday evening.

"Well," Emarthla said looking around the crowd, smoothing the gathers of her dress, then wiping her mouth with the back of her hand. "If that be a marriage proposal, I accept. Yes, sir. I sure do."

Green Brown's face dropped, as Emarthla gave him a slow wink.

Sput could not disagree with what the crowd had been saying. She'd been set free with nothing more than the clothes on her back, and the babies in her belly. Things were about to be different now, though, she believed. With no husband to look out for her, she had no choice but to believe.

Archie piped up. "But they're giving out money now, and Ma needs witnesses to get on the roll. You all need witnesses, too, the ones who was slaves, anyway. You gonna need to testify for each other." He turned to Famous Johnson. "Mr. Johnson, you know everybody."

Famous leaned back on one of the lakeside boulders and tapped his wooden leg with his cane. "I fought alongside the Cherokee in two wars. Lost this leg when we fought Texas back in eighteen hundred and thirty-nine." He took off his fraying straw hat and laid it next to him on the boulder. "Lost this eye in the Freedom War," he lifted his eye patch, exposing a shrunken eyelid barely covering a dark hole, "fighting with Stand Watie at Pea Ridge 'cause they didn't tell me I was fighting against the very people who wanted me to be free. And Watie kept us in the war, too, long after General Lee threw up the white flag. Didn't tell us we was free. Kept us out there to fight nobody." He shook his head. "Now they think about us coloreds like they think about a cow bone dry of milk."

Another asked, "That how you lost your ear?"

"Naw, sir," Famous replied. "That right there...was from a jealous husband." He winked his one good yellow eye at Emarthla, who promptly pruned her lips.

While some laughed, others grumbled.

"I put a lot of time and labor in clearin' this here land. Plantin' it, workin' it, buildin' things on it. I wants my due."

"All of us did," Emarthla added.

"Indian land was built on the blood and bones of African slaves," came a woman's voice.

Green Brown rejoined the exchange. "Tennessee land, too."

"They promised us."

"They promised everybody."

Archie rolled his newspaper up and slid it upright into his back pocket. "And now they gonna give you some money, and land can't be far behind. But it won't be easy. That's why y'all need to stand up for each other."

"Ya-huh," said Sput. "I'm signin' up for one of those affidavits as soon as they come to town and bring me one."

"Me, too," said Emarthla. "Plus, they makin' it too hard to just squat on the land now, always uprootin' the colored folks." Her eyes darted to Sput Louie.

Some of the others chimed in with sentiments of agreement. But not all.

"What about them other rolls they done made before now?" said someone. "Nothin' never come of them. They foolin' with us."

"Well, don't you see?" asked Archie. "Cherokees were supposed to give y'all that money a few years ago, same time they got theirs. When they didn't," Archie blew out a whistle like he was proud of what he was about to say, "our people went and hired a lawyer. And I hear tell he's colored."

"What?" asked someone in disbelief.

"He colored? A colored Negro lawyer?"

Archie gave a low chuckle. "Of a darker hue. Man by the name of Turner.

"Attorney Turner," someone said, like they were not only shocked at the idea of a Negro lawyer but fascinated by it.

Archie continued boastfully. "Attorney Turner is the reason there's gonna be a new roll. He filed a petition."

"Just for the coloreds?"

"Well," Archie twisted his lips to one side. "For the Shawnee and the Delaware, too. Cherokee gypped them out of their fair share just like y'all."

Famous Johnson opined once more, "I declare one more again, it ain't gonna happen. Indians got a cast-iron prejudice against the peoples what used to slave for 'em."

Sput cleared her throat. "They gon' come through on their promise to us with this one. I just have a feelin'. Besides, we been here all this time waitin' on this very thing."

"Yeah," Archie said. "This roll is from the federal government."

"Where was them other ones from?" someone asked in earnest.

Sput sighed. Who knew and who cared? "This a new one. Anyway, it cain't hurt nothin' to try."

Famous put his hat back on, and pushed himself up with his cane. "Fine. If any of y'all wanna waste your time, I'll be a witness for you. I knows each and every one of you." He turned his one good eye to Green Brown. "Even know this *wachina* here. I think it's gon' come to nothin', but if you need me, I'm gon' be there." An arrow of brown spittle again hit its mark in his spittoon.

Archie cleared his throat. "And if you can get an Indian friend or relative to vouch for you, that's gonna be all the more better."

"Ya-huh," Sput said, and turned her attention upstream to Two Bird and Aunt Rogers.

Chapter Sixteen

Sput Louie jumped back as Two Bird slashed his hatchet down on the devil's shoestring.

"*As long as grass grows and rivers flow,*" he said in response to Sput's broaching the subject of enrollment, "*that is how long ghost-faces promised the Cherokee would have tribal sovereignty.*"

She had never known her friend to be careless with his hatchet. Rattled, she wondered whether it was she who—blinded by her eagerness for his help—had gotten too close to the targeted plant. Or maybe it was Two Bird who, blinded by his own concerns about enrollment, hacked his hatchet too close to her.

Having severed the weeded top from its stringy bottom, he snatched them up, hastily divided them, and shoved the smaller share towards Aunt Rogers. Rogers jumped back as well. Had he not, the strings would have muddied up his white shirt and marred the delicately slim figure he cut. Not to mention, his gray Sunday-go-to-meeting suit pants made of the thinnest wool Sput had ever seen. He was dressed too fancy for a lakeside outing, but then so was Two Bird in his lace-collared blue-gingham dress.

Sput had wanted to talk with him out of Roger's earshot, but Rogers was never out of earshot.

"*Cherokee,*" Two Bird said, "*should say how Cherokee money is spent. Not the Great White Father. Why should coloreds get Indian money?*"

She thought about it. Not only were the Cherokees not saying and not doing, she wanted to say, but they were also not honoring their word. *"Because the Cherokees signed that treaty."* Her voice inflected up as if it were a plea instead of a reply.

He shrugged, and then lifted his chin. *"Cherokee signed the white man's treaty, why?"*

"Because it was the right thing to do for those that Cherokee kept as slaves, the black Indians."

"Shuh," Two Bird said. *"There is no such thing as a black Indian."*

Rogers looked up from his squatting position where he was bundling the strings together. Even though he had come from neighboring Creek country, he was nearly fluent in Cherokee. *"Two Bird never owned slaves. What is more,"* Rogers pinched his lips together, *"niggers are of no concern to Indians."*

She cringed at Rogers clapping hands on the white man's word, but Two Bird glossed right over the snub. It occurred to her that this wasn't the first time he had allowed the use of such a disparaging word in his presence.

"Owning slaves," Two Bird said, unflinchingly, *"was a misguided notion by those of thin blood to appear civilized to the Great White Father. 'Own slaves, become* Christians," he mimicked. *"'Have command of* En-glish *words. Adopt* En-glish *names. Have knowledge of the economy of the white man.'"* He dredged up phlegm from his throat and hawked out a plug with so much blood and thunder that Rogers flinched as he watched it miss his shoe. *"I will tell you what white man's economy is,"* He declared. "Greed."

"Greed," Rogers echoed."

Sput Louie seconded the sentiment. *"Like one panther eating two sheep at once."* By which she meant to malign the Cherokees as well as whites, but neither man seemed to pick up on it.

"There comes now this new enrollment campaign."

"Ya-huh," Sput said, *"so each will get bread money, maybe have use of their own parcel of land without fear of being turned off it on some fool notion by some fool man."*

But her effort to bring it back around to the plight of the Freedmen also went unnoticed. Two Bird was suddenly gazing across the lake. His expression was so curious that she turned to see the cause, as did Rogers.

On the far side of Lake Watanuga, Goliah Lynch huddled with Agent Talbot. A narrow plume of white smoke swirled between them, and Sput wondered what deviltry they were up to now. At the last fish-kill, they had plucked the wings off of butterflies to use as bait.

Two Bird scowled. *"Those of too little Cherokee blood fall prey to the white man's trap,"* he said, refocusing on the matter at hand. *"We were once hunters and warriors. Now we are farmers and merchants."*

Chiming in with his amen, Rogers said, *"Instead of warrior chiefs, we have mixed-blood politicians with white-man names and ghost-faced features."*

Sput raised one eyebrow at the only man in the conversation with a white man's name.

Two Bird stayed the course. *"Instead of ceremonials and peace councils, we have railroad deals and cattle* syn-di-cates."

The more frequently she heard Two Bird use English words, the less surprised she was. She wondered if he was aware of just how much English he actually spoke.

He went on. *"We surrendered land to allow for the railroad."*

"We give our all. What more do they want?" asked Rogers.

It sounded like the two of them were singing a song. A well-learned, well thought-out, well-practiced song. She glared at Rogers for using yet another term he had no right to claim, "we." She angled her back to him in an exaggerated fashion, making it clear her business was with Two Bird and only Two Bird. Rogers was a walking tale waiting to be told, true enough. Sput had heard he'd been run out of whatever town he was from, and was curious as to why. But right then, she didn't want to hear another word from him. *"The locusts are rejoicing today,"* she declared.

As soon as she did, she regretted it. Hopefully, Rogers had not yet learned of the saying the Cherokee used when loud-mouthed people spoke out of turn. Offending the mate of the man whose help she needed was ill-advised.

Barreling ahead, Two Bird said, *"We Cherokee are the sovereigns of this land."*

"Legal owners." Rogers pulled himself up to his full height, which was still a whole head shorter than his husband.

"I am speaking," Two Bird said with a glare.

Rogers looked down and away, like a chastised child bearing the sting of his father's scorn.

The Cherokees were known to show emotional restraint, and Two Bird was the finest example of such. Until today. His usual quiet dignity had become loud and derisive, and his scorn misdirected at those in closest proximity. The fact that Rogers was not exempt did not bode well for Sput Louie. She had not seen her friend so riled, so stinging, so cold as she had that day.

And she had never been so desperate.

"What about the treaty and the land promised to those who never asked to be slaves?" she asked. It always came back to the treaty, and why tribal leaders would sign such a thing if such a thing were not their intent.

Two Bird's face reddened anew. *"What about the treaty and land promised to the Cherokee who never asked to come here? What about the Trail Where They Cried?*

"Cherokee slaves marched along with their masters on The Trail Where They Cried," she reasoned, *"died along with them, cried along with them. They were one people suffering the same thing, Two Bird."*

"The Great White Father has changed the treaty many times. What is to say he will not change it further?" Two Bird shook his head no. *"Cherokee are the sovereigns of this land. We Cherokee can work out our own destiny."* For just a moment, his expression softened a little. *"You tossed off the land does not please me. Benjamin accused of theft does not please me, for I know it is a lie."* He rested his hand over his heart. *"I wish harmony for you and your family, Sput."* She held her breath then, hoping the next words out of his mouth were ones of action. Then he flipped his fingers up with a flourish. *"But this I cannot do."*

Sput's own hand withdrew to her heart, clutching her amulet at the finality of his words. She gripped it so tightly the cord strained against her neck.

"Forget about other Freedmen," she said. *"What about me, Two Bird? Benjamin would want you to help me. It was you who brought us together."*

Many years after she and Benjamin had married, she found out that Two Bird had been the one who'd sent Benjamin to find her that day at the Ugly Tree. Two Bird had seen her roaming around town looking like "a bundle of babies and bones," Benjamin had recounted to her, and suggested that a union between the two might be advantageous to them both.

"Now the family you helped create," she continued, *"are left to blow in the wind like a dry, stale tumbleweed."* She could feel her eyes tearing as her thumb searched the back of her amulet and found the soothing polished turtle bone. *"Freedmen need more than a sunny slope to sleep on."*

This concept seemed to give him pause. It was the only thing she'd said all day to do so. By his thoughtful expression, it appeared Sput had created a rip in the fabric of his argument, a crook in the seam, an unraveling of the hem. She decided to press on. *"Freedmen, too, are looking for that pearl of great peace."*

The "pearl of great peace" was a saying of Two Bird's, and she had just used it to accuse him.

His jawline tightened, while his eyes drained of all kindness. *"I will tell you how it is,"* he said evenly. *"I will not play the white man's game that is designed for him to win."*

With that, Two Bird let out a deep sigh, then angled towards the shore. Rogers bustled to trace in his lover's footsteps, while Sput stood stiff and silent. She tried to absorb the shock of Two Bird's dismissal of everything she wanted and needed, rightfully and legally. What was she to do now?

"The honey hole is beyond that boulder," she heard him tell Rogers gingerly as if Two Bird hadn't just upbraided him and downgraded her in one foul swoop. *"It is full of your favorite mooneye fish."*

Sput stood there like a plucked feather tossed to the ground and forgotten. She understood his allegiance to the tribe. They were as much a part of her life as his. She knew of his distrust of the white man's government, but they were trying to do a good thing here, weren't they? Enrollment was a way for everyone to be guaranteed a stable future, not just the Indians. She let out a trembling breath and shook her head.

Given his bent, Two Bird was supposed to be able to see the female side of things. Didn't he see that she was now a woman alone? Her sons would soon be going their own way, save for L.B. Hunter was already heading away from her, forging his own life. She had no doubt Archie would soon follow. She also knew that an egg could not butt heads with a stone, for it would break every time. There seemed to be nothing more she could do or say to change Two Bird's stubborn mind.

That left her with only one task.

She retrieved the kerchief from her bosom as she trailed the couple down to the lake. When she caught up to them, she tapped Two Bird's shoulder, only to have both men turn around.

"Benjamin left this for me to find at the Ugly Tree." She shoved the open kerchief close enough for both of them to see. *"Why would he leave me fruit from pawpaw tree?"* she asked deceptively, with a small smile curling the corners of her mouth. She waited for their reaction.

She didn't have to wait long.

As Two Bird looked at the items, his nose turned up. His body went rigid.

Rogers backed up one, two, then three steps, while his eyes remained fixed on the kerchief.

Two Bird gawked at the objects, then squinted, then gawked again. "Eee-yah," he yelped in high-pitched recognition. His chest began to heave in small breaths.

Sput held her hand steady, fixed, firm. Her expression was fearless and unflinching.

Then Two Bird began to back away, too. *"Those...are...not pawpaw."* He shuddered. *"Those are—"*

CRACK. BOOM. THWOOSH. A roar rang out from the opposite shore.

The ground beneath their feet jerked and jolted Sput forward into Two Bird's chest. She tried to grab hold of him with her free hand to keep from falling, but he hurtled to the ground too quickly. He covered his head with his arms, leaving her to fall over his back and flat on her face.

As water blasted out of the lake and straight into the air like an upside-down waterfall, she saw Rogers crawling on all fours. Bits of fish flew out from the cascade of water and plummeted back down. Sput let out a sharp scream. She didn't know whether to get up and run or stay put and take cover. Silvery flesh that didn't thlopp back down into the lake showered down in thuds onto the shore, into people's hair, smacking them in their faces. Some people ducked and dodged the fleshy bullets, while others ran to the water's edge in twos and threes to see what had caused it all.

People pointed fingers across the lake where Goliah stood amongst men, women, and children who were holding their ears, turning in circles, completely discombobulated. Goliah, in contrast to everyone else on the scene, looked calm, pleased even. He stood upright, arms folded across his chest.

"Giant boom powder," Sput heard someone near her say in disbelief. A chorus ensued.

"...killed all the fish..."

"...trying to kill us."

"...scared them away..."

"Fish-kill ruined."

"Ghost-faces," someone yelled.

There were screeches, shrieks, whoops and wails coming from every direction.

Sput Louie—kerchief somehow still in hand, gobs somehow still intact within—stared at the head of a spotted bass on the ground next to her. It had ricocheted off of her elbow when she'd fallen. "Damn bastards." Still, she had the presence of mind to pick it up and slide it into her apron pocket. Fish heads made a tasty soup.

Two Bird made his way to his feet. After he had helped Rogers to stand, he kicked a catfish torso that had landed near him. *"Leave it to blond-hairs to fish with dynamite."*

"And they call the Indian crude," Rogers added, as he picked fish bits from one of Two Bird's long braids.

Turkey vultures whined overhead as they descended on the lakeshore, swooping up and down, scavenging fresh chunks of fish flesh.

Sput Louie cupped the kerchief in her hand and shoved it high into the air. *"Two Bird,"* she yelled and nodded at the bundle in her open palm.

His face suddenly resumed the look of horror it held just before the explosion. He shook his head in disbelief anew, and said, *"That is not fruit from the pawpaw tree."*

Rogers agreed. *"Those are stones,"* he said, and shuddered.

Her hand stiffened so that the objects rolled apart like two giant marbles, saved from falling to the ground by the curled edges of the cloth.

Two Bird concurred by the way he stared at them, then jerked his head away as if by force, peeling his eyes off of them.

"Those are the stones of a man," he said, there being no Cherokee equivalent for the word "testicles."

Chapter Seventeen

"*I know just who they belong to,*" Sput Louie said, as she gazed at the stones like they were shiny baubles.

Two Bird, however, averted his eyes from the severed body parts. Just in time to catch a glimpse of Rogers easing towards a group of men migrating to the haphazard seating circle. Even though the blast ruined the fish-kill, the social hour still stood. Men were firing up their wooden pipes of tobacco, and filling their tin cups with coffee, the favorite drink of the Cherokee. Ready, no doubt, to castigate the blond-hairs for the day's undoing. Since Rogers had never been one to mingle, though, his fraternization sparked Two Bird's curiosity.

However, he was ultimately more curious about who had been stripped of their stones.

"*They belong to who?*" he asked, turning his attention back to Sput Louie and her declaration.

Sput rocked side to side like she was revving up for a stomp dance. "*One* Goliah Lynch," she said with relish, then carefully retied the kerchief and returned it to the safety of her bosom.

As Two Bird let out a long-held breath, his mind began to turn and click.

If you wanted bulls turned into steers, Snipping Ben McClendon was the man to hire. Everyone from east of Feather Falls to west of Going

Snake knew it. He could castrate a calf from California, a Longhorn from Texas, or a Brahma bull brought in from Mexico.

But could he have done this to a man, Two Bird wondered?

"That area will heal quickly, if done right," Sput said, as if she'd read his mind.

He considered that idea. *"Benjamin would often brag that it took one nick only."* As long as the cow chasers held the ropes tight and the animal still, Benjamin professed to be able to snip their sack and squeeze out their stones with his thumb and forefinger faster than you could say "stone gone." The nick would be small, neat and nearly bloodless. *"Like squeezing the eyes out of a pig on a spit,"* he had once told Two Bird. *"And just as slippery,"* he'd added, with a wink.

"Ya-huh," Sput mumbled. *"Said bulls never even slowed down after."*

A familiar whistle sounded from afar, drawing Two Bird's attention to a stand of trees behind the seating circle. Was that from where the bird-like trill sprang? When he looked, though, he saw nothing unusual.

Turning back to Sput his mind clicked again. *"At the marriage ceremony of Sky Spirit, Goliah tugged at his private area more than once. He walked like a redheaded woodpecker was lodged in his* ass." Two Bird tugged uncomfortably at his own private area. *"Hobbled like a cripple."*

Sput's lips curled into the faintest of smiles. "Ya-huh. *Maybe Goliah was scratching at a healing itch."*

Two Bird shook his head. *"What is to say the stones are not those of Benjamin?"*

She shrugged her dismissal of such a possibility. "Benjamin *has the skill to remove stones."* She nodded in the negative. *"Not* Goliah."

"For what reason would Benjamin...*would* Benjamin..."

"Snip them?" she asked, finishing his thought for him. *"And then hang them from a tree?"*

"Shuh." His eyes brightened, his mind clicked again. *"That would explain the horse. Ben* would need a horse to flee after such a deed."

Another click.

"But why go to Goliah's at all? Ben hates him more than Stand Watie hated Chief Ross, more than the south hated the north during the Big Feud."

Sput's mouth contorted to the side like she was about to say something distasteful. "Well," she began. *"We had an argument."*

"Ugg," Two Bird grunted. *"This again? About Goliah fathering him?"* He hadn't meant for it to sound like an accusation instead of a question, but he was as tired of hearing about it as he was sure Benjamin was. For years the couple had had this same argument. Still, he was bewildered by this whole new bent on the situation, and he did not like the feel of bewilderment.

Two Bird continued to try to figure it out. *"Goliah went to his blood father,"* he recounted as if he'd been there himself. *"Angry words were spoken."*

Sput nodded her assent.

"What could have been said that would make him do such a thing to his own father? At that time? Why not do it all the other years before now? What would vex him so?" He frowned in thought. *"Goliah is no match for Benjamin fist-to-fist. If there was a disagreement between them, they could have fought as men do. Not this lechery."*

Sput's nostrils flared as her eyes narrowed. *"I will not judge him like you."* Her expression then softened. *"But you have asked a question for which I have no answer."*

Ignoring the charge laid against him, Two Bird scratched his jaw, then reasoned aloud, *"What would make a man whirr up and wing off like bird?"*

"Goliah would know."

The familiar tune whistled through the air again, and this time a man called Bill Dollar emerged from the trees and approached the passel of men in the seating circle. Two Bird kept his eye on the *wachina* because he knew how he had earned his name, but he was not yet done with Sput Louie and her puzzling predicament.

"Ben did not flee with his family, why?"

"Another question for which I have no answer," Sput said. *"I intend to find out,* ya-huh."

Two Bird raised a brow just as he glimpsed Bill Dollar share what seemed to be quiet words with Rogers, then skulk back into the trees.

Rogers slunk in behind him. *"You will do that how?"* The words tripped out so fast they bumped up against one another, making it sound like one long word instead of one short sentence.

"I will show Goliah his stones," she stated as plainly as if she were announcing her intent to show him a pair of shoes.

Two Bird grimaced. *"A butterfly cannot do the job of a buffalo."* He crossed his arms defiantly and angled his body towards the trees. In his mind, he was already on his way to the wooded area Rogers had disappeared into, though he still stared at Sput.

"I have found who and what," Sput said, with a lift of her chin. *"This,"* she patted her bosom, *"is not the way of Benjamin. He is not one to drive a sharp stick into the eye of his enemy. But now he has done even worse. I must find out why."* She turned on her heels and walked away.

In Two Bird's estimation, Sput Louie was as stubborn as a sore-head bear. She was half the reason Benjamin was on the run, Goliah being the other half. Two Bird didn't know what had been said or done between the two men, but he did know that they would have to work out their own problems. Just like he had to do with Rogers right then.

Chapter Eighteen

With broad strides, Two Bird bypassed the circle of men, without so much as a salutation, and slid into the trees at the very spot where Rogers had disappeared with Bill Dollar. The trees were not so thick that they precluded sunlight. Still, it took a moment for his eyes to adjust. Spotting two figures in the dimness amongst the fauna and flora might not be so easy. He crept forward like an opossum. Slowly, so that the sunbaked leaves and dry twigs that carpeted the forest floor didn't crackle beneath his feet. A flowery scent floated past his nose as he edged by first one linden tree, then another. Up ahead and to his right, he glimpsed something that brought his brief search to an abrupt halt.

There, behind an unusually thick tree trunk, Bill Dollar crouched down.

Quietly widening his approach to catch a better angle, Two Bird recognized the elbow of Rogers' crisp white shirt peeking out as he leaned his back against the bark. By the looks of it, they were about to do the same thing they had been doing the very first time Two Bird had ever laid eyes on Rogers, and the very first time he'd ever encountered the name Bill Dollar.

It was two years prior, and it had happened on the plank board landing of Nevin's Ferry.

Two Bird was returning from a trading trip to the tribe's capitol where he'd bought the latest in dress goods; two bolts of French chintz, twelve yards of striped cloth, a package of needles, and a box of Boss ball thread. Per request, he'd also purchased a couple of cans of lemon sugar to make soda for his nieces and nephews.

Hidden underneath it all was a small supply of whiskey.

Though he did not partake himself, he kept it on hand as a neighborly treat for anyone who might come calling. It had to be secreted because federal law not only prohibited the selling of liquor to an Indian, but it forbade one from giving it away, as well.

Sitting atop his buckboard on the stage plank, Two Bird hastily counted out the fifty-cent fare charged for a wagonload. He was anxious to get back home and breathe life into the dress designs he had already drawn, but the man ahead of him was holding up the line, squabbling with the runner over the fare.

Because of the many canebrakes that filled the Grand River, only by flat boat could one navigate across the mouth of the waterway. To use the ferry, you had to pay the fare. The man ahead of him didn't seem to understand that, or didn't want to pay it, or didn't have the fare. Two Bird doubted the latter, though, because the man sat stately atop a black stallion and wore a finely tailored suit over a well-proportioned body. Not everyone had buckskin calf gaiters like this man wore. The skin of a stag was the best material to protect the pant legs from the wear and tear horse riding rendered.

The spiffy man oozed big city from every pore, yet he didn't have the twenty-five-cent fare required for a horse without a buggy?

"I can pull cable lines for my fare," the rider offered to the woman who ran the ferry in a language Two Bird recognized as Creek.

When she responded in Cherokee with *"This is not a line ferry, this is pole ferry,"* the rider then began to speak Cherokee as well, although haltingly. Maneuvering in and around Indian Territory where each tribe had their own lands and their own language, it behooved one to have a working knowledge of more than one tongue, especially if one was intent on doing commerce. Or crime, for that matter. Two Bird wondered which one this stylish man was here for, as he obviously was neither farm hand, nor ranch man, nor cow chaser.

The man turned his head towards a scattering of crates haphazardly stacked on the shore and cut a winsome profile in his broad-brimmed hat. Two Bird forgot about counting money and openly stared, unapologetic for his ill manners.

"Need help loading boxes?" the man asked, then eagerly dismounted his horse, ready to be put to work.

"No," the weathered white woman said. She then nodded to two colored men just beginning to load the boxes on board. *"Got help."* She shoved her open palm towards his chest. "Twenty-five cents," she said switching to English.

Two Bird stepped down from his wagon and approached the stalled negotiations, looking every bit the contradiction of a man in women's clothing. Sometimes, he enjoyed the bit of fame his choice of attire snagged, the shocking stares he would draw the further away from Feather Falls he got. Today was no exception as the fancy stranger gave him the usual once-over, only this time it seemed to be tinged with a patina of awe.

Instantly snatching his hat off, the man did a disbelieving double take from Two Bird to the ferrywoman. His expression pleaded with her for some clarification as to what he saw, as if to say *who is this man, or does this man dressed as a woman not shock you? Look at him...her...him.*

Two Bird was all too familiar with such reactions and found them amusing.

The ferrywoman, whom Two Bird had known for years, answered the fancy man's quizzical expression by remaining steadfast in her stance and stiffening her open palm. Clearly, there would be no verbal commentary forthcoming from her.

Fancy Man's lips widened ever so slightly into the smallest of smiles as he returned his stare to Two Bird.

"His fare I will pay," Two Bird said, as he strode up and plopped seventy-five cents into the ferrywoman's hand. She seemed happy to be able to move on to the rest of the passengers lined up behind his wagon.

"That you do not have to do," Fancy Man said, tipping his hat as the lady shuffled wearily away.

"I desire very much to get home before winter," Two Bird said, as the summer sun beat down on the dock.

While Fancy Man walked his horse on board the ferry, and Two Bird drove his wagon right behind him, there seemed to be a second squabble brewing back on shore. After they both had found spots against the railing next to each other, they turned to determine the reason for the ruckus.

A man with a marshal's badge pinned to his shirt was loud-talking the ferrywoman.

"A couple of moonshiners were headed this way with a load of white corn whiskey. One of them was a colored by the name of Bill Dollar. And if you allow either one of them on board, you're operating against the law as well. It's called abetting a criminal."

"I allow anyone on board who got coin, whether they have a stupid name or not," the ferrywoman said. "Go on and check the line yourself, if you'd like. Have at it."

While she moved down to the next patron with her palm out, the marshal moved up the line in Two Bird's direction, questioning first one person, then another.

The only thing that Two Bird gleaned from their exchange were the words *white corn whiskey* and *bill dollar,* though he'd always heard it as *dollar bill*. But that, coupled with the marshal's scrutinizing eye, was enough to spike the hair on his arms. What if the lawman looked in his wagon and found his hidden stash?

Apparently, it alarmed Fancy Man, too, because Two Bird saw him reach into his saddlebag and push whatever was inside it deeper down. Then he hurried around to the bag on the other side and did the same thing. Now, though, both bags bulged like a squirrel's cheeks swollen with nuts. If the nuts were rectangle instead of round, that is, and made of glass, which was Two Bird's educated guess.

"Here," Two Bird said, alighting from his wagon on the far side next to the ferry rail. He reached into the back of his wagon, lifted a bolt of cloth, and pointed to the gaping hole down its middle. *"Hide it here."*

Fancy Man reared his head back and scrunched his eyebrows together.

Two Bird did the same. He could see the distrust in the man's eyes and didn't blame him. He shrugged and offered up the hiding place again. This time more forcefully.

The man finally nodded his understanding and accepted Two Bird's offer. He quietly eased four bottles from one of his saddlebags, and quickly stashed them inside Two Bird's roll of chintz. Pretending to rub his horse down, he eased around to the other saddlebag. Emptied that one, smuggled the bottles around and tucked them deep inside the bolt of orange striped cloth.

By the time the marshal reached them, they had both come around to the near side of the wagon—away from the wealth of whiskey—as if they'd been whiling away in that position the entire time.

The marshal took a long gander at the length of Two Bird before he spoke.

"Nice dress, Matilda," he said, and moved on to Fancy Man without questioning Two Bird or searching his wagon.

Two Bird stood stoic while his partner-in-crime stood stiff-necked.

"You." The marshal pointed at Fancy man with a lift of his chin. "What's your name?"

"Rogers."

"Is that your first name or your last?"

"Just Rogers."

The marshal shook his head. "You people with no last names are uncouth." He shook his head in disgust. "Raised like wild animals, you are," he mumbled, then squinted at Rogers. "Take your hat off."

Rogers doffed his hat, revealing the slicked back hairstyle of the modern day man. He scratched his chin, unintentionally luring Two Bird's eyes to his lush lips.

"You're not Bill Dollar?" The marshal studied him with a skeptical side-eye.

"Rogers."

"Do you know Bill Dollar?"

"No, sir."

"Haven't seen him around these parts?"

"Don't know."

"Don't know what?"

"Don't know who he is, so I don't know if I've seen him."

"Smart ass."

After the marshal had questioned the other people already on board, ransacked a few wagons, he left without collaring his criminal.

As the ferry pushed off, and its passengers were settling in, Two Bird reached into the back of his wagon for some *kawhesti* and offered it to Rogers. He always traveled with the dish of roasted corn pounded with sugar because it didn't easily spoil. *"Bill Dollar, you may not be,"* he said, as he watched Rogers nosh on a bit of the mixture, *"but you do his bidding."* He appraised the man to be as graceful as a lynx, even while eating with his fingers.

Rogers stopped mid-nibble and landed a curious leer on Two Bird, who met his gaze. *"A woman you may not be, but you wear a dress."*

While his face appeared unmoved, Two Bird's heart smiled. Was that wonderment he saw in the man's eyes? With a tickle of intrigue? It was far and away from disapproval. He'd seen that enough to recognize it. But this, this was something else. It smacked of praise. Perhaps even admiration? It had been a long time since he'd seen anything even resembling that looking his way, so it was hard to know. In Cherokee lore, to dream of a lynx meant that a great secret would soon be revealed. This was no dream, but Two Bird was of the mind that this lynx-like man did indeed have a secret.

At least he hoped so.

Exhilarated with anticipation, he invited Rogers to his home for supper that evening. Rogers discreetly accepted with a curt nod of his head, and a shrug to the side-glances that surrounded them.

For months after that, whenever Rogers did Bill Dollar's bidding in and around Feather Falls, he would stay at Two Bird's home. Each stay would be longer than the last, until one day, Two Bird looked up and realized Rogers hadn't left in weeks. Even though he had been dry of his wares for a while. He had moved in. And when he did, he took on most of the daily duties of a wife, and all of the nightly pleasures.

Occasionally, there would still be a whistle heard from the trees behind his house announcing Bill Dollar's presence. Rogers would disappear into them and come back fully stocked with spirit water. That is, until Two Bird picked up the gauntlet Tiger Tee Hee had laid at his feet to spur the tribe back to the traditions of yore, long before the European invasion. That was when Two Bird forbade the selling of spirits by Rogers. And anyone else, for that matter. He no longer tolerated those kinds of harmful hijinks going on within a hair's breadth of his presence. Not if he knew about it.

Seeing Bill Dollar turn up at the fish-kill, lure Rogers into the forest and crouch behind a thick tree trunk, he suspected that was precisely what they were about to do.

Two Bird marched towards them with all the fervor of a soldier leading a battle charge. The closer he got, the harder he stomped, the sooner they looked up.

But it was too late.

There was a huge tin can next to a smaller tin can, connected to each other by what looked like a coiled copper pipe of some sort. Without a word, Two Bird hiked his dress up and kicked the whiskey-making contraption over. Fermented mash oozed out, the spilt blood of a felled enemy.

Bill Dollar jumped up and nearly tumbled backward from the fright. "What the hell..."

Rogers, with his mouth agape, whipped his head around.

Two Bird had eyes only for Bill Dollar. *"Spirit water is forbidden in Indian Territory."* His gaze was steadfast, his tone unwavering. *"And wachinas are not welcome."* He kicked one of the tin cans even further away.

Once he righted himself, Bill Dollar's shoulders reared back. His chest heaved with each breath like a wildebeest was trapped inside fighting to get out. His arms were so muscular they looked as if he had been trundling wheelbarrows every single day of his life.

With his fists balled tight, Bill Dollar inched towards Two Bird in a step so tiny it was nearly imperceptible.

Rogers quickly tried to warn Dollar off with a jerk of his head.

Two Bird's eyes were fixed with flames.

Yet, they didn't so much as scorch Bill Dollar.

Dollar wiped beads of sweat from his top lip with the back of his hand, drawing attention to a three-cornered scar on his left cheek that looked like it had been left there by a kick from a colt. Without breaking his gaze on Two Bird, his face suddenly, inexplicably relaxed.

The sudden calmness prickled the hairs on Two Bird's arms. Dark clouds began to form in his mind, shaped by a mix of anger and distrust.

"You come in like a tornado," Bill Dollar said in flawless Cherokee, *"spilling my load of liquor, wiping out a week's work and a month's pay."* A mischievous grin began to grow. "So *I will spill my guts now."* His face went from a silky smile to a steely glare.

"Don't you dare," Rogers pleaded in a gust of eye-popping bravado.

Bill paid no heed. *"Know this about me, Two Bird,"* he spat. *"I am no wachina."* He lifted his chin. *"Though I am half-Colored, I am also half-Creek, born and raised."*

"Shuh," Two Bird said. This man's lineage carried no weight whatsoever with him. Be it Creek or colored, he thought, whiskey laws were whiskey laws. They applied to everyone. Except for the blond-hairs, but that was a matter for another day.

Bill Dollar continued. *"And this dandy man right here?"* he lifted his voice as he raised his outstretched finger towards Rogers, *"is my little baby brother."*

Two Bird stiffened. A coldness shivered up his spine. His brother? A wild torrent of thoughts flooded his mind like a flash. Not the least of which was why Rogers wasn't refuting this smiling pig, this trickster, this outlaw. This liar.

Instead, Rogers stared at his own feet.

"What?" Bill Dollar asked, in the voice of a sweet innocent. *"You did not know his mother was from* Africa?"

Two Bird shook his head in disbelief, as he took a step back.

Bill tsk-tsk-tsk-ed. *"If you look close enough, you will see his hair is one slave ship manifest away from shrinking back to kinky if he ever runs out of bear fat pomade."* A wicked laugh, a guttural laugh, a laugh filled with triumph spewed forth. *"I bet he never runs out, huh?"*

It took all of Two Bird's strength not to turn his head and look at Rogers' skin the color of pale wheat, and hair that he—just at that moment—realized he'd never seen in its natural state.

Two Bird stood stock still amidst the torrent of falsehoods and untruths whirling around his head. Were they untruths, though?

Colored.

Kinky.

African.

Mother.

Brother.

Negro.

Those notions pelted him like balls of hail, one after the other, unable to be dodged, unable to be swatted away, unable to be absorbed. The sound of them shrieked through his ears like a screeching wind of words, a rattling rain of lies, and there was no safe port to turn to avoid their squall.

He was not prepared for the storm that had just blown into his life.

And neither, it appeared, was Rogers.

Chapter Nineteen

To Sput Louie, Old Crow's house looked like a hibernating bear. The two-story home made of bricks the color of raw meat was trimmed with a tint of hardened frost. The windows were closed. The curtains were drawn. All was as quiet as the dead of night. Except it was the break of dawn, and Sput was about to wake the beast of a house up from its slumber.

The sleeping giant—that most townspeople considered garish and gaudy—hunkered atop a hill sprinkled with Catalpa trees. At each of the four corners of the yard was planted a fruit tree; orange, apple, peach, and paw-paw. It gave the air around the house a sweet smell, though Sput was sure the inside must reek of burning brimstone.

Laughing to herself, she opened the gate and entered the yard like she lived there. Having the upper hand for once in her life made her rather giddy. She couldn't wait to see the look on Old Crow's face when he saw his stones in the middle of her palm. She knew she would replay that image in her mind for the rest of her days. He probably would as well. So she was going to take it all in slowly, calmly, completely.

No ideas had yet come to her as to exactly what she should say, how she should broach the subject, though she'd spent the previous couple of days thinking of little else.

Should she say something like, *did you lose anything?*

Or, *are you missing something?*

Or, *do you feel lighter? More barren? Less manly?*

It didn't matter. Sput just wanted Goliah Lynch to know that she knew Benjamin had snipped him. Just like a *ganali,* an animal. And what did he have to say for himself?

Hopefully, he would tell her what he had said or done to make Benjamin finally snap and do such a treacherous but—she was sure—warranted thing.

She took a deep breath and knocked on the front door that was as wide as she was tall.

Nothing.

She knocked again. This time she rapped so hard her knuckles turned white. Where was Little Fancy, the Lynch house girl? Sput almost yelled her name out. Little Fancy was from a long line of women called Fancy, none of which were related to the other.

The original Fancy, who was a vague part of Sput's childhood memories, had been one in a gaggle of slaves Philura Comstock Lynch brought to the marriage with her. The story was that she loved First Fancy—as she later came to be known—so much that when First Fancy coughed herself to death, every house girl thereafter had to be called Fancy in her honor. There had been Fat Fancy, Old Fancy, Black Fancy, and Yellow Fancy who, according to consensus, was there to service Old Crow in addition to serving Philura.

After serving several rounds of steadfast knocking on the big oak door, Sput finally heard the faint shuffling of feet. Inch by inch, the heavy door whispered open and what Sput saw through the slowly widening crack was not a Fancy, but a fright.

Philura Lynch was pale and frail in her nightgown and slippers. The cane on one side and the doorjamb on the other seemed to be the only things holding her up.

"Sorry to disturb you, ma'am." Sput tried not to stare, but the woman looked like a wilted rainbow. Her pupils were small blue dabs surrounded by a sea of yellow, hooded by red puffy lids, all of which was topped by a nest of gray hair tinged pink, the obvious result of a bad dye job. "Is

Fancy here, ma'am?" Sput wasn't sure she wanted to talk to Philura. She was innocent in all of this, at least as far as Sput knew.

"Fancy?" Philura's voice creaked with a sing-song lilt. "Fancy died years ago."

Sput rolled her eyes then peered behind the woman who was just as short as she was. If Little Fancy couldn't answer the door, surely Old Crow would be coming up behind Philura soon enough. They certainly wouldn't leave this woman alone and on her own. Would they? "No, ma'am," Sput said, returning her gaze to the source of her irritation. "I mean Little Fancy."

Too many drops of laudanum or paregoric was Sput's cursory diagnosis of Philura's current state. This woman needed help. She probably had brain fever or something. Was this how Old Crow kept his wife out of his business and her money? He kept her stewed?

"Is Mr. Lynch here, ma'am?"

Philura's eyes went blank like her mind had drifted before they lazily came back into focus. "He's gone, too," she said, thick-tongued.

Swaying back and forth, Philura squinted at Sput, then widened her eyes when they landed on the amulet. She dragged her eyes all the way back up to Sput's as if unraveling a thread of recognition. Sput barely recalled her, so she was sure Philura wouldn't remember her, either.

"I remember you," Philura said. "You're that gal married to that boy that came here a while ago," she swallowed slow and hard, like her throat was in a drunken stupor, too, "fighting with my husband."

Sput's expression froze in place. Only her eyes moved about, running rampant, sharp and newly inquisitive all over Philura's face.

She knew.

This woman knew about Benjamin. But how much did she know? Did she know why they fought? What happened? Did she know about the stones?

Sput slid her hands into her pocket and cupped the kerchief.

"That boy took advantage of my husband being up in age, and beat him so bad," she said, not so languidly now, but with a wash of irritability, "he had to go see a doctor. But my husband is one strong man."

Sput eased her hand out of her pocket and decided to let the woman talk. She might learn more.

"Stronger than his age should allow. Yes, sir. He drove himself to the doctor's over in Going Snake," she slurred. "I told him, 'Let Senix take you,' but, well, he's a stubborn one, that one." She resumed her distant look.

"Do you know why they was fightin', ma'am?" Sput could see the old woman was drifting again, and she wanted to keep her there and focused.

A fleeting ripple of lucidity crossed Philura's face. "Because he wants my money, that's why. He should be in jail. Is he in jail, girl?"

"No, ma'am, he ain't in jail. Missin', though," she said, in case that would prompt Philura's memory even more.

"Well, then, he's hiding so he won't go to jail. He's never going to get my fortune, you know. Nor you. Nor your idiot son. Oh, yes, I know all about you." She tried to spit, but the white foam just bubbled down her lip. "You're a dirty little whore, aren't you? Marrying that man when you knew who he was. Don't you know who he is? Of course you do. You disgust me." She began to back up, loosening her grip on the door, but leaning harder on her cane. "Men will be men, but us women— well, but then you're only three-fifths of one aren't you? Niggers aren't people. Not really."

"Ma'am." Sput put her foot in the doorway in case Philura tried to shut it. "You need to get rid of that medicine dropper and get you some damn sunlight."

Sput turned to leave but stopped at the edge of the porch and waited until she heard the door creak shut.

"That woman must be swimming in that paregoric instead of taking it," she muttered under her breath. She just stood there at the top of the stairs wondering what Philura Lynch meant by all that she'd said.

What did she mean by "dirty little whore?" Never heard of a married whore before. And why was Sput the disgusting one and not Philura's dirty-dealing raper of a husband?

An inexplicable chill shivered up Sput's spine.

What if the answer was more troubling than the question?

Chapter Twenty

In an act of both cruelty and grace, and in the wake of hurt and humiliation, Two Bird banished his lover from their house.

His lover, however, refused to go beyond their yard.

Two Bird peeked out of his window to watch Rogers trifling amongst the yard shrubs and jonquils roughhousing with their ragtag menagerie of animals. It was like he hadn't a care in the world. Like the white shirt he'd worn every day since the fish-kill wasn't now rumpled with grass stains smeared on it and cockleburs stuck to it. Like it wasn't his third day in exile. Like his hair hadn't puffed up and fanned out while Two Bird held his pomade captive inside.

Like he wasn't as lonely as Two Bird.

To get a better look, Two Bird parted the curtains that hung from a rope of twine, and recklessly bumped his elbow on the hot stovepipe that snaked up from the cook stove next to the window. He didn't even wince at the burn.

Cursed it, though.

The stove had been a compromise purchase. Two Bird liked cooking in an open hearth, but Rogers preferred the more citified cast iron stove, which meant Two Bird also had to buy new pots and pans because the round-bottomed ones that hung from a hook over the hearth would not sit on a flat-topped stove.

The concessions he had made to that man made him shake his head in disgust.

While his chief thoughts were on Rogers, they should have been on the five full bloods now seated at the supper table behind him.

He'd already plated and served them a meal of skillet bean bread, poke sallet, and parboiled possum he had cooked himself. It was a job Rogers normally would have done. The possum, he had not-so-mysteriously found on his doorstep that morning already skinned and primed, along with some wood for the stove already chopped and chipped. He did not fix a plate for himself, though. Neither did he fix one for Rogers.

Strong coffee well sugared was all he wanted. Needed, really. He grabbed the kitchen cloth from the sideboard next to the stove, and used it to lift the tin urn from the burner, then poured himself a cup of the brew. He quietly carried his matching cup and saucer and resumed his seat at the head of the table with his cohorts that were all drinking from tin cups.

"*The others must be persuaded not to help coloreds enroll in the blond-hairs' scheme*," said Big Smoker, who sat to Two Bird's right. Finished with his meal, Smoker took a long drag on the wooden pipe that always hung between his rotten teeth.

Sitting next to Big Smoker was Tickeater, whose eyes swept around the table. "*More big bloods need to be here.*"

Two Bird gave a curt nod as he reached for the Blue Willow sugar bowl sitting at the center of the table. "*A single arrow is easily broken,*" he said, "*but not ten in a bundle.*" With his fingers, he shoveled loads of the sweetener into his cup, thinking that Rogers would have chastised him for not using a spoon. That was one of the things he shouldn't have missed, but did.

"*And five?*" asked Tickeater, appearing to do a visual count of those at the table.

"*Five here,*" Two Bird said. "*Ten from the next town, fifteen from another. Soon we will be a thousand strong.*"

120

Big Smoker spoke from behind a cloud of tobacco. *"Negroes are like baby birds. They want to have food put in their mouths. Why should Cherokee money be given to them? They did nothing to deserve it."*

"Negroes already have use of Indian land," said Cabbage, sitting at the end of the table, loudly slurping his coffee. *"Why do they not go where they belong?"*

"That is where?" Tickeater asked as he pushed his plate away, and cleared a spot center stage for his coffee. *"Some of them have been with the tribe longer than us."*

Across from Cabbage sat Widow Hawk, who'd earned his name by seeking to marry every available widow because he said it took five old women to do the work of one young girl. Widow Hawk shrugged. *"They badly want to be in the tribe. Why?"*

"They want to have a vote."

Widow Hawk sucked his teeth. *"Even I do not vote."*

"They want to have a say in tribal doings. Like the Great White Father.

"Land," said Tickeater. *"The land is what they want."*

Two Bird pondered this. That could be the ultimate plan. Once coloreds were enrolled and paid bread money, would land allotment be next for them? That was surely what Sput Louie expected, and had even said so. However, he quickly dismissed the idea. First things first and one thing at a time. *"What new trick is behind this new scheme, I know not. If we snap bread money like a twig and toss it in the wind, that will be the end of that."*

"Not so. They hired one-who-constantly-argues on their behalf," added Big Smoker.

"A-ttor-ney it is called," corrected Tickeater. *"Colored A-ttor-ney."*

Two Bird spit out his coffee, spraying it across the table. *"Colored,"* he said, wiping his mouth with the back of his hand. *"The a-ttor-ney is colored like them?"* What Goliah had said was true. Only he failed to mention that the Freedmen's attorney was colored.

Tickeater dipped his chin, and each exchanged a knowing look with the others.

"Seeing a Colored a-ttor-ney is like seeing a dog ride a horse," said Big Smoker.

Widow Hawk concurred. *"Backwards and up a hill."*

"Why do the Cherokee not have an a-ttor-ney?"

Two Bird raised an eyebrow in feigned annoyance, and to hide the fact that he hadn't taken more seriously the issue of a Freedmen attorney. Knowing now that the lawyer was colored and might fight harder made the situation more urgent. *"Try to keep up, Cabbage. The Cherokee have an* at-tor-ney. *He does what the Cherokee council says. Not what the Cherokee people say."*

"The newspaper says the colored at-tor-ney *filed a* pet-i-tion," Tickeater added.

Cabbage frowned. "Pet-i-tion *is what, Tickeater?"*

"It is a paper where they complain about us to the Great White Father."

"That they were not born Cherokee? It is not our fault they are Negro."

"Too bad for them," answered Big Smoker in between coughs from one of his frequent hacking fits.

Tickeater's lips curled into a half smirk. *"That is what ghost-faces say about Indians, 'not our fault they are Indian.'"* He shook his head. *"Who says that about ghost-faces?"*

A veil of smoke swirled up from Big Smoker's pipe. *"Everyone else."*

Cabbage pitched forward in his seat. *"Negroes did nothing to earn bread money."*

Two Bird glared across the table at his comrade. *"You did what to earn it?"*

"I was born Cherokee."

"That is no feat of yours," said Two Bird, straightening his dress over his knees. *"But of your mother."*

"The Cherokee had their homeland stolen, then we were given this land."

Tickeater's hands fidgeted. *"Negroes were taken from their homeland, and given what?"* he asked defensively. Before anyone could answer, he shook his head in the negative and added, *"Too bad for them is right."*

Two Bird cast a suspicious leer at Tickeater. *"You take the Negro's side, why? The Cherokee did not take them from their homeland. Cherokees do not have a big boat."*

"Cherokees had a hand in it, though." Tickeater folded his arms across his chest. *"They held them captive, too. Made them break rocks, clear land, plant seeds."*

"Cherokees owe them nothing," complained Cabbage. *"Next bread payment for us will be smaller because of them."*

"That be the truth," agreed Widow Hawk.

Folding his arms across his chest, Tickeater proffered a declaration. *"So now Indians adopt ghost-face greed."*

Two Bird put his palm in the air and interrupted the exchange of his brethren. *"Do not scratch the shoe when it is the foot that itches,"* he chastised. *"This is what blond-hairs want the Cherokee to do, fight over Negroes,"* he suddenly understood. *"Our concern is blond-hairs. Blond-hairs are tricksters, not Negroes. They are not smart enough."* He tried not to think about the smart, deceptive Negro romping in his yard instead of frolicking in his bed. *"Greed is not the problem. Sovereignty is the problem. The Cherokee should say who gets paid what, when, and where. Not blond-hairs."*

They all raised their coffee cups in agreement. "Yuh," they said in unison.

Widow Hawk rubbed his chin. *"The Negro is but a small warm ember in a big ghost-face fire."*

Two Bird agreed, though he had to give Freedmen credit for hiring their own lawyer. *"Still,"* he admitted, *"the ember must be doused."*

"To fight the Great White Father is like trying to light a fire in a snow-storm," said Widow Hawk.

Tickeater finger-tapped the tabletop. *"If Negroes are in our tribe, our tribe is made bigger. A bigger tribe will fight the Great White Father better. We will win."*

It was Two Bird's turn to fold his arms across his chest. *"Tickeater does not listen,"* he said. *"Negroes are not Cherokee. Negroes do not enroll if the Cherokee say Negroes can not enroll. We need to show the blond-hairs we are a sovereign nation. We must spread the word that we will not help them one i-o-ta. That is how we light a fire in a snowstorm."*

Tickeater leaned forward. *"Can a battle such as that be won?"*

Two Bird again leered at his friend who had been antagonistic throughout, and wondered why he showed such a lack of faith in not just himself, but in his people.

Tickeater shrugged. *"Marmots should not chuck at eagles,"* he explained.

"Shuh," Two Bird grunted. *"Steel teeth can eat an iron eagle."* He bared his gritted teeth in a stunted smile.

Tickeater scrunched up his nose as he suddenly whipped his head around and glared at Cabbage to his left. *"What smells like a rotting corpse?"*

Widow Hawk put his hand over his nose and mouth. *"Can you not go outside when you let loose the wind, Cabbage?"*

Cabbage smiled. *"That bean bread I ate is having a disagreement with my gut. Gut is winning."*

"But if Negroes enroll," Tickeater said, steering the conversation back, *"Negroes will then be Cherokee. It is not a puzzle."*

Two Bird slammed his hand on the table so hard, the coffee cups rattled. *"Cherokee is by blood only."*

"Puzzle is solved," declared Big Smoker with a nod.

All raised their coffee cups in agreement.

All but Tickeater.

Chapter Twenty-one

From the cooking spot she'd staked out in her new front yard, Sput Louie stirred the cauldron of stew that hung from the wooden crane over the fire pit. She hoped the thin medley of squirrel meat and sassafras shoots would be enough to feed the half-dozen or so workers who'd volunteered for the go-doo.

The go-doo-ers were able to amass only enough wood for a one-room house, but Sput was grateful they were still able to fashion her much-wished-for crawlspace underneath. It was the little things that counted, and she took her joy where she could find it. She was accustomed to taking the good with the bad.

One of the good things was the fact that they were constructing the house in a clearing not far from their hillside dugout. Being near a creek lent itself to the potential for a well source to be divined once the house was completed.

One of the bad things was that red cow-ants and green blowflies infested the area, which lent itself to a rough time come planting season.

Still, it was raw unclaimed land, and that was a good thing.

Another bad thing, though, was the ditty L.B. had been singing incessantly for the past few days. It screeched against Sput's eardrum like a knife scraping across glass.

I thaw Pa
Pa comin' home
I thaw Pa
Pa comin' home

Pa wasn't coming home, Sput thought, as L.B. droned on. How could he? The Anti-horsethief Society was still actively looking for him. Albeit less fervently for sure. Sput hadn't seen them hovering around and about for a while, but she figured they were still out there.

"What are you singing about," Archie asked as he hammered a board into place.

L.B.'s only response was to repeat the refrain.

"A true tonsorial artist of the highest order," Archie said sarcastically, dismissing his little brother and his annoying ditty while also showing off his extensive vocabulary.

So L.B., with his Mason jar in one hand and the lid in the other poised to capture any fly slowed by heat or hunger, continued chanting the lyrics as he darted around the workers.

He zipped past Green Brown, and practically tripped over him as he sawed puncheon planks for the floor.

Then he zoomed past Lee Ray who was mixing a mud and stick concoction that would be used to build a fireplace. Hunter Big tried to shush him up and shoo him away by playfully wielding a hammer his way. Each of the workers at one point or another told him to scram, scoot and skedaddle.

All to no avail.

As soon as he ran too close to the cook fire, though, Sput clapped her hands to get his attention. "L.B., no," she yelled.

Immediately, she was blinded by visions of little Lily flashing in her head. White lights that were her daughter's blistering skin streaked across Sput's mind's eye as she rushed forward to block L.B. from the fire.

"No," she yelled again, and charged at him the same way she'd charged at her daughter years before.

L.B. was oblivious. His eyes were trained on the swarm of flies as his left foot nicked the right leg of the sawhorse-shaped cooking crane.

Sput screamed.

The crane's leg buckled just as she reached out to grab the back of his overalls. All she managed to clutch was a hand full of his shoulder strap, but she gripped it with all her might and yanked it as hard as she could. The crane fell forward. The cauldron spilled out sideways. L.B. tumbled backward, landing flat on his back and on top of his mother.

Sput screamed out in excruciating pain as the weight of him pressed the back of her left shoulder into the jut of a rock.

She thanked the Lord she was able to save L.B. unlike the time Lily had caught fire.

Five-year-old Lily had gotten too close to the fireplace and the fire did what fires do. Once it caught the hem of her dress, it quickly scorched its way up the dry cloth. Sput had been so busy tussling with baby L.B. trying to tie a diaper on him, that by the time she turned around to see why Lily was yelping, smoke swirled around her.

Sput tried to grab her, but she was too late. Lily took off running around the room fanning her smoldering dress. The whipping air sparked the fire into full-fledged flames.

As the flames lapped up her dress, Lily tore out of the house. The force of the wind from her flailing arms whisked the flames up her sleeves. Trying to outrun the fire, she fled towards the wheat field.

Sput snatched L.B. up and ran after her.

By the time the three of them reached the wheat field, Lily's hair had caught fire. Flames engulfed her

In a frenzy, Sput tossed L.B. to the ground and rolled him away to safety, then frantically dug at the dirt with her hands. She mucked up fistfuls of dry earth and desperately tossed them onto a now fallen but still blazing Lily.

Archie, Hunter, and Benjamin had been working the wheat field that day and must have seen or heard the commotion. They came running as fast as they could. Following Sput's lead, they, too, gouged up mound after mound of dirt and threw it over Lily until finally, they'd snuffed the fire out.

But not before it jumped to first one wheat stalk, then three, then four more until the entire field was afire. While Benjamin and the boys tried in vain to douse it with dirt and pails of water, Sput tended to a whimpering Lily.

Her baby girl, her only daughter lay on the ground curled into a raw-skinned ball, the fabric of her dress singed to her flesh, her hands fisted like she'd been fighting off a person instead of a fire.

Sput wrapped her in her apron and carried her inside the house, where she stayed with her for the three days it took her to die. The entire time she held Lily in her arms trying to comfort her as best she could, the child looked up at her wide-eyed and accusing, her eyelids having been burned back.

That was the nightmarish image Sput saw as she lay there in pain with L.B. on top crushing her shoulder.

"You could have caught fire, boy," Sput shrieked, while L.B. worked his way off of her and to his feet.

All of the workers were agape at what they probably thought was a hysterical woman making much ado about nothing. Or maybe they were lamenting the loss of lunch.

"And stop singin' that stupid song." Sput grabbed her shoulder and tried to get up, but the pain pushed her back down. "Why you singin' that, anyway? Your Pa ain't comin' back."

"Ya-huh," he said, usurping her favorite word.

She gave him a side-eye, even though she knew he hadn't done it with malice. Mimicry was simply the way L.B. learned.

"I thaw Pa." He shrugged. "Pa comin' home."

Sput pressed lightly on the top her left shoulder, then down her arm in self-examination. If it wasn't broken, it sure pained like it was.

Her shoulder throbbing, Sput managed to say, "And you ain't seen him."

"Ya-huh," L.B. said again. "I did, too."

Sput squinted at him. "Where you see him at, then?"

Hunter came over to help her up while at the same time motioning for the men to continue with their work. "You gon' need a sling for that arm?"

"I'm alright," she announced, as she stood and shooed him back to work.

Somehow, L.B.'s bug jar was still intact, and he stared at the fly he'd managed to capture despite all of the commotion.

"I said where you seen him at, then?" she asked again.

Laughing Boy widened his eyes and gleefully declared, "I thaw him at the creek the other day. He waterin' hith horth. He thay," L.B. put a finger to his lips, "'don't tell nobody.'" His finger came down. "But you ain't nobody, Ma."

Surprise widened her eyes. Had L.B. overheard the conversation about Old Crow's missing prize horse? She couldn't remember.

Holding her left arm in place with her right hand, she glared at L.B. "Don't tell nobody what?"

"That he comin' back."

Sput rolled her eyes.

"And..." L.B. added but didn't go further.

It was a good thing Sput's arm was in such pain. It made it easier for her to resist the urge to wallop him upside the back of his head.

"And what?" she demanded.

"Only a fool look for dung where a cow never grathed."

And just like that, the pain in her arm became an afterthought.

Chapter Twenty-two

Goliah stood as steady and still as the juniper tree he hid behind. Slowly peeking from around it, he eyed his destination in the clearing up ahead. The Gooseberry Primary School.

Just as he felt safe enough to advance, the snort of a horse that sounded nearby stopped him. Was it his roan, he wondered? He had tied Ephinetta to a tree at the far end of the woods to be discreet as directed. Could she be heard from there? He froze stiff, listened hard, but heard nothing more. Maybe Ephinetta was just clearing her nose of dust, he thought.

Before creeping from the shadows, he gave one last visual sweep of the woods.

Nobody.

Nothing.

Naught.

Inhaling an anxious breath, he got an unexpected whiff of the blue Juniper berries used to make gin. It stirred up a thirst for a jug of it right then and there. Or at least a swig in celebration.

He didn't want to rejoice just yet, though, because what was he celebrating? Or why? Or maybe even who? Indian Agent Talbot had surreptitiously summoned him there. He'd cornered his skull Senix in town the previous day while loading farm supplies in the wagon and gave him a message to deliver to Goliah. The dispatch implored Goliah to meet secretly at the Gooseberry School, which was used as the agent's office in summer when school was not in session; and that if he did, it would change his life for the better.

This news intrigued Goliah so much that he couldn't sleep that night. That, coupled with the lingering pain in his groin. He scratched at the area desecrated with debauchery by Benjamin McClendon. He felt violated anew every time he thought about that depravity. He may as well have been raped. Thank God, no one knew about it. Even through the pain of that perverse night, he'd been able to keep his wits about him and see to that.

Deftly pushing those thoughts aside, he entered Gooseberry through the back door as instructed. The school was located just south of town. He'd never set foot inside that particular schoolhouse before. As a youth, his father had sent him away to boarding school once his mother had discovered Goliah's carnal activities with the slave women. From boarding school, he had matriculated to law school in Lebanon, Tennessee.

Crossing the threshold of Gooseberry, he was somewhat surprised to land in a vestibule instead of an actual lecture room. There were no pupillary desks to sit at, no slates to write on, no windows to look out. Though he supposed all of that to be beyond the inner door opposite him.

The walls of the small anteroom were the silvery color of timeworn teak. On the wall to Goliah's left was a bookshelf housing titles like McGuffey's Spellers, Franklin readers, Reed and Kelloggs Graded Lesson in English.

In the corner of what Goliah ultimately decided was the teacher's private office sat a desk. Behind that desk sat Agent Clem Talbot. In front of that desk, much to his dismay, sat long, lanky Tickeater with his leg jiggling up and down at a fast clip.

What was that babble mouth doing here if the meeting was so secret, Goliah wondered?

"Come on in, Goliah," Talbot said, without rising, or extending his hand or, indeed, barely looking up from his paperwork. Tickeater gave a negligible nod.

Almost immediately, Goliah's eyes were drawn to the dark gray double-breasted suit coat hanging on a wall hook behind the Agent. It had a black velvet collar with wide lapels just like the light gray one Goliah himself was wearing. He mentally patted himself on the back for choosing his attire well that morning. Big Bugs from Washington had a style worthy of emulation.

He took the only empty chair in front of the desk next to Tickeater, though he hadn't yet been asked to sit.

"Now," Talbot said, as he pushed his paperwork aside. "I understand," without glancing at Tickeater, "full bloods are against this new Wallace Roll for the Cherokee freedmen."

Goliah shifted in his seat. "All Cherokee are against it," he reported, and then thought if that was what this little meeting was going to be about, he might as well leave now.

"I am not," said Tickeater.

Just as Talbot raised a silencing palm to Tickeater, Goliah slouched back in his chair, perplexed as to when this full blood next to him had learned to speak the Queen's English.

The agent leaned forward and rested his elbows on the desk, bringing his hands together in prayer pose. There was a curious shine to his eyes as he stared at the mixed-blood, a flicker of something Goliah couldn't quite put his finger on just yet.

"Well," Talbot nodded slowly, "I'll tell you why you shouldn't be, either." He reached towards the end of the desk where a rusty tin can full of pencils sat. He plucked one right out. "Listen closely, now. This is how it's all going to play out."

How what was going to play out, Goliah wondered? It sounded like some plan was already in play, and he was just now finding out about it. He eased forward slightly to listen intently.

"Freedmen will get some money. Seventy-five thousand dollars has already been set aside for them to split with the Shawnee and the Delaware. After that, all land across these United States will inevitably be spoken for. Indian land will be no exception. It will be allotted. In severalty." With his elbows resting on the desk, he propped each end of the pencil between each of his index fingers and twirled it back and forth with his thumbs. "That means individually."

"I know what *severalty* means," Goliah said in a sharp tone. "Land will go to the freedmen as well, I suppose?" But he already knew the answer to that.

"It's what's best for the tribe and the rest of the country, I might add."

Goliah harrumphed. "But will the rest of the country give freedmen part of their land?" He already knew the answer to that, too. "I think not."

Talbot snapped the pencil in two. "You people act like you didn't sign that damn treaty. Can we move past that? It's a done deal." His eyes flicked upwards. "Freedmen will be a part of this tribe, and you might just like the reason why." He stuffed the now split pencil back into the can. "Now hear me out, Lynch. When this land is ultimately allotted, everyone," he looked from Goliah to the strangely silent Tickeater, "is going to receive one-hundred-sixty acres. That's what Tickeater here will get." Then he turned his focus back to Goliah. "But you, you have cattle. Any Indian who has cattle will get additional land. It's not yet settled, but right now, they're saying upwards of three hundred acres for grazing. How about that?" He slapped his palm down on the desk like he'd just won a bet.

With a stony stare to hide the fact that Cherokees presently only allowed him the use of a fraction of that for pasturage, Goliah shrugged. "I control nearly that much already."

"Control? Can you sell it? Lease it? Drill on it?" Talbot shook his head. "Not without the tribe's permission, and you of all people know they are giving no such permission. That's why you have to claim that new herd is yours, when everyone knows it's not."

Goliah shot Tickeater an icy glare, suspicious that he was the source of Talbot's all-too-accurate information. Then he thought about just how right the agent was. Tribal laws governing land usage were tougher than a nine-wire fence. If there was a way to get around that, he could make more money than he ever had.

Talbot continued. "Now, after this Wallace Roll goes through, it will be combined with that Cherokee By Blood Roll you all made a few years back. That 'by blood' part is what gave rise to this whole need for the Wallace Roll in the first place." His face softened a little as he smiled. "You bolted your door with a boiled carrot on that one. If you wanted to keep the freedmen out, you shouldn't have excluded them in such a blatant way." His expression turned serious again. "Anyway, the combination of those rolls will be the list from which all Cherokee land and monies will be allotted.

"So freedmen will eventually get land, too." Goliah cast his eyes so far down, they nearly closed. "If you give them land, next they'll be voting in our elections, and maybe even running for office, even those niggers that helped the Yankees during the war." If they were smart enough to hire a lawyer—as he had heard from his friend at the Sentinel—they might think they're smart enough to try and run for a seat on the council.

A garish grin spread across Talbot's face. "Why Goliah Lynch, you have political aspirations, do you? Think the coloreds might not vote for you?"

While Talbot smiled broader than Goliah thought the jest warranted, he kept his face non-committal. He did have aspirations, economically and politically. He wanted to be on the Cherokee National Council so he could vote on life-changing laws, profit-making laws, laws affecting the entire tribe and maybe even the entire country. He might even worm his way onto a seat in the U.S. Senate. *Senator Goliah T. Lynch* sounded good to him.

He gave Talbot another shrug. "Why, you must have taken a drink from the fountain of enthusiasm. I've never given much thought to politics, really."

"Well, you should. I'm sure you'd go far in the Cherokee government. Maybe even principal chief some day."

Goliah felt a flush of heat creep across his cheeks.

So this was how the world saw him. Not as half white with all the privileges attended thereto, but as half Indian burdened with the seemingly unshakable images of savagery and un-scholarliness, of weak minds and no ambition. Had not his unmistakable acculturation made a bit of difference? His education? His prestige here in Feather Falls? His standing amongst his peers? Why should he be limited to only tribal politics?

Talbot's eyes flicked upwards again. "Anyway," he continued, "For the good of the tribe—"

Again with the old good-of-the-tribe ploy, Goliah thought. Though intended to open doors, it threw up walls instead.

"—- there will be restrictions placed on the land," Talbot finished.

And there was said wall. "I thought we were getting rid of restrictions, not adding new ones."

"You know, so land speculators can't come in and gyp the—oh, let's call them the less sophisticated of your bunch. But that will only be for full bloods. Part Indians, such as yourself," he pulverized the *P* with lips and spittle, "will have no such restrictions."

The wall began to crack, but would it tumble all the way down?

"Freedmen will be unrestricted as well, eventually," Talbot continued.

It seemed to Goliah that this land allotment ploy was as much about the freedmen as it was about the Indian. But was that a deal-breaker? Or was it a crack-closer?

He stole a peripheral glance at the full blood sitting next to him, wondering but not really caring what he thought of his land being restricted and freedmen's not. "How will they know who is mixed-blood and who is full blood?" he asked, not adopting Talbot's characterization of "part" Indian. It sounded so slight, so unpleasant, so pejorative. In his mind, Goliah pulverized the *P* in *pejorative.*

"Good question," Talbot answered. "Now, this is at some point down the line, but we'll take a family history of each individual, and also give them a visual test to judge blood quantum. Full bloods have a certain look about them, you know." He seemed to avert his eyes from Tickeater, who wore a bandana tied around his head while two long braids lay across his shoulders.

Tickeater pushed his bandana up so that it rested more evenly between his hairline and his brow line. "I will claim to be only half Cherokee since my father was Comanche," he said.

"And that's how he'll bypass these restrictions," Talbot explained.

"But why do this now?" Goliah asked.

"That's the question of the day." Talbot paused as if garnering fortification for what he was about to say next. "One day soon, this whole territory will become a state. There's an act coming down the pipeline, so to speak, that will give the U.S. power to divvy up these lands." He shook his head resolutely. "It's just a matter of time."

Goliah understood his words and the idea behind it, but he took a moment to try to decipher the ramifications, if any, to the whole tribe when Indian land became a state. Tickeater interrupted his train of thought with a pronounced clearing of his throat.

Talbot seemed to take that as his cue. "And speaking of pipeline..." He gestured his open palm towards Tickeater as if he were on stage introducing the next act to perform.

"Prospectors came by," Tickeater began slowly. "They knock on my door twice now. Say river of oil flow beneath my land and my neighbor's land." He pointed at Goliah with a lift of his chin.

Goliah wanted to jump up right then and there and celebrate that little morsel of good news. He'd always felt, or maybe it was hope, that some mineral or another—preferably oil—ran under his land. He was just sorry now that he hadn't claimed Tickeater's land, too, when he'd had the chance.

Tickeater continued. "I have no proper tools, no proper skill to dig myself. So I will lease to them when time come."

And so will I, thought Goliah. But he still didn't see why freedmen should get money and land, same as him.

He leaned forward, both hands on his knees. "Alright, then," he quickly agreed.

Goliah may not be able to stop the Wallace Roll, but surely he could keep its numbers down. There was still a trick or two up his sleeve. He just had to put his own ploy in place. For the good of the tribe.

Chapter Twenty-three

Sput Louie found a carnival atmosphere when she arrived in town to sign up for the Wallace Roll.

Not the kind she had heard tell of with a fat lady kept in a cage, or where a penny would buy a gander at a dog-faced boy, or a bearded girl, or a fire-eating man. But the kind where you had the hustle and bustle of people—a few of whom were colored strangers in the citified dress of *wachinas*—milling about town, selling wares, holding foot races, sneaking sips of whiskey. There was even a man she didn't recognize who played guitar with his hat laid belly-up on the ground to catch any coins tossed his way.

Fighting her better judgment, she looked for Benjamin amongst the crowd. Although his promise to L.B. had apparently been an empty one as it had been several days since the boy's disclosure and Ben still hadn't come home. Moreover, the puzzling words he'd told L.B. had not been such an enigma after she'd given it some thought. That Anti-horsethief Society was looking for Benjamin at a place where, in actuality, he'd never been. Exactly like searching for dung where cows had never grazed. This assumption sent her back to feeling a loss of hope.

Benjamin may not have been hiding in plain sight amidst the hullabaloo going on in town, but there were plenty of strange white faces hanging around. They were likely illegal squatters, unrecognized claimants, or hopeful profiteers. Some were huddled together talking, while others played games of chance where you could lose your money, your horse, or whatever were the stakes of choice.

What Sput thought would be a minor affair had turned out to be a major event. She regretted having sent L.B. with Hunter to track down something for supper instead of bringing him here to see the spectacle. He would have loved it.

Most of the hubbub centered in an area that was a rock's toss from town. The half-acre space was commonly called Buffalo Wallow. It was a dusty depression left long ago by wallowing buffaloes after they'd eaten the tall tangles of grass that once grew there.

The dent they left in the earth was where the Methodists would raise their tent each summer and hold camptown meetings. They used the nearby creek as a baptistery to save the souls of those they considered heathens. Now, though, there were two tents for one purpose. One was for the Shawnee and Delaware Indians who'd also been excluded from the Cherokee By Blood Roll to fill out their affidavits for bread money, and a smaller tent for Freedmen to do the same.

That was where the real show was, the tents. There you could get two feats for the price of one. You could enter the "Coloreds Only" tent a castoff, and exit an official applicant. That was the closest they'd ever gotten before to inclusion in the tribe.

Inside the tent, Emarthla and a host of other Feather Falls' Freedmen excitedly signed affidavits for themselves as well as for each other. Even Famous Johnson.

With the hand that wasn't in a sling, Sput Louie scratched out an "x" on a piece of paper for the very first time in her life. That simple act gave her pause. It whipped up within her an inkling of what it felt like to be a person of some means, in charge of your own destiny and not be beholding to the whims of someone else. She wanted to hold onto that feeling for as long as she could. Then she thought about Benjamin. He should know that feeling, too. They should share it together.

With that thought, the feeling of privilege died as suddenly as it had been born.

Something else, though, quickly reared up to take its place.

In the full face of noonday, as she exited the tent with Archie in tow, the crowds parted to reveal a spectacular bit of fortune. From on high, this blessing beamed down on her like a ball of light.

There, at the outer edge of the press of people, leaning against the wall of Gooseberry School was none other than Goliah Lynch, looking meaner than a barbed wire fence.

"Look," Archie spoke in a loud high-spirited manner, like the ballyhoo of a carnival barker. "There's Two Bird."

Sput swiveled her head around to where Archie pointed opposite of Old Crow. "Whuh?"

"See him standing on that tree stump?" Archie motioned to the middle of the crowd where Two Bird stood unusually taller than normal, speaking to a group of Indians.

What was he doing here? What was he saying? Sput wondered.

She was too far away to hear much of it, but she wrinkled her nose when she heard something about *"when elephants fight, the grass suffers."* That immediately brought up thoughts of Ma Bay and her descriptions of all the different animals from Africa. Sput had never seen an elephant, and could not picture such huge animals fighting. Nor did she want to. She had bigger fish to scale and fry.

Stretching her neck long like the graceful giraffe of Ma Bay's homeland, she held her head high and strode towards Goliah Lynch.

Just as she did, Archie—probably thinking she was behind him—wended his way towards Two Bird, the speechmaker.

As did Goliah. He seemed to be concentrating with a hard ear and a tough stare trained towards the big Indian.

Inexplicably, though, he stopped just short of the listening crowd, and turned towards her with an odd expression that took her aback, gave her footsteps pause, and caused her to nearly trip over one of the many remnants of buffalo bones that still marked the wild beasts' former territory. She caught herself and stepped over a hollowed out skull that still had its horn.

Old Crow stood there looking annoyed. He began to scan the crowd as if he were searching for something.

Glancing in the direction he was looking, all Sput saw was Sheriff Hitchens in conversation with someone she didn't recognize. No one could help Goliah now, not even the law. Old Crow was a sinner in need of a sermon, and she would be his preacher.

That, and so much more.

The closer she got to Old Crow, the bigger his smile grew. The bigger the smile, the bigger the knife, but Sput wasn't worried one bit. She had a knife of her own in the form of testicles tucked into her sling.

So she rivaled his smile.

Suddenly, Goliah veered left, away from the crowd, like he wanted to lead her away from other people.

No matter. Sput neither needed nor wanted anyone else to hear what she had to say to Goliah. Not yet, anyway.

She mirrored his movement and veered right, positioning herself directly in his path.

Stopping no less than a foot from her, Goliah pulled his lips back and bared his teeth into a smile of superiority. He'd probably worn that same smile each time he'd bought another human being like he was buying a horse, Sput thought.

Her eyes widened with disdain. Old Crow had no idea what was about to happen to him.

"Where is my Benjamin?" She was closer to his face than she'd ever been in her entire life. She could see his yellow teeth, smell his loathsome breath. If a hungry wolf bares his teeth, then she was going to feed this one a taste of his own flesh.

Old Crow snickered. "If I knew where he was I'd have him arrested."

Again, he looked in the direction of Sheriff Hitchens and opened his mouth as if waiting to say something as soon as the sheriff looked his way. Hitchens never did.

"I know you had something to do with his leavin'." She gave a cocky "Hmmph."

His eyes flashed with relish and delight. "I had everything to do with it," he said, a little too calmly.

She was beginning to feel comfortable in the coat of superiority Old Crow had probably worn his whole life. "At first I thought you done killed him, got rid of him somehow," she said, not giving him a chance to respond. "Ya-huh. Wouldn't be the first time you took somebody away from me. But then you wasn't in no position to do no harm to him, was you?" She paused and glared. "Didn't have the stones."

With a quick sideways glance, Sput caught a glimpse of Archie who was now staring at her from afar. She trained her eyes right back on Goliah.

Goliah's right hand twitched by his side like it itched to reach down and make sure whatever he had left between his legs was still there, Sput supposed.

"I didn't have to kill him," he said with a shrug as if he'd been blessed with an out just short of murder.

"He coulda killed you, though," she said, reaching her free hand into her sling, ready to grasp the kerchief and whip it out at just the right time, the perfect moment to steal the crown and claim the glory. Victory and vengeance would finally be hers.

Goliah snickered again. "Nearly killed him, though, when I told him the truth." He tilted his head back and squinted down at her.

Curious, she held her flaunting of the stones in abeyance.

"What truth would that be?" she asked, doubtful that he had any-thing worthwhile to say, but she did want to hear the whole story of what had happened between him and Benjamin.

Goliah rubbed his hairless chin. "You ever wonder why your boy L.B. is simple?"

In an odd way, it struck Sput that this was Goliah's version of kindness. He might have called L.B. the town idiot, or the local loon. She'd heard worse before. This time, though, he called her baby boy by his given name.

"I ain't followin'," Sput said.

"Just like your little girl. What was her name?"

"Don't you bring Lily into this." Sput balled her fist at her side. This man was evil and had done many devilish deeds. That much she knew. But a vile disease could not be cured with sweet medicine. "Get to it," she said, because she would soon shine a light on the darkness of his heart and the blackness of his soul.

"She wasn't normal, was she?" he asked. "And I mean that in the kindest way."

She was not impressed by the way he could feign graciousness. A steel hand in a silk glove was still hard and cold.

He continued. "But thank God her skirt caught fire, was it?" he asked like he wasn't sure. "And she burned to death."

Sput Louie's gut twisted into a knot.

"But then, she wasn't just your daughter, was she?" He seemingly took in the whole of her face inch by inch, from top to bottom. "And she wasn't just Benjamin's daughter, either, now was she?"

Her whole body began a slow tremble as she felt the spirit begin to drain from her. It pooled all the way down and settled around her feet like so much blood.

"That's not just an old wive's tale, you know. Sometimes, those old biddies know whereof they speak."

The wheels in her mind began to turn. She thought about the words Philura had used with her a few days prior. Could that have something to do with this?

"They got this one right," Old Crow said, "Didn't they? You see, she didn't stand a chance of being sane."

Sput Louie stopped breathing altogether. Her body went so rigid that she could have been snapped in two. She tried to follow his words, but they no longer sounded like English.

In her peripheral vision, Sput thought she saw someone on approach, but she couldn't be sure because she was concentrating so hard on the patchwork of words coming out of Goliah's mouth.

"So after all these years," Goliah continued, "I confessed to your husband that, yes, I am his father." Then he eyed her with villainous glee. "And I'm your father, too."

Chapter Twenty-four

At the center of Buffalo Wallow, in front of the two white tents, Two Bird found himself standing atop a sycamore stump.

He had come to Buffalo Wallow to warn any of his brethren who would listen about what had hit him in the middle of the night, in the middle of his head like a well-aimed bullet.

"Shiny bauble," he began, just loud enough to get the attention of a couple of Cherokee milling nearby, and just soft enough for them to have to move in if they wanted to hear more.

Hiding one hand behind his back and waving the other across the flurry of activity that had been whipped up around the wallow, he continued. *"Look at the shiny bauble belonging to the tribe, but given to those who are not Cherokee. That is what blond-hairs want Indians to do."* He paused for dramatic effect, anticipating more spectators might migrate over. *"But what is hidden in the other hand?"* He let his waving hand drop by his side to draw focus to the one hidden behind his back.

Not only did a few more tribal members join his growing gaggle, but also a few intruders stopped their clamor with one another to stare at the commotion this native in a dress was kicking up. That he had piqued their interest fortified his grit.

He just wished they understood Cherokee, too.

"*When elephants fight, grass suffers,*" he declared. "*While our tribe concentrates on a shiny bauble over there, the Great White Father plots to kill the tribe over here.*" He brought his hidden hand out front and displayed his yet unfurled palm to the group that was fast becoming a crowd.

"Iyee-Iyee," one of the crowd members whooped. "*Is the Great White Father making war with the Cherokees?*"

Two Bird had little patience for questions that day, and no desire for interruptions while he sounded the drum and rattle for his people. He did not want it to be a give and take, question and answer, call and response. But he supposed he must, as part of the problem was that Indians were too straightforward to discern the subtle ways the federal government could use their power, their influence, their laws to destroy a people.

So he explained as succinctly as he could.

"*Those who are not Cherokee will have bread money given to them. After the bread money is given away,*" he jutted his chin sharply towards the tents, "*land will be given away. After land is given away, Indian Territory will become one of their states. Statehood is dressed up to look like a privilege.*" He pounded his closed fist into his other palm. "*Be certain it is a curse.*"

And then as if on cue, as if providing a living example of his words but in a personal context, Two Bird spotted his former lover standing next to his stallion at the back of the crowd. Rogers donned the same suit he'd worn the first time they'd met. Only this time his hair was wild with a roar of curls. He found this bewitching. Wobbling atop the stump and in his mind, too, he quickly righted himself both physically and emotionally. Yes, he counseled himself, Rogers was alluring, enthralling even, but he was still a curse dressed to look like a privilege, much like the prospect of statehood that he had just maligned.

"*When this land becomes a state,*" Two Bird said, regaining his composure and trying to ignore the shudder that rippled down his spine, "*blond-hairs will be free to come here. Not so now.*"

He gulped down too much air and tried to blow it out by clearing his throat.

"*When this land becomes a state,*" he continued, voice cracking, "*Indians must pay taxes to the Great White Father. Not so now.*

"*To pay taxes, Indians will have to use the land for profit. They will have to make money.*"

"*Not so now,*" someone in the crowd picked up his refrain.

"*Worse,*" asserted Two Bird, beginning to hit his stride, but as he scanned the crowd, giving their curiosity time to peak, he caught sight of yet another distraction. Sput Louie and her son Archie emerged from one of the tents. While Archie bustled over to the crowd, Sput Louie stopped dead in her tracks and gave a hard stare to someone or something. When Two Bird followed her gaze, he saw it, too.

Goliah Lynch.

Two Bird had no time to wonder why her arm was in a sling, but he knew immediately why she made a beeline over to Goliah.

Nevertheless, he had to get back to his people who were becoming impatient with him.

"*You say there is worse to come,*" someone bellowed.

"*What is worse than taxes paid to the white man on land Indians own?*" another asked.

Exactly, thought Two Bird. "*If Indians cannot pay taxes, Indians lose their land. Not so now. When Indians lose their land, a long line of blond-hairs will be there to find it. Soon more blond-hairs than Indians will own Indian land. Not so now.*" He paused to let sink in the image of a never-ending ribbon of whites coming to take their land.

Returning to his first and foremost refrain, he went in for the kill. "*When this land becomes a state, Indians must abide by state law, not tribal law. The state will take away Indian sovereignty, rule over Indian land, rule over Indians.*" He raised his arm again, and slowly unfurled his empty palm for all to see. "*With tribal sovereignty no more, our tribe will be no more.*"

When someone said, "*The shiny bauble is rusty inside,*" it let Two Bird know that at least some of them were getting a grasp on the situation, understanding the ramifications to the tribe upon being sucked into the white man's world, their independence abolished, their power usurped, their tribe all but dissolved.

"*When Indian sovereignty is taken away,*" he said to those who still might not understand the severity of the situation, "*Indian land will become the white man's land.*"

Mumbling hummed in the air all around him.

"*Where will the Indians go? What will happen to our tribe?*" a woman asked.

Then a ruckus was heard, and everyone momentarily turned their attention towards the commotion at the back of the crowd where Sput seemed to be in a heated conversation with Goliah.

Two Bird grimaced as he turned his attention back to the crowd, and answered the woman's question. "*Indians will go nowhere. Indians will stay. Fight. Fight statehood. A danger foreseen is half-avoided,*" he declared, head tilted back, chin in the air. "*There is still time to act.*" Though some had resumed their interest in his speech, others' attention was still drawn to Sput and Goliah.

He spoke louder. "*What is coming, we now know—*"

Gasps went up.

Everyone, including Two Bird, gaped as Sput Louie began to yelp. She slapped Goliah's face in full view of everyone.

Goliah grabbed her hand, but she wrenched it loose.

He pushed her back. She did not retreat but charged forward again. This time she pounded his chest with her one good fist, yelling words Two Bird could not make out.

The crowd began to abandon him and scuttle towards the fighting duo, with Archie leading the charge.

"*Wait,*" Two Bird yelled to his fleeing crowd.

Goliah whipped Sput Louie around and tried to grip her in a bear hug to seemingly halt her assault. She ducked down and worked her way out of his grasp.

By the time Archie was halfway there, Two Bird had decided he'd better follow suit before one or both of them did some real damage to each other.

Goliah spun Sput around by her shoulder so that her back was to his front. She screamed out in pain, but that didn't stop her assault. She squirmed and kicked.

He then wrapped his arms around her chest and seemed to clamp down on her good arm as well as her slinged arm.

A horrifying screech again shrieked out from her as she strained against him.

Suddenly, inexplicably, her body went limp. As soon as it did, Goliah let her drop.

Archie arrived just in time to catch her fall.

Chapter Twenty-five

The putrid smell of fresh vomit stung Sput Louie's nose.

Was it hers?

She didn't remember retching. She didn't even remember eating. But the stench was as thick as a brick wall, nearly suffocating her as she lay on her side.

She struggled to catch a clean breath.

Where was she? And why was it so dark? Were her eyes open? She couldn't tell.

Was she still asleep? Maybe.

Perhaps she was dreaming?

It seemed like there had been a dream. She remembered L.B. being in it, but what else had happened? Who else had been there?

Her body ached too much to think clearly, especially her arm. Her bones were as heavy as iron, stiff, tired, like she hadn't moved in days. Maybe she should turn over and at least change positions, get off the sore arm, get a whiff of clean air so she could go back to sleep if she were even awake.

As she tried to move, a bolt of lightning shot through her arm and pierced her mind.

Her senses dimmed. Her thoughts faded into the dark.

#

Ma.

Mama.

Sput Louie McClendon.

Sheriff Hitchens.

The muffled words seemed as though they came from way yonder somewhere rousing her from her slumber.

Rain falls on the just and unjust.

Was that Two Bird talking?

A flickering light filtered through her eyelids and rolled past.

But her lids, so heavy, just would not open.

She gave in again to the darkness and let it swallow her whole. Down, down, down she went until she was no more.

#

UM-BET, UM-BET, UM-BET. The sound of tree frogs woke her.

A balm of sycamore wafted up her nose. Lily had loved the sweet earthy scent of sycamore leaves. She always had Sput add a dash of it into a bar of soap made just for her. No one else was allowed to use it, not her brothers, not even Sput.

Sput snuffled again to get a bigger whiff of the minty smell. Not enough to mask the remaining stench of dry puke, but enough to let her know the trees must be nearby. She wanted to go to them if only she could see them.

She wanted to play amongst the treetops. Skylark from branch to limb, from pine to sycamore, swooping, swerving, dipping, soaring. Wings spread as wide as a breeze. No hunger, no thirst, no care, no sorrow. Lily, Lily. Sorrowful Lily. So sorry, little Lily.

But Lily wasn't there anymore, was she? Burned to death right before God. *Good thing, too,* she heard someone say before everything went to black again.

Chapter Twenty-six

The loquacious Doctor Vernon L. Farley settled his black medicine bag on the nightstand next to his patient lying stiffly on the bed. "Let's see now," he said.

With his wrinkled hand, he rubbed his bearded chin while giving his subject a visual once-over. "This is the second time I've seen you in as many months. First time, you came to my office in Vinita when that nigger boy gave you an orchiectomy."

Farley laced his fingers together and twisted his wrists outward. Knuckles cracked. Elbows popped. Lungs deflated into a loud sigh.

"Did they ever catch the boy that?" the doctor asked.

Clad only in thin linen undergarments, Goliah turned his head away and pressed a hard stare at Philura's ornate chifforobe set against the wall of their bedroom. "Just get it over with," he said. He neither needed nor wanted further discussion of his genital mutilation.

The doctor refused to disembark from his train of thought, though. "That nick was so neat and clean," he blew out a whistle, "looked like a trained professional did it," he said, almost admiringly. "That's why you lost so little blood and had so little residual damage." He shook his head. "Except for, er, uh—" he paused abruptly.

Except the damn thing doesn't work anymore, Goliah finished in his head. So far, anyway. Goliah figured he was well past the child-producing stage so that part had been easy to accept, but he still wanted to take pleasure with a woman from time to time.

His neck went rigid with a sudden realization. Maybe Benjamin had done it to be both prohibitive and punitive. It wasn't just punishment for past deeds, but a bar from future ones. Or both.

Bastard, he thought, as his stomach knotted to match the pain in his leg.

Pinching his eyebrows together, he garnered enough vigor to bark at the doctor. "I don't need a blow by blow of my miseries. Just get on with it." He rolled over onto his good side and offered up the injured one. He didn't know which hurt more, the reminder that someone else knew of his humiliation, or the sharp spasm shooting down his right leg.

"So what happened this time?" Doc Farley asked, undaunted.

Before formulating an explanation, Goliah steeled himself against the hurt by concentrating on the angels hand-carved into the chifforobe's door. That's what his children should have looked like, he thought. Chubby-cheeked cherubs instead of half-black bastards. He couldn't deny that Benjamin McClendon favored him in appearance. Somewhat. But that Sput Louie was the ugliest woman in the whole of Going Snake District. And that had to be one of his daughters?

Why was he thinking about her, though? Because that's how the whole fiasco had begun, that's why. He flicked his eyes up as part of his answer to the doctor's question. "I fell."

While the doctor began his examination, the pain pushed Goliah back to Buffalo Wallow where the incident had started.

The day could not have gone worse.

He'd first spotted Two Bird standing on a stump looking every bit a politician. Who knew he could pull a crowd together and hold their attention so rapt? Who knew a man in a dress could make a man in a suit teeter between jealousy and envy, finally pushing said-suited man into a full tilt loathing?

Two Bird had been railing against everything Goliah was now for, and that must stop.

Since Goliah had accepted the freedmen's ultimate enrollment in the tribe as a necessary evil that would clear a path to increase his coffers, he needed everyone to be on board, especially the full bloods. He just wanted to keep the colored count down as much as possible.

Before he could make his way over to the seemingly spellbound crowd to try and stop Two Bird from messing with his money, his livelihood, his life, Sput Louie put her scrawny carcass directly in his path and demanded an audience.

He'd squelched that right quick, though, hadn't he? He revealed the truth of her life so he could get on with the lie of his.

That had certainly whirled her measly spindle of a brain.

After a minor dustup where he blocked more swings than she landed, Sput Louie had gone as limp as a bruised peach hanging from a dead tree. Passed out cold, like she was surprised at the news. Like she hadn't ever even suspected.

Maybe she was surprised, though.

Benjamin certainly had been.

A slow, weak smile spread across Goliah's face. Sput's reaction was proof that Benjamin hadn't shared with his wife what Benjamin had done to him in the barn. He wouldn't have been able to bear not even one more person knowing what that boy had done. Especially not a woman, albeit a nigger woman.

The pain from the doctor pressing on his leg brought him back to the present. Goliah groaned. Less at the misery in his leg than at the memory of Benjamin's actions.

To Goliah's mind, he bore no culpability for that fiasco of a coupling himself. If Sput and Benjamin, he thought, weren't so dim-witted, they could have figured it out before they'd said their *I do's*.

Now Benjamin was—by the looks of it—gone for good. Surely, Sput Louie would follow his lead sooner rather than later.

Not a chance, his mind cautioned when he remembered that she'd come from the tent and had probably already signed up with that Wallace fellow. With any luck, though, her affidavit might be adjudged invalid, or faulty, or incomplete, and they would place her on the Doubtful List.

She would surely leave Feather Falls if that happened, and he would see to it that it did.

"Mr. Lynch," the doctor said impatiently.

"Yes," he answered in a sharp tone.

"Seems like you did more than fall. I see the scratches all over your face, and there's a bruise reddening your temple."

Bringing his hand to his temple, Goliah brushed past his cheek and was surprised to feel what appeared to be a raised claw mark.

"Looks like war paint," the doctor said, chuckling. "I'll put some salve on it before I leave."

Goliah flicked his eyes upwards. "Don't need your salve."

"Looks like you got the worst end of that fight."

"I said I fell," he fumed. Or rather I was pushed, he thought. A golden nougat he didn't feel the need to share with the nosy doctor.

"You're going to need a splint for this sprained leg, too." Doc Farley said. "I have one in my carriage. I'll go fetch that and the salve."

As the doctor left the room, Goliah closed his eyes again and resumed reliving the incident at Buffalo Wallow.

After Sput Louie's son had hauled her away, Goliah found himself in the middle of a crowd that suddenly looked like a mob led by a formidable foe.

He'd arched his silver brow at that foe, as the eye below it twitched.

"*You fight with a woman, why?*" asked Two Bird, whose light pink lips had pressed into a thin white slash.

"*Sput Louie got the better of you,*" said someone from behind him. Others made their consensus known by mumbles and nods.

Goliah paid them no heed and glared only at Two Bird.

"*A deranged slave woman is no concern of yours. What is of concern is—*"

"*Shuh.*" Two Bird interrupted as the crowd around them began to grumble. "*Do you not mean freedwoman?*"

The sweat that had been collecting on Goliah's forehead began to trail down to the tip of his nose. He resisted the urge to scan the area for his hat. He'd probably lost it in the scuffle. Instead, he thumbed his nose dry and cleared his throat.

"*Slave, former slave, freedman, freedwoman,*" Goliah said, then noticed that he was standing next to someone's wagon. He climbed atop it with more strain and effort than was desirable in front of an audience. Once on top, though, he outstretched both of his hands commanding the grumbling crowd to quiet down.

They didn't.

He knew he had to speak to them in a way they would understand. "*Listen, or your tongue will make you deaf,*" he yelled, invoking an old Indian adage. In Cherokee, as was expected. Not expected in an anticipatory fashion, but expected in a mandatory fashion.

The press of people stilled ever so slowly. First one, then two, then another two or three.

Goliah began deliberately.

"*They want us distracted,*" he paused. "*Not by this* Wallace *Roll. By talk of statehood. The Shawnee and the Delaware, did we not adopt them? Are those small tribes not our brethren? Do they not deserve our loyalty? Our protection?*" More of the crowd quieted to a whisper. "*Should we not honor our word to them? Freedmen are a bitter tonic that we must hold our nose and swallow. Do not look over there when they are not the trouble.*"

Just then, seemingly not to be outdone, Two Bird climbed atop a buckboard. Goliah loathed the ease with which he did so. And in a dress, no less.

"Sput Louie *gave you trouble not one minute ago,*" someone in the crowd yelled, but then Two Bird gave the group a stony stare that shushed them forthwith.

"*And the stream of whites,*" Two Bird said, "*that will come to our land and overrun it, what do you say about that?*"

Goliah could not say that whites wouldn't invade the territory. And he couldn't think of any advantages of them coming in such numbers, except it would improve the sophistication of the town with more businesses, better industry, higher commerce, not to mention more opportunity for intelligent conversation for himself.

The crowd would care not one whit about those kinds of things.

So he explained, "*Even if that were true, which it is not, the Cherokees are not going anywhere. We will still be here. We will still be governed by tribal laws, because the tribe will still have sovereignty. We could lose that, how? It will always be that we are our own nation.*"

Two Bird responded as if Goliah had said nothing true. "*Swifter than the shuttle of a weaver come your lies.*" He flipped his hand up as if to shoo him away. "*You forsake your own people.*"

"*Help is what I am offering,*" Goliah protested. "*A learned opinion.*"

Two Bird stiffened his arm and pointed at Goliah. "*The land -rich will forever be beseeched upon by the land-hungry, and bore upon by the land-greedy. Our leaders allow such? People are no match for a government that deceives its own. It is time now to infiltrate. They will hear a learned opinion from me. That is why*" and here he paused, "*I will try for a seat on Cherokee National Council.*

But the crowd seemed to have a better idea. "*Chief,*" someone immediately yelled. Others quickly picked up the call.

"*Chief, Chief,*" they began to chant in unison.

So there it was, thought Goliah. Two Bird's plan. He almost chuckled. "*A chief who wears a dress, has anyone seen such a thing?*" he asked above the din.

The words fanned out across the crowd, the import of them slowly covering the mass one by one. While some stopped chanting, though, others continued.

"*Just remember,* Lynch," Two Bird said, rising to the challenge, "*those who have one foot in the boat and one foot in the canoe will soon fall into the river. One cannot serve two masters.*"

One man angrily shoved the side of the wagon Goliah was standing on.

Another on the opposite side followed that idea and began to pull it.

As they began to rock the wagon to and fro, back and forth, side to side, it forced Goliah to bow down to one knee. He latched a hand to each sideboard to keep from being knocked around.

Still, the wagon teetered and tottered, while the horse hooked to it snorted in complaint.

"*Traitor,*" someone yelled.

"*Wait,*" Goliah shouted," "*we can beat them at their game. I can help. If you think the white man will veer right because a big Indian in a dress is on the left—*"

But no one paid attention. One by one men and women made their way over to the wagon and joined in pushing this way, pulling that way.

Goliah tried to climb out, but someone shoved him back in.

The horse blew out a fluttery snort.

As the snort grew into a full on squeal, someone unhitched the animal from the wagon and led him away. The crowd then revved to a feverous pitch of ridicule, shouting over and over, "*Traitor, traitor.*"

Goliah looked left, then right. He crawled to the side of the wagon to find a way down, off, or out. The surrounding mob blocked all four sides. Their hands gripped every inch of the side panels, their faces filled with anger, their mouths spewed one barbarous insult after another, their eyes shot daggers of loathing and hostility, scorn and animosity. Unable to find a way to dismount to the safety of solid terrain, the wagon tipped on its side, and a stunned Goliah toppled to the ground.

Chapter Twenty-seven

"Ow," Sput Louie moaned.

Pain pulled her out of her slumber yet again. She tried to reach for her elbow to rub it but, to her surprise, her knuckles scraped across something directly overhead. Felt like wood. A wooden lid?

If she could just open her eyes.

She heard movement.

A door slammed.

Footsteps scuttled.

Where the hell was she? Was she dead? Such close quarters. Was she in a casket?

"Mama," a muffled voice pleaded from somewhere. "'Neither do I condemn you, Jethtuth declared.'" It stopped. Then reverently resumed. "John 8:11."

She tried to open her eyes to see Jesus coming to get her, but her lids would not cooperate.

Here I am, she wanted to say. *Right here.*

When she reared up to go to Him, though, THWUMP, she hit her head on something. She moaned loud and hard as she laid back in defeat. She straightened out her cramped legs, which opened up a flood of ease.

She melted back into the darkness.

#

The next time Sput stirred awake, something yanked on her foot. What was it? It tugged at her like a hand trying to latch on, desperate fingers cleaving to her ankle.

Who was it?

With her free foot, she kicked at the hand, but she was so weak, so feeble that her efforts were futile. Still, she managed to get away, though she lost her moccasin in the scuffle. A cool breeze swiped at her toes.

But where was she scooting to in the dark?

Towards the light, the light that filtered through her eyelids.

One of her arms wouldn't move, couldn't help her. It was dead to the world. It was as crestfallen as she was.

Using the fingers of her good arm, she tried to grasp whatever she was laying on top of to get some leverage. The substance crumbled in her hand.

Dirt?

Pressing her hand up again, cautiously this time, she latched onto something overhead. A knurl? A knob? Dirt beneath her. Wood on top.

Then the hand at her feet was back again, straining at her. She fish-tailed onto her side in the tiny space, and wriggled, writhed across what smelled like damp earth, going deeper into the cool, the dark, the safe.

"Ma."

The voice was familiar this time.

Finally, she was able to will one eye open. She craned her neck towards the sound coming from the direction in which her head lay. The faint smell of vinegar tapped her on the nose before it breezed past.

Focusing through the slit, towards the familiar voice, she saw two eyes come into view. Fearful eyes. In a terrified face. But why were they afraid? She wasn't trying to get them. They were trying to get her.

Another voice called to her, and then a third. They outnumbered her. One was ahead of her reaching for her outstretched hand. She recoiled and tried to retreat, but the other person clawed at her feet. She had nowhere to go.

"Come on out." The voice at her head with the frightened eyes she now realized was Hunter Big.

"The sun's nearly up." Archie. Archie was the someone at her feet.

"Ith Ma comin' out now?" L.B.

And then it began to wash over her. Little by little, thoughts and images seeped across the crags of her memory. Ebbing here, Flowing there. Or were they dreams, too?

In what seemed like a far away land, an image danced in her head. She was fighting Old Crow, striking out at him like a captured cat, even though her arm was in a sling. But why was her arm bandaged like that? She couldn't remember.

She just remembered flailing her one good arm in every direction, wanting to connect, needing to connect, aiming to connect her fist to Old Crow's mouth so that he would just stop talking, just stop laughing.

Liar, liar, she recalled yelling over and over. It seemed to be the only word her mind could form.

I'm your father, too.

"Liar, liar, liar," she mumbled again now in rhythm with the um-bets of the tree frogs.

That didn't last long. Pretty soon Sput Louie petered out. Her mind muddled again. Thoughts crashed into one another. A mishmash of lies with sharp edges sliced at her life. Shards of words filled her head until all she could see were what looked like bolts of lightning.

And then a flashback of Two Bird's words cut a shock of colors into the sea of white. "The soul would have no rainbow if the eye had no tears," he'd said.

But there was no rainbow there in the dark. No tears.

"Where am I?" she asked Hunter, and turned her head so that he could not see her eyes and she could not see his.

"Come on out, Ma," he said gently, sweetly. He reached out his hand towards her as if she was in the middle of a rushing river, and he was trying to guide her to the safety of the shore. "You don't know where you at?"

Sput shook her head, making sure to keep him relegated to her peripheral vision.

Her first born, a man now, gulped like a little girl.

"You under the house."

Chapter Twenty-eight

Under the house?

The tension in Sput's body collapsed under the weight of her confusion.

To drown out the chorus of pleas from all three of her sons revving up to a roar now, she closed her eyes and fought through the fog in her mind, struggling to make sense of her circumstances. She swished the dense mist this way, threshed it that way until she forged a clearing where she remembered arriving home in Two Bird's coverless wagon with Rogers at the helm, and her head in Archie's lap.

But why had Rogers been driving? And why was his hair so big?

He'd halted the horse right in front of her house. As soon as it stopped, she'd wordlessly lifted her head from Archie's lap and alighted with his help.

"Wait right there for me, Ma," he had said then.

But while he leaned into Rogers and exchanged whispered words, Sput dragged her feet towards the front door until she spotted before her a gift from God. A sanctuary, a hideaway, a haven where she could hole up away from suspicious eyes and questioning lips. God had delivered to her a saving grace in the form of a crawlspace.

Before anyone knew what she was doing, she wormed herself into it and let it cover her like a blanket. Tucked away in the safety of the dark, Sput had nothing to explain. She didn't want to look into Hunter Big's eyes and see what he saw, what any of them saw when they looked at her.

So she had folded into herself upon reaching the underbelly of the house. Scrunching her outsides into her insides, she melded them together until she felt so small as to be completely indiscernible in the deep dark crevice of her fractured mind. She was far away from the brutal light of Goliah's words and miles away from the moment when she'd tried to scratch a hole in his face and rip out his tongue.

In the comfort of the crawlspace, she had willed herself to die.

For a while, she thought she had. But here she was countless hours later—or maybe even countless days?—still besieged by the incessant pleas of her sons.

"Ith you comin' out, Ma? Pleathe, come out."

Sput was helpless, though, to stop the unraveling of her life that had begun at Buffalo Wallow. She was incapable of getting away from the awful fact that she had married her brother.

So no, L.B., she wanted to say, she wasn't coming out.

Not only had she married her brother, but she had also joined blankets with him. That was the bigger sin.

But had she?

A tiny spark of reason reared its head and asked the question. Of course, she had, was the answer. But she hadn't done it knowingly. That was a fact.

How could she have let this happen? Shouldn't she have known? Shouldn't she have felt something...something so wrong, so awfully, horribly, disgustingly wrong?

She pinched her eyes even tighter and prayed to God to let it not be true, to let it not have happened, to let it all have been a dream. But when she opened them up and reasoned it out, the spark in her mind flashed larger, lighting the way to a barrage of facts that could not be dodged, ditched or sidestepped.

Not the least of which was L.B. and Lily.

They were the only live births from her union with Benjamin and were in fact born dull-minded. Just like Old Crow had said. She'd heard the old wives' tale, too, and knew it to be true. That's why Cherokees forbid marrying within their own clan or that of their father's. Clans were simply an extension of a family from brothers and sisters to nieces and nephews to cousins and more cousins. In the old days, one would have to go to the next village to find a mate.

This was modern times, though, wasn't it, Sput reasoned? Families spread out now. Especially after slavery. How could she have known?

And what about her other precious bundles that had all fallen still-born? Something must have gone so wrong with them that God took them from her before they'd even taken their first breath.

Why hadn't she paid attention to that?

Another thing staring her in the face was the fact that Goliah was a known liar. Why he would make up that particular lie confounded her. Why wait until now to tell her? He could have made up anything else. He could have denied all of it, said he wasn't anyone's father. There was no getting around the Lynch resemblance between Benjamin and Old Crow, though. That was as clear as a cloudless day. They both had the same long nose and the same copper-colored eyes.

What was less obvious, what went against the argument that she was a Lynch was how she didn't resemble either one of them. She was not as dark as some coloreds. That was true. But nowhere near as light-skinned as those who claimed mixed. Sure, her hair was a strange cross of tightly curled strands jumbled together with wiry, straight ones, like it was at a fork in the road and couldn't make up its mind which way it wanted to go, heavy and straight or light and coiled.

That brought to mind another piece of the puzzle. Boslan, her Pa. Or the man she knew as her Pa. He had never liked her hair. Ever.

"Tie that gal's hair up. She look like a hedgehog," he had said once, with a disgusted look on his face.

It occurred to her that to this day, that might be the reason why she always wore her hair hidden under a scarf. Her Pa's disapproval. Even though he was long dead, she still never let her hair out, never thought about letting it out. Why would she? It was ugly, according to him.

Maybe it was a reminder that she was not his.

Why hadn't he just told her? For that matter, why hadn't Ma Bay? Benjamin's Ma had told him, hadn't she? How was Sput to know if no one told her?

As she pondered this question, she ran her tongue across her teeth to conjure up moisture for her dry mouth.

Would she have understood even if she had been told? Maybe. But maybe she had been too young. Goliah wrenched her from her Ma and Pa at, what, about age ten or eleven? Perhaps they had intended to tell her, but she was swiftly banished to Texas before that could happen.

How hurt her Pa must have been to have known his wife bore another man's child. She was sure it had happened the same way as it had with Benjamin's Ma, too, because a leopard doesn't change his spots, and rapists don't stop raping.

But there was something else, too.

One undeniable thing that held sway, had supreme power, mastered over all of the arguments for or against such a sin. And it wasn't just the fact that Benjamin had come to believe that his love for her was so abhorrent that he didn't want to lay eyes on her ever again, or even be in the same town. No, the biggest tell was the fact that Benjamin—a man of soul, truth, and feeling—had such a violent belief in the truth of Goliah's words that he'd crudely, cruelly, viciously ripped out the man's stones.

And then gifted them to her to do with as she wished.

The spark in her mind flashed into a full-on fire as she reached down and patted her skirt pocket with her one good hand. It was flat.

She hurriedly slid her hand into her bosom. Empty.

Then she felt a lump in her sling next to the killing pain in her shoulder. She breathed a sigh of relief. When she reached in, she carefully withdrew the kerchief that had somehow miraculously survived all the chaos at Buffalo Wallow, all the commotion in the crawlspace.

Old Crow had been in her life since the day she was born, and now he was in her blood as evidenced by the stones in her hand. The blood of the devil coursed through her like a cancer.

Those stones were the proof.

She clutched her stomach as it roiled like it wanted to throw up her very existence, vomit out the vileness that had become her.

But wait.

Another thought occurred to her. It bugged her eyes wide and to the side where she saw morning light creeping around the eastern edges of the crawlspace. As the thought roamed around her head, looking for a place to fit in, she realized all was quiet again outside. She breathed out a long slow sigh of gratefulness that her sons had, hopefully, finally given up and gone back inside the house.

In all that quiet, though, the one thought rang out.

If she had Goliah's blood, if she was truly his daughter, an Indian man's daughter, didn't that now make her Indian, as well?

It was all beginning to make sense. Maybe that was why Sput had always felt in her heart, her skin, her bones that she was Cherokee. It wasn't just because she was raised to forget her African-ness and forced to celebrate the Indian-ness of the people that had enslaved her; it was that she had had Indian blood all along. Other slaves felt the same way, but they didn't seem to have the same strong desire to be Cherokee like she did.

All her life she'd wanted to be accepted by the tribe as one of their own, a real *adonisgi*, not just a freedwoman cast aside and of no further use. Now she understood why. It turned out she was Cherokee. By blood, for those who counted blood.

And didn't everyone?

She thought it odd how Indians and whites alike measured blood. Half-bloods, full bloods, mixed bloods, a drop of blood. Indians should have learned by now that measuring blood divided them. Weren't people just people? She guessed not. There had to be a difference made because otherwise, how could one bring their might to bear on the other if everyone was equal? The white man had made sure to not only conquer but to also crush the Indian. Which made it all the more strange that the Indian would so willingly turn around and bear down on Africans until they were on their knees and at their mercy.

It made no sense. Why would she want to claim heir to people like that?

Inhaling deeply, she let all of the ills that plagued her fill her chest. Stay there. Fester there. Blister and burn there.

Then she let it go. Eased it out. Purged the pain. Snuffed out the burn. It cleared her mind to a vision of sweeping freedoms, a full range of opportunities and privilege. She would make lemonade out of buttermilk.

Most of all, she was done with being the weight of a feather with no power to move on her own, going wherever the winds of life blew her. Her skin prickled. The world could no longer confine her, nor would she let it destroy her.

The way of the troublemaker is thorny, pricking and piercing anything with which he comes into contact. But Sput Louie had in mind a precise plan on how she would de-thorn that evil bastard Lynch.

Stretching out her good arm, she had just enough space to use it as leverage to turn over onto her stomach. She was careful not to crush the stones of redemption.

Stretch, scoot. Stretch, scoot, until she bumped into a glass jar filled with dead fireflies. She figured that must have been the light that rolled past her in the dark. A gift sent in the night by L.B., no doubt.

She silently thanked him and kept moving. She was anxious to get out and implement her newly formed plan of three ultimatums, one demand, and no other choice. That sense of urgency pressed down on her mind. She dug her good elbow into the dirt once again and drew herself towards the light. She could almost feel the warmth of the sun and how it would wash over her, invigorate and fortify her.

As soon as she reached the precipice that separated asylum from exposure, she paused. Hearing nothing but hushed voices that sounded like they came from inside the house, she snaked her head out and squinted through the glare of the sun.

It took a moment for the man's shoes to come into view. They were dark, dusty and store-bought. Her body froze, her breathing stopped, but her eyes crept up from the shoes to the trousers. And then to the gun cocked and pointed at her head.

"Sput Louie McClendon," Sheriff Hitchens said in a southern drawl. "I'm gonna have to arrest you."

Chapter Twenty-nine

A pinched-mouth Sheriff Hitchens used his hip to push the table he typically ate his supper on across the room. The teakwood legs scraped and screeched until it was cater-corner to his desk. He used the back of his hand to sweep away the leftover crumbs, used his knee to push a chair underneath it, used his foot to shove the three extra chairs haphazardly against the rear wall.

When he finished, he looked around with a satisfied smirk. The Feather Falls Sheriff's Office had become a courtroom simply by rearranging the furniture.

"That good enough?" Hitchens asked the three men who stood around watching while he did all the work.

Goliah, leaning on his cane, stood with his back to the only window in the room and shrugged his answer.

Paun Big Bee, sober since it was not yet noon, signaled his assent by taking a seat behind the desk that now doubled as a judge's bench. He had become a local judge simply by having an arrestee crop up outside the months of May and November when the official District Judge held court. Otherwise, Big Bee was the proprietor of a rundown cotton gin and frequenter of an illegal gin mill.

Billy Bean Stick promptly took his seat at the supper table that now stood in as counsel table. He had been pulled away from his duty as the Sentinel's editor to serve as prosecuting attorney.

Both men had been appointed by Goliah to be the town's legal system, though he had no such authority. Since no one ever saw fit to lodge an objection to the appointments or cared enough to complain, Goliah took it upon himself to be the hands on the clock by which Feather Falls justice system was set.

The three men all hailed from prominent mixed-blood families and were the town's only educated elite. They had been childhood friends at the Peavine School, then later at the Male Seminary just outside of Tahlequah.

While Goliah and Bean Stick ostensibly matriculated to law school, Big Bee's family pockets went empty from his father's gambling debts, and he matriculated to the distillery. He became the meanest, most ornery drunk. When he wasn't using prairie dogs for target practice, he was swinging stray cats by their hind legs. When their bones snapped, he'd toss them away just to watch them drag around until they either died or someone put them out of their misery. That someone was never Big Bee.

People thought he was crazy and so they feared him. That fear is why Goliah sought to appoint him as a judge. Local judgeships did not require a law degree but did require the person to be a respected member of society. To Goliah's way of thinking, crazy bred fear, and fear was the highest form of respect. Therefore, Big Bee was revered.

"Bring the prisoner in now," Goliah ordered the Sheriff. "And hurry up." He knew they needed to get this thing done before Sput Louie's sons showed up. He smiled inside knowing that their only mode of transportation was shod feet. It would take them until noon to get there. He never underestimated Big Hunter, though, or whatever his name was.

The sheriff cocked his head to the side. "Don't she need a liar?"

Goliah raised his brow. He was reminded yet again of full blood Cherokees' inability to pronounce certain combinations of letters once they learned English, especially when they picked it up around town instead of at school like Sheriff Peacheater Hitchens had probably done. That glitch made the word *Tom* sound like *tome* and *lawyer* sound like *liar*.

"We only need one law-yer—" Goliah took his time pronouncing the word, "—for this." Then he shot a bold stare at the man wearing a tin star and dared him to continue questioning procedural issues that did not fall under a sheriff's purview.

Hitchens was either too dumb to decipher Goliah's glare or he didn't care. "This is a tribal court, though. For Indians, not Negroes. Ain't we gonna wait on the District Judge? And what about a jury," he asked?

Bean Stick and Goliah exchanged glances. Big Bee rolled his head around and cracked his neck. "Why, a District Judge doesn't get summoned for nigger shenanigans. She-nigger-gans." Big Bee chuckled. "Sheniggergans, get it? I believe I have coined a phrase right there." He reared back with laughter.

Goliah fought the urge to exchange yet another glance of irritation with Bean Stick lest Big Bee caught sight of it.

Hitchens' eyes narrowed. "Uh-huh."

"Hurry on up now," Goliah said as gently as his limited patience would allow. "A hungry stomach makes for a short prayer, and we've got to get to the meat of this meal right now. I don't have all day for this. Got more important business to attend to."

While the sheriff sauntered out of the room slower than a turtle mired in mud, the venerable local judge cleared his throat and looked sheepishly around the room. "There's more than one way to skin a polecat, you know."

Everything about Big Bee said thirsty. From his big round eyes that looked like a pair of giant snake bites, to the dry skin crusting on his lips. Goliah was glad that he'd been able to round him up before he got wet with whiskey or some other kind of moonshine. He knew Big Bee didn't have an innovative bone in his body. He was a follower, not a leader. Goliah had already given him the plan for the day, and they'd all put paid to it. So whatever he was talking about now was superfluous. "She should be sentenced to a more than adequate amount of time," Goliah reminded him.

Big Bee leaned his chair back on its two hind legs to the point where only a fraction of an inch touched the floor. Goliah feared the skinny man would fall and break his back. Not today, he prayed, not when he was counting on him, and not when they were just about to drive the final nail in Sput Louie McClendon's coffin.

With the aid of his cane, Goliah turned his back to the room and looked out the window at the accused currently tied to a tree. Sput Louie had her arms wrapped and tied around the trunk of the old post oak that served as the Feather Falls jail. He rued the fact that the large and leafy canopy provided so much shade for her, and silently vowed to see to its pruning as soon as this business was over.

Hopefully, it would be the shortest trial on record. Goliah and his cohorts had already discussed that. The sentence would be long and served far away from here. Hopefully Fort Smith, but Tahlequah would work just as well.

Sput Louie looked up at the window as the sheriff untied her from the tree. Goliah saw fear in her eyes, but surprisingly no tears, and certainly no remorse for ruining his crops. If he could have added in the assault at Buffalo Wallow, sure, that would add some time onto her sentence, but it would also open up questions as to the reason for her attack, which might then shine a light on that whole nasty business with Benjamin.

Goliah would not, could not suffer that.

Once the sheriff ushered Sput Louie into the room looking lost and forlorn, Big Bee cleared his throat and began what Goliah hoped would be the end of this whole McClendon saga.

"Now Sput Louie McClendon, since there's nobody here but us chickens, so to speak, let's get right to it." Big Bee smiled broadly.

The smile quickly melted when the rear door flew open and hit the back wall. A gust of hot air swooshed in carrying Hunter Big and Archie, with L.B. riding their tailwind.

Goliah jumped to his feet and shuffled sideways.

Bean Stick's face contorted like he'd swallowed a curse.

Sput Louie brought her bound hands to her mouth and bit down on her knuckles.

A sly grin spread across Sheriff Hitchens' face. "Well, you boys sure got here fast."

Chapter Thirty

With the hasty appearance of her three sons, the temperature in the makeshift courtroom rose through the roof.

Archie panted like a rabid dog. "I – I did it," he said, his words launching a string of spittle from his mouth.

Hunter, sweating like a man in the throes of Choctaw Fever, zeroed in on his mother. "You all right, Ma?" His eyes still held the look of terror Sput had seen from the crawlspace.

It wasn't until Sput Louie got a glimpse of L.B. looking dazed with broad shadows under his eyes that her chin undertook a tremble and her knees began to weaken. It took every bit of fortitude she had left to remain upright.

Judge Big Bee raised both hands in the air like he was the one under arrest. "Whoa there, boys."

All of this, Sput saw in her peripheral vision, as she still did not want to look her sons in the face for fear they would be able to detect her dark secret, see it in her eyes, read it on her face, feel something awry in their hearts. She'd gotten somewhat of a reprieve during her capture when Hitchens had placed her in the back of his wagon just as her sons emerged from the house. "Your Ma's going to jail," he said when they came running out. "Lynch is pressing charges of vandalism against her." Then he'd hurriedly driven her away.

Now, here her sons were boring into her with their eyes, fully capable of detecting the hole in her heart the size of a cannonball.

Bean Stick bounded to his feet with a quick glance at Goliah. "What is the meaning of this? Barging in here like animals."

Archie took a slow deep breath. "I did it. I pulled all the nails out the floor."

"Did what now, boy?" Judge Big Bee asked, looking perplexed from Goliah to Bean Stick.

Hunter's legs were planted wide, his chin high as he whipped his head around to face the judge. "He ain't your damn boy."

Sput did not need to look at Hunter to know he had his fists balled. She bowed her head in prayer but kept her eyes open and her feet light.

Hitchens movement to the row of chairs that lined the back wall momentarily distracted everyone. He swung a chair around backward and sat astride it like he was front and center of a minstrel show.

Goliah glared at the sheriff. Receiving no apparent response or even acknowledgment from the law enforcer, he then turned his glare on the McClendon men. "Now hold on there. You are disturbing official court business and disrespecting an official court judge. This is a court of law."

"Then where the jury at?" Hunter asked, his gaze bouncing around the room from man to man to mother.

Goliah's cheeks flushed red, as did Bean Stick's.

"I was the one that vandalized your place, Mr. Lynch," Archie repeated. "I pulled the nails out the floor. Every single one of them. Ma didn't know nothin' about it."

The three friends looked at one another.

A hard smile crept across Goliah's face. "Did you poison the crops, too?"

Archie's face contorted as he swung his head toward his mother, then quickly jerked it back. "Huh?"

A thick silence blanketed the room as everyone turned to Sput. She was caught dead to rights. No need in thinking how did I get here? No need to look where she'd fallen, but where she'd slipped. And where she'd slipped was in choosing to poison the crops in the first place. It had been her choice to travel down a road greased with vengeance. "I'm the one done it," she said in a voice almost too small to hear. It was the first time she'd spoken out loud since the crawlspace. "I killed your crops." She finally raised her head towards her sons and shrugged. Confession was good for the soul, even a partial one. Her boys had tried to rescue her, and she was thankful for the effort, but they may as well have been trying to bite the sun.

As small as Sput's voice was, Bean Stick's boomed in response. "See there, a confession. And you all," he pointed his finger at each of Sput's sons, "are witnesses to it. You heard it right here. That's why we don't need a jury."

"For I tell you that out of theethe thtoneth God can raithe up children for Abraham. Luke three, chapter eight."

All eyes turned to L.B. None, though, were as surprised as Sput was at hearing the word "stones" come out of his mouth. He didn't even know what he was saying. Or did he? She swiped a peek at Goliah who must not have understood L.B.'s words nor the riddle they were wrapped in, as he showed no reaction whatsoever.

She felt herself drift far away from her body, outside of the flesh and bones that had given birth to a son that was also her nephew. She floated a far piece until she could see the entire room and everyone in it from somewhere on high.

Judge Big Bee cleared his throat and yanked her back to her body with the words he spoke.

"You boys are welcomed to sit qui-et-ly," he said, staring pointedly at L.B., "and observe proceedings provided you don't speak." Then his eyes raked across all three of Sput's sons. "You cut no figure in this court."

"Let us proceed, then," Goliah said, and resumed his seat.

It was Big Bee's turn to glare at Goliah with a look that said *I am the judge here*. "Let us proceed."

As Hunter pivoted away from his Ma and confronted Goliah with a seething scowl, Goliah rose halfway out of his armchair and nodded his chin towards Archie. "Oh," he said, seemingly ignoring the hostile stare slung his way, "and thanks for making it easier to raze that dilapidated old shack. Didn't know it had no nails." He smirked as he plopped back into his chair.

The judge cleared his throat even louder. "Now, Mrs. McClendon."

It was not lost on Sput the change in Big Bee's demeanor as evidenced by the formal way he now addressed her. Maybe things would not go so badly for her now that her sons were there. She smiled wanly at the only people left who loved her. Would they still love her if they knew she'd joined blankets with her brother? She frowned at the memory that thought evoked, then quickly cast it from her mind.

"You have now confessed to destroying the property of one Goliah T. Lynch. That," Judge Big Bee paused, "amounts to larceny. Do you know what larceny is? Thievery," he answered for her. "Since this is your first appearance before a court—is that right?"

Sput answered with a small nod. She just wanted this over and done. She would go away to jail where she wouldn't have to face the prying eyes, the accusatory leers, the disgusting looks that would surely be in the offing. Her boys could make it without her. In fact, they'd be better off that way.

"Since this is your first offense, that draws a fine of—how much is the fine, Mr. Prosecutor?"

Bean Stick was ready with the answer. "Sixty dollars or a year behind bars.

Sput Louie's chest tightened, igniting a slow burn.

"Plus," Bean Stick continued, "we have to add in the money the victim would have profited from the crops had Sput—Mrs. McClendon not been so decidedly malicious." He turned to Goliah. "How much would you say that would be, Mr. Lynch?"

"Oh, quite a bit," Goliah said, rising from his chair once again. "I expect those crops would have been quite remunerative. At market, I might have garnered seventy or eighty dollars."

While Archie's mouth slackened, L.B. scratched his cheek; Hunter stood his ground, and Sput bristled. She and Benjamin had never grown enough crops to sell, only enough to feed the family for two or three months. Yes, they had traded a bushel here and there in kind, but she doubted they could have gotten anywhere near seventy dollars if they'd even thought to sell it.

"That comes to one hundred and forty dollars. Now, if you'll just pay the fine," Big Bee said, "you can be on your way."

Sput didn't even have it within her to muster up amusement at the notion that she would have any money, much less one hundred and forty dollars. They knew her pockets were as dry as a dead well.

"Do you have the money?"

Her voice vacant, she simply did not answer. She just looked at Old Crow, who smiled at her confident and cocky.

"Then you'll have to do time."

Ordinarily, when Sput found herself in dire times, she would reach for her amulet. She only pretended to reach for it this time. She pressed the flat of her bound hands over the amulet to feel the small cloth clump that rested in her bosom. It was still there. But what now? What would happen to the stones in jail? Would she be able to secret them away so as to go unnoticed? She didn't know how she would keep them or why she wanted to. She did know that the fact that they were still there gave her some hope. She was ready for her sentence.

Big Bee gave Goliah a crisp nod, but Sput saw a glimmer of something suspicious hiding behind his eyes.

"Now, typically," Big Bee said, "we'd have to send you over to the Tahlequah jail because, of course, we can't keep you tied to that tree for a year." He chuckled looking directly at Goliah, whose eyes suddenly narrowed into an expression of confusion. "I know you don't want to be that far away from your family. That's a two-day ride for any visitors provided you're allowed them."

Bean Stick's face contorted in puzzlement as he mouthed the word *what* to Goliah, who cleared his throat like he was about to answer.

Big Bee beat him to it.

"I hereby sentence you to be indentured for the term of three years to Goliah T. Lynch." He banged his fist on the desk, which not only served to highlight his lack of a gavel but also offered finality to his words.

Sput's hands flopped down as her mouth dropped open. She looked at her three sons who looked just as confused as everyone else, except for Goliah. His face gnarled into a menacing scowl.

"Starting tomorrow," Big Bee continued, "you can work off the damages you have caused this man to suffer. You shall do anything and everything he asks you to do from sunup to sundown."

When his eyes flashed Goliah's way, a sudden look of uncertainty crawled across Big Bee's face. "Now, I know Mr. Lynch doesn't want to pay for your keep so, um, after each day's work, you may go home to your own bed and eat your own food, but you must return promptly at dawn the following morning. This you shall do day after day, after day, for three years."

With that, Big Bee looked dubiously at Goliah, whose face tightened and twitched like he'd just been offered a bottle of whiskey for the price of a cow. The judge's bottom lip stretched into a grimace as his eyes scanned the room in confusion. Big Bee seemed not to understand the problem nor what to do about it. "I, um, I—I guess we'll release you for today?"

Chapter Thirty-one

Goliah was not a man who pivoted east to keep from hurting west's feelings, but he did not say one word to Big Bee after the sentencing debacle. He couldn't. Words had failed him.

He had, however, kicked the chair over in a conniption fit as he left the surrogate courtroom. He didn't even glance Sput Louie's way as he brushed past her and her scrappy sons.

Sitting atop his coverless wagon heading home down Rabbit Run Road, though, he cursed Big Bee. Loudly. "Dumber than driven cattle," he yelled to the birds and the trees, the clouds and the sun. Goliah had expected to be salivating lickspittle right about then thinking about Sput Louie locked up and far away. Instead, his tongue was as dry as deadwood at the thought of her being underfoot. Every day. For three years.

All he could do was shake his head at Big Bee and his big idea as he turned his wagon and took a shortcut through a stand of Hemlocks. That would be his last time giving Big Bee free rein. Getting through to Big Bee was like trying to wet a greased pole. His friend needed reeling in. Although, how much of a friend he would still be remained to be seen in the face of such a stupid—

WHIZZ BLAP

The sound interrupted his thoughts and Goliah ducked instinctively. His head swiveled to his right, then around to his left looking for the winged nuisance.

WHIZZ BLAP

This time Ephinetta snorted and pricked her ears.

"Steady, steady, steady," he commanded, scanning his surroundings with even more scrutiny this time. Increasing his pace would only serve to rile up any potential pests, so he slowed to a two-beat trot.

Scouring the branches above, he saw no beehive or wasp nest from which to steer away; just the flicker of a squirrel's tail as it scurried up a tree trunk. The only sounds he heard were the click and crack of dead twigs and dry cones crushed under the weight of the wagon wheels.

He sucked in a whiff of the sharp odor the crushed hemlock cones released and soon went back to damning Big Bee to hell for not doing what they had distinctly discussed. He would have to continue dealing with Sput Louie McClendon. His only recourse now was to feed her a box of grave worms. Or something like it. He did have one option left in his bag of tricks, and he couldn't wait to pull that off. But right then, he just wanted to strangle Big Bee for all of the—

WHIZZ THWAP.

Ephinetta let loose a roar this time and yanked her head to the side as if she'd suffered a blow to her muzzle.

"Whoa, girl." Goliah tugged on the inside rein and came to a complete stop. "Stand," he commanded. He surveyed his surroundings again looking for the ghostly culprit. What the hell had lit into her? If it was large enough to make her wrench like that, it should have been large enough to be seen.

WHIZZ BLAP.

This time, the something lit into his hat and knocked it off his head and into the dirt.

WHIZZ THWAP

That one hit his neck; then another hit his jaw in rapid succession. Its pointy edge stung as he ducked and rubbed his cheek. Whatever it was had hit him with the force of an arrow shot from a bow. Only it felt more like a rock from a slingshot.

WHOOSH

The projectile whizzed in front of his face barely missing his nose.

Goliah hunkered down deeper inside of the footwell of the wagon. What was happening? Was he under siege? From who? From where? And why?

Not having the time or the ability to investigate given his out-of-commission hip, he quickly reached for the whip lying on the bench seat. "HA." He quickly poked his head out just long enough to yell at Ephinetta.

Before she could heed his command and before he could snap the braided lash of rawhide above her head, another WHIZZ BLAP hit, and she reared back violently.

Goliah raised his head for another quick peek.

WHIZZ CHINK

The propellant ricocheted off of the buckle on Ephinetta's belly band and struck Goliah's temple forcing him to drop the reins as he fell backward. He caught himself on the railing before falling completely out of the wagon.

His mind raced. His hands shook. Ephinetta bucked.

The missile had come from his right.

Was it too late to get Ephinetta under control and get them both to safety? From his crouched position back in the convulsing foot well, he stretched his bum leg down the side of the wagon and searched for the metal mounting step. As soon as he put his weight on it, though, his foot slipped off.

"AARRGGHHH." His sore hip hit the ground first.

Ephinetta reared back a second time, then took off through the trees dragging the wagon behind her and leaving Goliah exposed and without his cane.

He scrabbled towards a wide tree trunk a few feet away. Before he could get within hiding distance, a shod foot came from out of the blue and kicked him straight up the center of his backside.

Goliah curled up in blinding pain.

The foot then pressed into the back of his neck and forced his face to eat dirt. Whoever it was weighed as much as a bull and wore moccasins instead of boots. Goliah felt the man's toe knuckles pressing into his scalp and his heel bearing down on his spine.

"My money's in my pants pocket," Goliah pleaded through the grit pushing its way past his lips and onto his teeth. "Take it," he managed to spit out.

His assailant's foot relented just long enough to draw back and kick him in the ribs this time.

The full weight of who Goliah decided must have been a bushwhacker then trounced on his torso. He felt his shoulders being squeezed between his foe's knees as the man straddled his back.

Was he going to kill him? Was his throat about to be slashed? Was he going to be strangled?

The answer came as a thrashing began at the crown of Goliah's head.

When he turned his head to the right, a punishing blow landed on his left ear.

He turned his head to the left, and the man bashed his right ear.

A barrage of blows pounded the top of his spine, the bottom of his neck, the back of his head.

With his hands pinned beneath him, he struggled against the pummeling with his body as best he could. He tried to worm one hand loose but felt his shoulder pop in the process. Heard it, too.

His attacker continued to hammer him relentlessly.

The fury of the blows caused Goliah to bite his tongue. A spurt of blood filled his mouth.

"Ahkkkk" dredged up from Goliah's gut and erupted from his mouth.

His body gave in, but his assailant railed on. Goliah's mind melded into the flurry of fists. He began to whimper.

"Please," he begged through welling tears.

It didn't work.

As the beating went unabated, something deep within drove his whimper into a full-fledged wail.

Suddenly, the beating ceased.

The man was gone. Without a word. Except for what he had communicated with his fists.

Goliah lay there a moment before he could roll over onto his back. When he heard Ephinetta neigh in the distance, he raised his silver brow. Clearly, robbery had not been the motive. Whoever had attacked him reeked of retribution. For what, though, he hadn't a clue.

What he did know were two things.

One, that his attacker had hornswoggled him by using an old Indian war tactic; if you would shoot a general, shoot his horse first.

Two, before the man left, he'd stood over Goliah, one mocasined foot planted in the dirt on each side of his victim's head. That's when Goliah had taken a chance and stole a quick peak. Embroidered on the right shoe were yellow beads. The awkward round shapes sprouted out from the crooked green line sewn down the center seam.

It was a crude likeness of a delicate sunflower.

Chapter Thirty-two

Early the next morning, Sput Louie snuck away from the house. She quietly bypassed her sleeping sons in the same way she'd sidestepped their probing questions the night before.

I don't wanna talk about it, she'd told them on the long walk home from town.

When they pressed her, *Grown folks' business* is what she'd offered up. To which the twins simultaneously replied, *But we are grown.*

When L.B. joined the inquisition, she thought she could put him off much easier. *Why don't you catch your Ma some fireflies,* she'd suggested.

To which he'd responded *Ain't no fireflies in the daytime.*

Then Sput doubled down with *some things are better left unsaid,* and that seemed to put an end to it. For the time being, anyway, which is why she'd felt the need to sneak away before they woke.

However, not before she'd pilfered L.B.'s bug jar.

She took the jar and went straight to Lake Watanuga before heading to Old Crow's place, the fading moon and burgeoning sun both lighting her way.

Once at the lake, she knew exactly which big boulder hid the most peat moss. Her sore arm was on the mend enough for her to lift her skirt as she waded into the cold water. With one shivering hand she fetched two handfuls worth of the squishy green substance.

Back on the shoreline, she wrung water from the moss into the jar, nearly filling it. She tossed in a couple of green clumps for good measure. If it worked to preserve fish until it was ready to cook, it would certainly keep a man's stones from drying out and shrinking up. She was just sorry she hadn't thought to do so earlier.

She'd had other things on her mind, hadn't she? Life had dealt her a near crushing blow.

She was about to fight back, though.

After cautiously unfolding the kerchief, she let the stones roll off the cloth and into the jar. Carefully screwing the lid back on, she set it down in the dewy grass.

She breathed a sigh of satisfaction that her plan was coming to fruition. With everything now in place, she snatched her head rag off, fluffed her hair with her palms, and let it fly free. The peeking sun shone red through her closed lids, and the chilly air felt fresh on her face. She could have stood there like that all day, but she had business to attend to soon. Did she have time to bathe first? Wash her hair? Probably not.

Before she knew it, she was naked. Her skirt, shirt, and bloomers were laid out on a rock. She wadded her uplift into a ball and used the undergarment as a washrag. The waters of Lake Watanuga were as calm as the day one of the pass-through preachers dipped her in it and washed away her sins without nary a chunk of soap. Maybe the lake would do it again.

Once out of the water, she dressed and dried her hair with her headscarf. When she got a glimpse of the rising sun reflected in the ripple-less lake, something told her to go over and get a gander at her hair. She couldn't remember the last time she'd seen it since the McClendon's had never owned a looking glass.

She climbed atop a medium-sized rock for better scrutiny.

The texture of her hair, its fullness made it look harder than it was. It was soft to the touch. Like damp cotton. Only instead of being cushiony white bolls, it was cottony black spirals. The coils sprouted outwards and were bedecked with crinkled slivers of gray that shone silver in the sun. It was different from Ma Bay's hair—hers had been more robust, more full-bodied—but it was of Ma Bay. Just as she was of Ma Bay, no matter the circumstances of how that came to be. Her hair was part of her heritage. Just like the color of her skin, the smallness of her nose, the thinness of her arms, the flatness of her chest, the way she could bend her thumb all the way back to her wrist, the way her smile hitched a little to the side, the way she hunched her shoulders and dipped her chin when she laughed. All of those things connected her to Ma Bay.

Why would she be ashamed of that? Why would she hide any of it?

Would doing so mean she was somehow ashamed to be like Ma Bay? Ma Bay had made Sput who she was by everything she had taught her, showed her, given her, by the way she had loved her and protected her as best she could. Old Crow hadn't contributed a thing outside of his seed, and there was nothing she could do about that.

Well, there was one thing. Or more exactly, three things. Prepared now for the day head, she picked up the jar and shoved it in her pocket where it was completely swallowed up into the folds of her skirt. She took a gander at the ever-rising morning sun. Where had the time gone? She was going to be late now.

Something in her peripheral vision caught her eye and gave her pause. Her ears perked up. Further down the shoreline, there was movement. It was a figure. A human figure. Her instincts told her to crouch down. One could never be too careful in a land where the pistol laid the law when the lawman was absent, and sometimes when he was present.

She squinted her eyes for better scrutiny, but then gasped when she realized who it was.

#

The man's hair was as big as hers, wildly aroused with the vitality of spring. Just like when he'd driven her home from Buffalo Wallow a few days before.

Rogers headed towards her.

"That's some nice hair," she said when he got close enough. She didn't hear the sarcasm in her tone until it was too late to do anything about it. Sput hesitated before braving the question that begged to be asked, though she already knew the answer. "Negro then?"

Although he did not look insulted as she had feared, nor surprised as she had expected, he still evaded the question. "Nice hair yourself."

She didn't know why she wanted to press her nose into someone else's business. That was so unlike her. She just knew she had to bow to her instincts. "Mulatto?" She frowned and cocked her head to the side.

Rogers stretched his neck back so far that his chin almost touched his collarbone. "No," he said emphatically. "Ain't carryin' no white blood. At all."

When had he gotten so down on white people, she wondered? She wrinkled her nose at this puzzle wrapped in a blanket of mystery laid across a bed of befuddlement.

"Thank God for small favors," he said, puffing out his chest.

And when, she mused, had he started sounding like a Negro? Probably about the same time he began looking like one, was her best guess.

"My father was Creek. Mama was African."

The two of them watched as a bale of green terrapins herded themselves out of the water and onto the shore. Rogers picked up one of the small smooth stones obstructing the turtles' path and tossed it. They both watched as it skipped across the lake.

"Father didn't see fit to marry Mama even after he gave her five children." He skidded another stone. "Took care of us, though. On the other side of town." He paused before adding, "Away from his real family."

Sput nodded her acknowledgment of not only an old familiar story but also of their newly realized connection. They were both African and Indian, though she supposed she must admit to a dollop of white blood as well, given Old Crow's father. Her and Rogers' commonality, though, parted ways when it reached their choice of mates.

Rogers hadn't married his brother.

She pondered whether she would now break the world into two groups, those who'd married their sibling and those who hadn't. So far, the former would be a group of one. She fixed her mouth to chuckle but caught herself. Would she one day be able to laugh at her situation?

Maybe. Probably not, though. Would she think of Goliah's dastardly act every time she saw someone looking at her with more than a passing glance? Probably so. But hopefully not. The despicable deed had not been her transgression, but Old Crow's. She had to keep reminding herself of that.

Their truncated conversation continued.

"Two Bird know," she asked?

"Does now."

Knowing how Two Bird felt about helping Negroes, Sput couldn't believe that he would ever accept a colored man as his *adalii*, even if that wife were as easy on the eyes as Rogers. Even with his hair looking as regal as a feathered headdress.

"Still together," she queried?

Rogers shrugged and looked into the distance. "Won't let me in the house."

"And you still wanna fool with him?" she asked incredulously. Then it dawned on her that Rogers' railing against Negroes at the fish kill had been all bluster. Just like the terrapins creeping past them heading back into the water, Rogers had a powerful jaw but no bite. His words had no teeth if he was half Negro himself.

"Don't let Two Bird soak up your sun. Learn from him and shine on your own."

"Learn what, how to look down on people who are different?"

God gives us all a song, Sput thought. My, how this one had changed his tune.

"They calls that prejudice, and it only goes one way, and that's down. People have to have somebody to look down on so's they can feel puffed up and highfalutin. Indians look down on coloreds. White folks look down on Indians."

"Who looks down on white folks," Rogers asked?

Sput flicked her head to the side. "Hard to look down on the people what run everythin'." She twisted her mouth into a thoughtful expression. "Folks sure do resent, 'em, though," she reasoned. "Funny thing is white folks don't even know it. They' heads' in a cloud and they feet's off the ground when it comes to seein' how what they do mess it up for other folks." She smiled at this new understanding she had gained at that precise moment, pleased with herself for teasing it out. "They mind is as blind as they skin is bland," she heard herself say, and decided to follow her mouth's lead. "Blind from all the lies they tell theyself so's they feel bigger and better than everybody else." My, her mind was keen this morning. Sharper than cut cane. All of a sudden she had thoughts on everything. Smart ideas, too. She wasn't accustomed to it, but she sure did like it, this newfound gall, this fearlessness, this daring to say what was on her mind. And she had plenty on her mind.

She waited to see what else she would come up with to impress herself.

"And another thing," she said, "By pretendin' to be somethin' else, you lost who you was. Look at Two Bird. He know who he is and don't care what nobody think about it. He made peace with hisself, and you should, too." She looked up at his hair. "You not packin' your hair with goop no more, so that's a good start."

Out of habit, she ran a hand through her hair to smooth it down. Rippled with pride, it spring back up. It would not be denied, and neither would she. She knew she should be on her way to Old Crow's by now, but she'd just at that moment decided he could wait. For her.

"You think Africans is somehow different from Indians," she asked? "They only difference is the customs, the traditions. For an instance, my Ma's tribe had their weddings at night under a full moon for good luck." She surprised herself by remembering that little tidbit from Ma Bay. "Cherokees treasure the circle. Everything that's important to them is round, ain't it?" She paused in thought. "I bet you cain't name one white custom."

Rogers rubbed his chin in seeming contemplation. "Stealing folks' land?" He smiled.

"Ya-huh," she said. "Be proud of who you are. Be worthy of your forefathers. The Indian ones and the colored ones, too. You both." Just like me, she didn't dare say out loud.

Sput Louie thought about her own forefathers and foremothers and how she must honor them. Cutting her eyes from side to side, she surreptitiously patted the pocket that held the jar of stones. "I best be on my way," she said. Not only would she be worthy of her past, but her past was about to be prophetic of her future.

Chapter Thirty-three

Sput Louie had a lilt in her step as she finally wended her way towards Goliah's place.

A bird flew overhead, its wingspan the most vibrant blue she'd ever seen. She heard a scarab burrowing into a tree as she passed. At least she thought that's what she heard. When she stopped to inspect the tree trunk to confirm it, maybe run her hands across the bark of the blackjack oak to feel its roughness, she found herself licking it instead.

Its scratchiness drew a loud yelp from her. Well, that was silly, she thought, amused at herself.

Why she would do such a thing she didn't know. All she knew was that after her talk with Rogers, all her senses felt magnified. She took this heightened spirit of awareness to mean that she was on the right track, albeit to do a bad thing, but it would be done in the best possible way, wouldn't it? Sometimes, she rationalized, a rocky vineyard needed not a prayer but a pick axe, and Old Crow was one rock-ribbed patch of work.

As she approached the path leading to his front gate, her jauntiness waylaid a bit. Senix Lynch stood sentry under the arbor blocking the entrance to her salvation.

"Hey there, Miss Sput." He held his hand up in a halting fashion, nearly dropping the deerskin passel tucked under his arm.

His dark skin glistened with sweat as if he'd already put in a full day's work as Old Crow's skull. His eyes, though, were soft in apology. *Sorry you have to go through a second life of slavery*, they seemed to say.

"Bossman say you gots to prune the apricot orchard," Senix said, getting right to it after a solemn round of pleasantries.

Sput had fully expected chastisement for her lateness but was pleasantly surprised at its absence. She took that as another sign.

"Workin' by yourself," Senix continued, "that might take a week. Maybe more."

Sput looked over his right shoulder towards Goliah's massive two-story brick house. Two of the upstairs windows bore down on her like a pair of evil eyes. Was the man who'd brought down the hammer that smashed the brick of her existence behind one of them watching her? She shot a wry scowl that way just in case, then turned back to Senix with a straight face. "By myself?" She tried to act like she was going to do the work he was assigning her. Old Crow had evidently planned to have her sweating out all but blood. She was not surprised.

She had a plan for him, too.

"Then you move on to the paw-paw trees, then the pear orchard. By the time you finish up with the peaches, Boss'll have more chores lined up for you."

Looking across Goliah's huge spread, she saw a horse barn, pigsty, corncrib, and what appeared to be a millhouse with open doors on each side. A handful of men were feeding logs in through one door while another team caught the boards coming out of the other. She wished Senix would oversee them so she could sneak over to the big house.

"Boss gave strict orders, now," he said as if he knew of her plan, "for you not to go anywhere near him or the house. If you see him comin', go the other way." He put one eye on her while he lidded the other. "You hear me, Miss Sput?"

"I got ears."

He one-eyed her a little longer, then turned and began walking towards a nearby catalpa tree, his parcel jingling and jangling with every step. She took her cue and followed.

Once under the shade of the tree's heart-shaped leaves and pearly white flowers, he squatted and unfolded the deerskin revealing what turned out to be a passel of tools.

Her eyes widened as she squatted beside him. There was all manner of shivs, shanks, and ticklers.

"Now, this one here," he picked up one of the smaller knives, "you fit this curved blade around the twig to yank it off." He made a jerking motion, then handed it to her to try.

She turned it this way and that, admiring its thinness, its sharpness. Sunlight flickered off of the blade and flashed in her eyes causing her to double-blink. This shiny tip, she thought, would fit nicely around the tip of Old Crow's nose.

She mimicked the yanking motion.

Next, Senix picked up a lopper from the neatly organized array of tools. "Now, this one here is only for branches no bigger than two fingers thick." He held up his index and forefinger to demonstrate. "You put the branch in between the two blades, squeeze down hard with both hands." The loppers went SNAP as he clamped them together.

It looked like an oversized version of the clothes-pegs she used when hanging wash out to dry, except it was sharp enough to snip off a finger. Goliah's finger? She pushed the thought from her head. Why did she have maiming him on her mind? That wasn't why she was here. Besides, her husband had already seen to that, and rightly so.

With that thought, she pressed her lips together in a grimace. It had almost slipped her mind that her brother was also her husband, and her nephew her son. She supposed she'd better get used to that thought cropping up when all she wanted to do was tamp it down.

Then just as unexpectedly, a new thought popped up. Sput put a finger to her cheek as that thought begat a wish, and the wish, in turn, gave birth to a new twist to her plan.

After Senix had shown her how to use the folding saw, the fixed-blade saw, and the folding knife, he bustled over to the cornfields while she ambled over to the apricot orchard. Once there, she immediately unrolled the passel, removed the folding knife and slid it into her skirt pocket, the one opposite the jar.

She took stock of her surroundings to be sure no one had eyes on her. Seeing no human impediments to upcoming victory, she marched towards the big house heedless of any danger that might await her there.

#

Hoping Goliah would be the one to answer the door, Sput took a few deep breaths before she poised her hand to knock.

The door swung open, so swiftly it nearly sucked her breath away.

Little Fancy's eyes bugged round and wide like she'd swallowed the sun and it was fighting to get out. Sput figured it must be her newly freed coils that fired up Fancy's face like that. Standing across from Goliah's housegirl in her clean blue dress with the starched white collar that accented her pressed white headscarf, Sput thought she probably still looked a tad more colorful than Fancy.

"Osiyo," Sput said, feigning politeness only because Fancy was not the object of her venom. Her manners wouldn't last much longer, though. Fancy was the second person to block her path that day.

Sput did not take that as a sign.

She did take a visual measure of the woman who was nearly the same height as her but twice as wide. Even though Little Fancy had a hearty bosom that was about to bust a button, Sput figured she could take her in a fight if it came to that.

Fancy took the smallest of steps forward. "You know I cain't let you in here."

Was Fancy citing a rule or making a judgment, Sput wondered? She searched the girl's eyes, curious as to whether or not she knew the McClendon secret, and if she did, did she know Sput was not to blame for it?

A loud, impatient sigh came from deep within Sput's gut. She looked from side to side, and then snatched Fancy by her buttoned-down collar with both hands. Their noses were so close together that sweat from hers dribbled onto Fancy's. This time, Fancy's eyes not only bugged but crossed as well. "Don't you have some goats that need milkin'?" Sput reached up with one hand and yanked the woman's tidy headscarf from her head. She chucked it catawampus into the yard behind her.

Fancy's mouth dropped open as her eyes slid sideways towards where it had landed. "Well, yes sir—I mean ma'am. Yes, ma'am, I surely does, uh-huh, yep."

As Sput released her, Fancy quickly put her hands up to hide hair that had been haphazardly parted, tightly plaited, and violently exposed.

"Barbarians," she thought she heard Fancy mumble on her way down the porch steps.

Sput cared not.

Passing over the threshold, she landed in a bounteous hall that had at its center a solitary round table bedecked with an elegant lace cloth.

Scanning the walls brimming with portraits, it transported Sput back to her childhood and the infrequent occasions she and Ma Bay had passed through this same vestibule. She remembered wondering at the time who all the people were in the paintings and thinking how grand and imposing a room it was, but now it didn't look so colossal. And the people were probably her ancestors.

She frowned in distaste.

The aroma of freshly baked biscuits curled around her nose and brought her mind back to her mission. She couldn't remember the last time she'd eaten or what the meal had been. But it hadn't been biscuits.

She followed the buttery scent to the back of the house.

It led her to a kitchen where a half-eaten plate of biscuits, bacon, and eggs sat on a small cloth-covered table directly in front of the man who had raped her mother.

"I'm done slavin' for you." Sput issued her decree with a coolness that showcased her confidence.

Goliah jumped up with such force that his chair flew backward, causing the cane leaning against it to hit the floor. The man himself nearly keeled over sideways but caught the edge of the table just in time.

"How did you get in here?" he demanded. His eyes, wide with surprise, quickly narrowed in anger.

Sput took her time in taking him in. His stiff white shirt and mud brown trousers somehow suited his character. A clean bright covering up top, but a mess of dirty evil-doing down below.

"Fancy," Goliah yelled as he looked beyond Sput to the doorway.

Her ears heard his words, but all she saw was a crooked man begging to be set straight once and for all.

She shrugged. "Fancy ain't gon' hear you." Sput slid her hands into her pockets. One gripped the jar. The other one, the knife.

"What have you done to her? Fancy," he screamed again like she still might come running.

"You need to be screaming for the Almighty."

Goliah straightened his body and let loose his grip on the table. "You think I can't handle a puny little negress like you? I've already done that." He laughed half-heartedly. "Niggers occupy the lowest rung on the ladder."

The first thing folks pulled out of their arsenal of hate towards colored people was the word *nigger*. They whipped it out like it was a loaded gun. Knowing this, Sput was not only used to it but was prepared for it.

"Ya-huh. Well, your ladder's 'bout to be kicked out from under you."

He lowered his silver brow. "You have the audacity to enter my house to try and raise riot?" He gripped the table again.

Sput Louie let out a booming "Ha." Then said, "You cain't hide behind your five-cent words 'cause you just a two-bit fool." She looked down the length of him and back up again with a smirk. "Minus the two bits."

Goliah sucked in a breath. "Why you little whore."

Hearing that word made her squeeze the jar tight and the knife even tighter. Goliah's eyes flashed to the movement of her hands inside her pockets. He hobbled back a smidgeon seemingly to give himself a wider berth.

Was that fear she saw in his eyes? Maybe he understood now that she was a worthy adversary. Or maybe he just thought she was crazy.

He was right on both counts.

"You tore me away from the only people what loved me," she began.

"Niggers don't love. They just fornicate. Like animals."

In that split second, she let loose the jar and gripped harder the knife. Could she cut a man, she wondered? What if that man was the devil?

"I didn't have nobody to look after me, protect me, show me how to be 'til I come back here and found somebody to do just that. But you found a way to ruin a thing that never should have happened in the first place. How could you let us marry knowin' what you knew?"

His eyes darted to her hair as he gave a half shrug. "Ain't my business what two niggers do."

Her eyes locked on his. "Well, you ain't never gon' repeat to nobody livin', dead, or dyin' what you told me the other day."

He harrumphed nervously. "You don't tell me what to do. Why, I'll shout it from the top of the town house if I want to. In fact," he straightened up and let go of the table again, "I'll tell everyone right now that you married—"

Before he could finish, Sput barreled forward and whipped out the content of her right pocket. It was like a bolt of lightning had stricken Goliah in the chest and shoved his back against the sideboard, causing the copper-bottomed pots hanging from the top ledge to rattle in complaint.

He flopped down to the floor like a wet rag doll.

Sput stepped back as his face went slack and all the color drained from it. All that was left was an expression of shock and recognition as he gazed fixedly at his testicles floating in a jar.

"W-where did you g-g-get—"

"Don't matter. This is you, you raper. In a jar." She swirled the contents around. "This is where they belong. And I hope you cain't rape nobody no more."

Goliah shook his head slowly back and forth, back and forth, never taking his eyes off of the jar.

For the first time in a lifetime of Sput Louie McClendon dealing with Goliah T. Lynch, he seemed at a loss for words.

She, on the other hand, was not.

"Now, it's three things you gon' do and one thing you bett' not."

She waited for a nod of understanding. Seeing none, she pressed on with a nefarious smile.

"First, you gon' claim Benjamin as your rightful heir. He probably don't want your precious Indian land now, but his son need it. So you gon' make sure the Cherokees know L.B. is your grandson and that you right proud of that fact. You gon' get him use of the land and any bread money that's due him."

Goliah's eyes remained fastened on the jar. Sput stepped closer until she was standing directly over him again. She shook the jar in his face for good measure, like giving a friendly warning with a meat axe. He recoiled like the coward she knew him to be.

"Next, you gon' call off them there Annie-Horsethief Society folks."

His eyes were as empty as two nutting stones.

"Number three, they say Freedmen is agitatin' for Indian land. Whatever that means, you gon' do it, too. You gon' agitate right along-side all the freedman what slaved for you. You gon' help 'em get what you all promised to give 'em all them many years ago. We coulda been doin' as good as you by now if y'all had lived up to your word."

Goliah cupped his hand to his temple and shielded his eyes from the jar.

It was Sput's turn to laugh half-heartedly. "Well, now I done put a worm in that shiny apple of a life of yours, haven't I? Didn't ruin yours, though, like you tried to muck up mine."

She shook the jar towards his face again. He turned and looked away. That's when she noticed that his ear was red and swollen. It looked deformed. And he had a knot on his forehead. A satisfied grin stretched across her face. Someone had beat Old Crow but good. She didn't know why or care by whom. She was just sorry it hadn't been a McClendon.

"Good Lord," she said. "Is everybody after you? You must not be livin' right."

She swatted his hand down from his face and forced him to look up at her.

"I ain't done yet. It's one more thing I bett' not ever," she paused, "ever hear from you or about you." She stopped. The words she wanted to say next felt like barbed wire on her tongue, so she just spit them out. "That you...are my father."

Her work done, her message delivered, her orders given, it was time to go. Just before she did, she drew her right leg back and swung it forward for one swift kick dead center of her former owner's crotch.

Goliah grabbed the area and groaned in pain.

Returning the jar to her pocket, Sput turned to leave, but couldn't. Someone was blocking the doorway.

How long had Philura Lynch been standing behind her, she wondered? Based on the way her eyelids fluttered like the wings of a hummingbird, it was long enough to have heard their conversation.

Just in case she hadn't heard, Sput decided to school her as well.

She looked Philura over from her frilly nightcap to her lacy nightgown. "I may have married my own brother without knowin' it, lady," she swallowed hard, "But you knew you was marryin' a raper, and the only children he ever gon' have," she paused to let the upcoming truth sink in, "came out of a abomination to the Lord."

She withdrew the knife from her pocket and slowly unfolded it. Philura shrunk back.

With the handle in her fist and the blade high in the air, Sput said, "'Oh, Lord, what wilt thou give? Give them a miscarryin' womb and dry breasts.'" Then she plunged the knife down and stabbed the kitchen table beside her. "Book of Hosea."

With that, Sput Louie left, leaving behind only the bones of the beast. She and Benjamin had slain Goliah.

Chapter Thirty-four

One year later, as Sput Louie scoured the chicken yard hunting down eggs for breakfast, she noticed her flock had increased by one.

Yesterday, she only had two dingy white hens, a spotted gray one, and a black one with yellow legs. Now, a winsome red had been mysteriously added to her flock. If she didn't know any better, she'd think her new hen was a Wyandotte, but that couldn't be. They were hard to come by.

Every few months, a new animal or two would appear out of the blue. One day, the McClendons would be down to three chickens from four because they'd eaten one for dinner. Then in the next couple of weeks, two more would mysteriously show up. Another time, L.B. had let their only pig escape. They looked everywhere for that pig, and had the neighbors on the lookout, too. Nothing. The following week, they woke up to a new and different pig in the pen.

Courtesy of Goliah Lynch, no doubt.

At first, her family turned to her for answers as to those strange occurrences. They'd peer at her with a silent curiosity that bound them to one another. Just like the day she returned home from Old Crow's without having done a lick of work, then announced that he had agreed to claim L.B. as his grandson and free her from her sentence. They looked at her with wonderment but somehow knew instinctively not to question her.

If these unexplained acts continued, one day she would not only have a bevy of hogs to fatten and butcher but enough hens and eggs for sale or barter.

Just as she approached the house with her arms full of brown eggs, Emarthla peeped her head out of the door. "Breakfast ready."

Great, Sput thought, biting her lip to keep the sarcasm from seeping out of her mind and into her mouth. Probably more kafir-cornmeal and dandelion greens, she silently bemoaned. That was Emarthla's specialty, and she had cooked it nearly every day since she'd moved in with Sput months ago, right after being turned off of her land by a Shawnee. The only way Sput could get what she wanted for breakfast without hurting her friend's feelings was to beat her to the stove. She had failed again that day.

"Now, Emarthla, I done told you you don't have to cook breakfast every day," she said as she reached the porch. Sput was very fond of Emarthla but less than elated at having to share the same bed. She regretted not having another bedroom added on when they'd built their new house on the new acreage, but she hadn't wanted to deplete the timber resources on land L.B. was granted the use of. And it was all his from the land to the houses, from the swine to the fowl. She was just the official guardian of it all. She had the papers to prove it.

"Oh, you wanted eggs?" Emarthla looked sheepish as she peered at the bundle in Sput's arms.

"Got an extra hen this morning." Sput eased into her favorite chair on the porch.

"Another one?" Emarthla asked. She looked at Sput with a curious side-eye but then nodded her acceptance of Sput's non-answer as she took the eggs from her. "Guess they droppin' from the sky," she wisecracked, then turned towards the front door but suddenly stopped short. "Company comin'," she said, eyes trained on a cloud of dust slow-rolling up the rutted road towards their house.

As Emarthla began to saunter through the door, Rogers came barreling out. Emarthla had to jump back to keep him from crushing the bounty of eggs.

"What kind of company?" he asked, gun in hand, ready for action. Rogers had moved in with the McClendons even before Emarthla had. At Sput's invitation and much to the chagrin of her sons, but she just couldn't abide the way Two Bird had mistreated him.

"Put that gun away," she said as the billows of dust began to dissipate, revealing an oddly familiar gentleman on an equally recognizable horse. She just couldn't quite place either. "Might be that tombstone salesman back again?" She didn't bother rising from her rocker for a better look. Travelling salesmen were fast becoming the norm in Indian Territory, in particular for those who lived in fine frame houses like L.B.'s. It drew all kinds of folks hawking their wares because they thought whoever dwelt there could surely afford them.

Rogers dropped open his revolver's cylinder, looked at it with an eye for counting bullets, then snapped it shut. "I told Tombstone Tom the next time he come back, he gon' need his own product."

Sput was amused. Rogers' growingly common usage of the Colored man's dialect still didn't sound quite right. He was in their fold now, though. She would get used to it just as he had.

The barrel of his gun pointed towards the horseman as Rogers squinted his eyes over the sight. "Jesus," he said, flicking his eyes upwards while letting his weapon drop down to his side in defeat. "That ain't no salesman, Miss Sput."

"Who is it?"

Curious now, Sput stood and squinted into the distance. The rider was still a ways away, but close enough for her to recognize him now. And recognize him she did. Even though she'd never seen him in men's clothing before.

She turned back to Rogers, but he silently retreated inside just as L.B. bolted out. He had his slate in one hand, a piece of chalk in the other, leaving only his forearms to hold up his beltless pants. He nearly tripped hurtling himself down the two stairs, but luckily caught himself and landed on his feet.

"Boy, come back here," his mother commanded.

"But imma be late for thkool, Mama."

He grudgingly obeyed his mother and stomped his way back. Sput pulled the two ends of his rope belt tight around his waist.

"Today, Archie gon' learn us to read writin', Mama."

"Read writin'?" Sput asked incredulously, knotting the belt twice.

"Uh-huh. I can read readin', but I cain't read writin'. Archie gon' learn me."

She presumed L.B. was referring to reading handwriting as opposed to reading the printed word, but couldn't be sure, as she could do neither. She was just happy her baby boy had the opportunity to do what he'd wanted to do his whole life, and that was to go to school and learn.

Once she finished straightening out his clothes, she patted him on his back, and he took off running across the yard towards Archie's house, which doubled as the schoolhouse. So far, Archie had only three other students. Their parents were supposed to pay one dollar a month for each child, but Archie had only been paid for one of them, and that had been in trade. The trade had been six months' tuition for one McGuffey Speller. Throw in the Bible, and that brought the number of books up to a total of two for the Panther Paw Primary School. "So named," Archie liked to say, "because I aim to show the world that the mind of a colored man is just as powerful as the claws of a panther's paw."

He would have to do that with someone other than L.B., though, Sput lamented.

L.B. must have spotted Tawny as he hurried across the yard to school because he doglegged towards her as she emerged from her and Hunter's house carrying a basket of something. Probably breakfast for her husband who was fast at work in the fields. L.B. gently patted her belly swollen with child. She rubbed his wooly head in return. Then he ran the rest of the way to school.

The hugeness of Tawny's belly reminded Sput that she would have her first grandchild soon. It might even be that very day. That grandchild would be part of the family's new beginning, a child who would never know of its Lynch blood.

Sput was still engrossed in the thought as Two Bird finally reached her porch.

"He-lo," he said in English, dismounting from his horse.

She smiled, proud of his progress at learning the English she had been teaching him. As soon as he'd won a seat on the Cherokee National Council, he vowed to learn the white man's words so he could better deal with the white man's ways. "You here to see Rogers?"

Just then, Rogers strode out of the house balancing in one hand a cup and saucer made of blue willow china filled to the brim with strong smelling coffee. He'd brought the delicate pieces with him when he moved in, and since he had not offered to let anyone use them, Sput had coveted them from afar. Until now.

He handed the coffee to Sput without looking at his former *uyahi*. She had suspected the china belonged to Two Bird all along, but being offered a drink from it—and in front of Two Bird no less—confirmed it.

Sput took it and immediately lifted the cup to admire the weeping willow painted in the center of the saucer.

Rogers may not have looked at Two Bird, but Two Bird fastened his eyes on Rogers. That is, until he peeled them away and went to his saddle bag. From it, he retrieved an item that turned out to be a comb. Sput could just make out the butterfly etched in the handle.

Two Bird extended the comb to Rogers like it was an olive branch. "To help with hair."

If looks could cut a man in two, thought Sput Louie, Two Bird would now be Half A Bird.

Rogers glowered. "My hair don't need no help," he said thrusting out his chest.

Looking flustered, Two Bird said, "*Help* is wrong word." He frowned like he was racking his brain for the right one. "Your hair," he said with a nervous smile plastered across his face, "it is like looking at music instead of listening to it."

Rogers' eyebrows angled downwards. Sput's lips pruned upwards.

"Shuh," Two Bird said in a tone of exasperation. "*Somebody these words understand.*" He cleared his throat and tried it again. "Like fiddle. Pluck fiddle with finger or use bow." He still held the comb extended out. "Still good music." He looked down and dejected. "Use comb or not. Still good music."

Before he dropped the arm holding the comb completely down to his side, Sput Louie stood up and took it. She set the cup and saucer down next to her chair to examine the wooden instrument thoroughly. The comb had only four teeth to its name and the handle goosenecked out from its center instead of from its end. "Now this right here is a comb." She turned it this way and that. "Colored folks don't need no tiny-tooth comb." She began to pluck at her coils with it. "Our hair is too strong for that kind of foolishness. This here will work right fine. Yes, indeed. Right fine."

Rogers gave her the peeved look of someone who'd just been about to shoot a deer until a man stumbled into his line of sight. Or a woman. He about-faced and marched into the house, letting the door slam behind him.

Two Bird heaved a heavy sigh as his entire body seemed to slump.

"Give him time," Sput advised. "He gon' come around. Grass don't grow no faster if you pull on it."

"I want to stop being about to constantly think of it."

Sput resisted the urge to roll her eyes. "*Worry.* The word you want to say is *worryin'.*"

Two Bird shook his head. "According-to-white words no good for Two Bird."

"English. *English* words."

"Shuh."

"Well, you got according-to-white clothes on. That's workin' for you, ya-huh?"

He narrowed his eyes "Council say dress is dis-trac-tion. I say Wa-shing-ton easy to dis-tract then." A proud smile played on his lips as he puffed out his chest. "I agree to change how I dress, not change who I am."

Sneaking a gander at his steel gray trousers and his buttoned-down shirt made of common brown domestic cloth, Sput couldn't help but think that if it were a dress, Two Bird would have spared no expense on the fabric.

"De-le-gate must go to Wa-shing-ton. Speak with man by name of Dawes about new Indian Roll."

"Another one?" Sput's voice went up a notch. "Is this one gon' take the place of that Wallace Roll I signed up for? I heard they broke into that Wallace fellow's house and stole the whole roll." Sput sighed. "Had my hopes all the way up with that one. Guess they had no intention of givin' Freedmen's they bread money." She thanked God L.B. had gotten his. She thanked herself for keeping Old Crow's stones still in the jar tucked among her winter blankets.

Two Bird mounted his horse. "One day Freedmen will be settled. Uncle Jerry Alberty and I will see to it."

Sput didn't know Jerry Alberty, but she had heard that a fellow freedman by that name had also won a seat on the Council. It gladdened her heart to hear Two Bird show his respect by addressing the man with the reverential "uncle."

"I am working with thin-bloods, too," he boasted, "to better understand them." He tugged on the reins to turn his horse towards the road. "I will arrive again in one month."

"Return. The word is *return*," she said, her words trailing behind him.

\#

After Two Bird had left, Sput decided then would be as good a time as any to gather some pain-relieving herbs for her grandbaby's impending birth. She thought she'd seen some raspberry plants near the Ugly Tree on her last visit there so she headed that way. She would need some of those leaves for her birthing brew.

Just short of the Ugly Tree, she spotted wild plum blossoms and thought they might look spiffy in her hair. She picked a couple, and as she wove the stem into her locks, she spotted spikes of white flowers jutting out of the ground, which meant rattlesnake root was underneath. That would work well for Tawny to chew on when the pains started coming fast and hard.

As she knelt down to start digging them up, she felt a presence behind her.

Before she could turn to look, a baritone voice said, "Sput Louie."

Her head whirled around so fast that her body had to catch up to it. When she saw who it was, her mouth dropped open, her breath caught in her throat, her heart throbbed in her chest. She stood up slowly.

"Benjamin."

Chapter Thirty-five

put Louie wanted to cry out. A thousand thoughts and ideas ran through her head all at once. Leading the pack was the notion of fleeing.

"'Siyo, Brother." She managed to eke out the word as she peeled her eyes away from him.

"So then you know." Benjamin released a seemingly long-held sigh riding on an undercurrent of relief.

Sput nodded looking at the ground. *That's why you left the kerchief at the Ugly Tree,* she wanted to say. *So you could tell me without having to say the words.* She quickly corralled those thoughts. Why was she mad at him? Neither one of them was to blame for this tragedy.

Unsure of where to look, she focused her gaze on Ferd's fetlocks. She was grateful for the horse as barrier. Ferd looked healthy, well groomed. It gave her great satisfaction to know for sure that Old Crow's most prized possession was in the hands of his most loathed son.

The growing silence between she and Benjamin cried out for words to fill it and put it out of its misery.

The only thing that came to Sput's mind was, "Guess I'll have to apologize to L.B. now."

Benjamin let loose another sigh, this one colored with curiosity. "L.B.?"

"Ya-huh. He said he seen you and Ferd. Said you was comin' back."

More silence. Sput couldn't help but wonder if Benjamin was avoiding her eyes like she was avoiding his.

"Sorry to you, too." Her eyes dared to creep up, but only as far as the knees of his trousers. His pants were worn thin there. Somebody needs to patch that before it grows into a full-fledged hole, she thought.

"Sorry for what?" he asked.

"For sending you to Old Crow in the first place." From the corner of her eye, she could see him rub the back of his neck.

"You didn't send me, Sput. I went on my own."

He was right of course, but she felt like she was the wheel that got this disaster rolling.

"And what if I wouldn't have went?" he asked. "I would still be married to my sister?" A hint of anger did a delicate dance on the edges of his words.

Ferd snorted his disapproval. Sput silently agreed.

She had no answer for his question, but she had a thousand of her own. Like where have you been living? What have you been doing this whole time? Why are you here now?

"*Uyo ayelvdi,*" Benjamin said.

A tear stung the back of Sput's eye. She fought to keep it there. "No need to apologize to me," she uttered quickly. "What happened to us was not our fault."

"Cain't argue with that."

Sput's eyes crept their way north of his knees, high enough to see that Benjamin's suit coat matched his pants. Fancy, she thought. Prosperous lookin', too. Archie's face would shine like a ginger cake if he could see his Pa dressed like that.

"I'm married now."

Sput's gut wrenched at the words.

Breathe, she told herself so that it would ease up. What did she think would happen? Did she think a man as beautiful as Benjamin would not be snapped up by some spoony woman? She hoped the woman deserved him. A throaty "Ya-huh," was all she could dredge up. What else could she say to that? She'd been washed out of his life like dirt from a shirt. If memory served, she was sure you had to officially end one marriage before you could legally enter into another one. It was easy for Benjamin to live a lie, though. He didn't have the truth sleeping in the same house with him. She would never have left her sons, and she certainly had no plans to remarry ever, though she guessed Senix could be called a suitor of sorts, as he was still sniffing around.

Sput cleared her throat. "Where she at, your woman?"

"Well, I works at the Topeka Carriage Factory now." He sounded almost boastful. "I paints the carriages after they build 'em. But on the weekends, I hauls water for a water delivery company. Anyway, that's where they at, back in Kansas."

"They?" Sput smiled weakly. She tried to sound indifferent, look unconcerned as she finally plucked up the nerve to meet his eyes.

"Got a baby now, too."

She had never noticed before how flecks of gold dotted his copper eyes.

"A little girl," she heard him say from what seemed like far away. "We calls her Lily."

Lily. The cragged boulder of a name slowly pierced her heart. She took a step back, then two, as she struggled to catch her breath and maintain her balance.

"Sput Louie?"

Sput Louie shook her head. "Lily," she muttered and took yet another step back. Not even their daughter had been spared from being erased and replaced.

"Don't be mad, Sput. That's just my run at honorin'—" he paused and swallowed. "—our Lily."

A tinge of anger wormed itself into her next words. "Your new wife, she know about me? About 'our' Lily?"

Benjamin didn't answer. He didn't have to. Why would he ever repeat the story of their lives? She never would. She was confident their story would die when they did.

Benjamin swung his leg behind him to dismount.

"Don't you dare get off that horse, Benjamin," she yelled louder than she had intended.

He quickly settled back in his saddle. They remained there in silence, Benjamin allowing Sput the moment he must have instinctively known she needed.

Sput shook her head in disgust at the turn their lives had taken. On some level, she understood his naming his new daughter after his dead one. It signaled a new beginning, a different life but one with a single invisible thread linking it to the old one. Something to say yes, it was real. Yes, you existed. Yes, we existed, but that life is gone now, bone dead and buried deep.

"Things sure do change, don't they?" Sput conceived.

"And time don't stop."

"Old Crow bent us," Sput said, looking into the distance. "Tried to, anyway."

Benjamin nodded. "By all rights, we should be as evil as he is."

"Ya-huh."

"It took me a while, but I finally come around to feelin' sorry for that man."

Sput harrumphed.

"That's how they raised him, Sput. To think his life is worth more than somebody else's. His Pa 'lowed him to hurt what was probably more than a handful of women slaves."

She didn't want to think about any other siblings they may or may not have from other rapes Old Crow more than likely committed, but Benjamin was right. Why would Goliah Lynch have stopped at just two women?

"As the twig is bent—"

"So shall the tree grow crooked," finished Benjamin. "Or somethin' like that."

How effortlessly they had fallen back into their old rhythm of talking despite their shared tragedy. Or maybe because of it.

"Yes, suh, Old Crow is one crooked tree."

A satisfied smile curled Sput's lips. "You unbent that tree, though."

"We unbent that tree." Ben paused. "Made him change his ugly ways."

"So far, anyway," Sput said.

"I wonder if he learned somethin' from it."

"Ya-huh. How to hide his hate better."

Benjamin chuckled. "Sho took a lot to unbend his ass."

"We'll see how that work out and how long it last." Sput folded her arms across her chest. "I'm comin' out the other side of this mess. Not all the way there yet, though." Then she thought, unlike you. You look well on your way to a better life.

"I just wanted to see firsthand how y'all was farin'."

"The boys don't know, you know. Never told 'em. Never will."

His face showed not a smidgen of surprise. "They always did know not to pester you."

"Hunter's gon' be a Pa," Sput added enthusiastically.

"I know." Ferd bobbed his head back and did a little three-step dance. "Rode by your place this morning. That's how I followed you here. Saw Tawny takin' breakfast to Hunter in the field." He paused. "Archie finally got his school, I see. I'm right proud of him. All of 'em really."

"It's not my place. Belongs to L.B."

"I knows that, too. A man from around the Nation passed through Lawrence where I live and told the story of a Cherokee who came forward and claimed his colored grandson. The fellow claimed the man was gon' help other colored folks get they land, too. Didn't say nothin' 'bout what happened to the grandson's Mama, though."

"Well, Old Crow ain't helped nobody else yet. But he will. I hear tell a new roll comin'." She had every faith Goliah would, and two stones to make sure just in case he didn't. Then she asked the question she'd wanted to ask for more than a year now.

"How'd you do it?"

At first, Benjamin looked confused by the question, but his face showed full understanding in the matter of a moment. Perhaps this was why he had come back in the first place. Maybe this was what he needed to say to slam shut the final door on his old life.

"I went there hat in hand beggin'," he began, "like no man should have to do, but he do it anyway. For his family. A man ain't a man if he don't look out for his family. I laid out the particulars to him. Told him we was tired of eatin' varmints and victuals." He swiveled his head to one side and cracked his neck. "Asked me was I tryin' to vex his wife with my visit. I said to him he done vexed me with his. So that's a turnabout. That's when he called me a ridiculous nigger." Benjamin frowned like he was getting riled anew. "Told me if I kept on with it, he was gon' tell you the truth. I said, 'What truth you got to tell my wife about?' And that's when he told me."

She knew he couldn't bring himself to say the words. She also knew she didn't want to hear them ever again.

"I asked him how could he let us marry knowin' what he know, and you know what he told me?"

Sput said, "'Ain't my business what two niggers do.'"

Benjamin blinked wide with surprise. "That's when I clipped him. Cocked him cold with my fist first, though. Snuffed him out like a candle. Yanked his pants down, lifted his sack, and snipped it. Squeezed the stones on out and left him there just like that. Pants down around his ankles, business bared to whoever might come up on him." He smiled wryly. "I didn't care if he lived or died. Ain't never snipped a man before. Come to find out the bastard lived."

"Good," Sput said. "'cause without him, L.B. never woulda got this land. And you woulda been strung up."

They both went quiet in contemplation of this fact. My how things might have turned out differently.

With seemingly nothing left to say, Sput offered a way out of their returned awkwardness. "You should bring the wife and baby around sometime."

He pressed his lips together. "I might just do that."

Benjamin could probably tell Sput didn't mean it. Sput knew for sure he didn't.

"Sput," he said hesitantly. "You know I still—"

Sput held up her palm to stop his words. "You don't have to say no more, Ben—" His name suddenly felt funny on her tongue now, like it didn't belong there.

Benjamin nodded, and after a moment's hesitation, he slowly turned his horse around to face away from Sput and the Ugly Tree.

Sput turned her back to him as well, though neither made a move to leave.

Nonetheless, reason won out over impulse, propriety over ambiguity, and principles over heart.

As she heard his horse saunter away, she spotted a bush of blessed thistle with its leathery leaves and prickly spikes a few steps to the left of the Ugly Tree. The herb would be good to help the flow of Tawny's milk after she gave birth. Sput ambled over and pulled a couple of the purple bulbs off.

She stuffed them in her possible bag alongside the plum blossoms and rattlesnake root, then headed home without ever looking back.

Author's Note

It happened around the same time that my mother died.

Why is it that we wait too late to be curious about our parents' past? Is it because they never talk about the things that happened to them, their parents, or their great-grandparents? Many family secrets are taken to the grave this way.

It wasn't until my mother began to get sick, that I began to wonder about her life, her family's story of origin.

So I began my research into our family tree. My mother's branch was easy to trace with her being Native American of Creek and Cherokee descent. The U.S. Government kept meticulous records on who they were allotting land to, which made it easy for them to know who to steal land from. There were many rolls for the Cherokee from Early Settler's to the Dawes Indian Roll. Although, I have blood ancestors on both Cherokee and Creek rolls, I chose to enroll officially in the Muscogee Creek Nation.

My African-American father's line was a bit more difficult to trace as genealogists usually hit a brick wall called slavery where records were kept on slaves, yes, but as property. Often, they were only listed by first name, and sometimes just by gender and age. There were no avenues to discover their ancestry beyond that.

Or so I thought.

A couple of weeks after my mother's death, and after many months of research, I finally found my father's great-grandmother enumerated on the Dawes Indian Roll. You see, my G-G-grandmother was listed there because during enslavement, she had been owned by Cherokee Indians.

That surprising fact gave me pause.

It was the first time I'd ever heard that Indians (and I use that term here because it was used back then) had owned slaves. Why would one oppressed people turn around and oppress another people? This was one tiny part of volumes of African-American history that to this day remains untold. It is not taught in schools and is almost never mentioned in books. I thought to myself someone should write a book about this.

No one had.

So I followed Toni Morrison's advice to "write the book you want to read."

Although Seeds of Deception is fiction, the spine of the book is comprised of facts. Such as the way Cherokee Freedmen (the term for former slaves of Cherokee Indians) lived in Indian Territory (now known as Oklahoma), the various and sundry rolls Washington D.C. used to count and keep up with Indians, the contentious relationship between the tribe and their former slaves that to this day still exists. Try Googling "Cherokee Freedmen."

The flesh of the novel, however, is pure fiction, a dark tale from my twisted imagination. As a nod to my forebears, I've used some of my ancestor's real names as characters' names, i.e., Goliah, Sput Louie, McClendon, and Archie. This is not their story, though, but mine.

Acknowledgements

The road to publishing this debut novel was peppered with people who shared my vision, not the least of which was my writing mentor, Pamela Samuels-Young. She taught me about story structure, book marketing, publishing, and keeping my "butt in the chair" to finish my novel. I couldn't have done this without her generosity. She pulled me into her writer's group and from there we created our own: Prize Writers, which also included Darlene Hayes, Mark V. Jones, and Dewayne Alexander Smith, all of whom were instrumental in bringing Seeds of Deception to fruition. Their input and guidance was sorely needed and much appreciated.

I'd also like to thank Book-a-licious Book Club for being my beta readers: Judi Johnson, Kamillah Clayton, Raunda Jones, Helen Jingles, Claudette Knight, Dianne Moore, Saba McKinley, Lesleigh Kelly and Lisa Kelly.

Two people that gave me invaluable insight into the Cherokee Nation were Jennifer Cain Sparks and Mark Harrison. I thank you from the bottom of my heart for your precious time and energy. That special gift Mark gave me will be treasured forever. Jeri Reed, you were with me from the start. Thank you for your friendship, insight and input.

A legendary shout-out must go to the Oklahoma Historical Society; the Pioneer Papers; Chronicles of Oklahoma; the American Indian

Resource Center and the Los Angeles County Library for providing forty plus history books and a place to do countless hours of research.

David T., I love you, and thank you for your ever-present encouragement. Press on.

To Michael, Marques, Ayla, and Sara, you are my reasons for being. I love you to infinity times forever.

BOOK CLUB QUESTIONS

1. How does the book's title relate to the book's content?
2. Did you pick up on any themes? If so, what were they?
3. Have you ever traced your family tree? If so, did you find any surprises?
4. Do you think family secrets should stay buried?
5. Does your family have secrets, devastating or otherwise?
6. Did you guess the big secret? What tipped you off?
7. Would you have reacted to the big secret the same way as Benjamin and/or Sput Louie?
8. Was Benjamin justified in doing what he did?
9. Did you ever think Benjamin was dead?
10. Did you know "Sput" was pronounced "put" only with an "S" in front?
11. Do you think Sput Louie should have handled Goliah differently? If so, how?
12. After Goliah delivered the devastating news to Sput Louie and she was in and out of consciousness, where did you think she was?
13. What did you think of Two Bird's reaction when he discovered Aunt Rogers was not what he thought he was?
14. Had you ever heard about two-spirited people in Native American tribes?

15. Were you surprised how readily Two Bird was accepted by his tribe?

16. Did you know that the Cherokee had signed a treaty at the close of the Civil War granting citizenship and land rights to their former slaves? Any thoughts on why white enslavers weren't required to give their slaves land?

17. Did you know about the largely untold history of Native Americans owning African slaves?

18. After reading Seeds of Deception, do you have a new perspective on the three major groups represented in the book: Native Americans, African-Americans or whites?

19. What other untold history would you like to see in a book?

20. Did you find anything about the book that was surprising, startling, disturbing or unique?

21. How well did the author build the world of the book?

22. Was the story believable?

23. Did you pick up on any symbolism?

24. Everyone has a favorite character and a least favorite character. What was yours and why?

25. Are there any quotes or passages from the book that you found particularly compelling?

26. What did you think of the author's writing style?

27. What main points did you think the author was trying to make by writing this book?

28. How do you picture the lives of the characters after the end of the story?

29. Were there any loose ends you would like to have seen resolved?

30. If you got the chance to ask this author one question about the book, what would it be?

Made in the USA
Las Vegas, NV
07 December 2024